MISS DESIRABLE

MISCHIEF IN MAYFAIR — BOOK FOUR

GRACE BURROWES

Miss Desirable

Mischief in Mayfair—Book Four

Copyright © 2022 by Grace Burrowes

All rights reserved.

CHAPTER ONE

"Elle est une veuve."

She is a widow. Xavier Fournier offered the observation quietly enough that the lady would not have heard him. He stood behind the beaded curtain that separated the wineshop's mercantile area from its private domain, while his sole customer perused the labels on some of the best Merlots ever to leave the Continent.

"She asked for you specifically, monsieur." Jacques spoke softly as well and also in French. "Is it unusual for a proper English lady to buy her wines in person?"

"Widows can become prodigiously fond of wine," Fournier said. "Some widows." Others became fond of laudanum, lusty bachelors, gambling... Interesting women, widows. "In general, the wine purchases are an errand for the butler or the first footman."

The woman moved between the racks of bottles with unhurried confidence, her steps silent on the Axminster carpets. Her ensemble was black velvet, a peculiar choice for mourning attire, because the fabric held a sheen. The cloak draped loosely over her shoulders looked to be a merino blend—excellent quality, warm, and light-weight, though at present, glistening with damp.

Black gloves, rain-spattered black bonnet, and a heavy black veil, but no wilted posture, no sense of soul-deep fatigue as she inspected the clarets in which Xavier took such pride. Her mourning attire showed off a rounded figure several inches taller than dainty perfection.

She would be an armful, this widow. Xavier mentally kicked himself for entertaining such a thought. He checked his appearance in the cheval mirror—halfway between dapper and dashing, as befit an émigré successfully navigating proper English society. Dark hair, dark eyes, slightly exuberant but fashionable attire.

"Look in on the clerks," Xavier muttered to Jacques. "Be sure the stove is roaring. This English weather is less obliging than a neglected mistress." What passed for spring in Albion's great metropolis frequently involved sleet, rain, and bitter wind.

And this widow, if she truly was a widow, had braved the elements, without maid, footman, or companion, merely to shop for wine? A puzzle, that.

"Madame." Xavier passed through the curtain and paused a good six feet from the lady, a friendly but not flirtatious smile in place. "Fournier, at your service. Jacques says you have some questions for me."

"Monsieur." Her curtsey was both correct and graceful, neither the nervous dip of a recent schoolgirl nor the creaking gesture of a matron with bad knees. "My thanks for your consideration. I am not familiar with the clarets on offer, and your expert opinion is needed."

She managed to make that most unwieldy of tongues—the king's English—sound lovely. So many Englishwomen either drawled their general disdain for life itself, *darling this* and *ever so that*, or they adopted such precise diction that they sounded annoyed even when they were not.

Warmth came through when this lady spoke, despite her weeds. Xavier would swear that behind her veil, she was smiling *at him*.

"I can but recommend, Madame. The ultimate decision must be yours. What sort of occasion inspires your purchase?"

"A beefsteak supper, informal, and the meat will be properly prepared."

"Will ladies be present, or is this meal for masculine palates only?"

She returned the bottle she'd been inspecting to the shelf, an unassuming Sauternes that would have been an abomination with beefsteak. "You choose different wines for men and women?"

"May I speak freely, Madame?"

"I much prefer honesty."

If so, she was different from the usual insinuating, innuendo-ing, *on dit*-ing proper lady.

"If the meal is for men only, Englishmen, then the meat will be charred on the edges and nearly raw in the center. No sauces will conceal this mortal sin against proper cuisine. No spices will soften the affront to the feckless creature who gave its life for human sustenance. To add barbarity to insult, a lone, shriveled potato will accompany the steak, and if *le bon Dieu* is merciful and the heifers have not all gone dry, then butter will render the potato alone nearly edible."

"And if ladies are present?"

"Then the diners have a prayer that proper care will be taken with the menu." Not being able to see the woman's face had become irksome. Was she amused at his tirade? Insulted? Xavier passed her a bottle of decent claret. "That one is heavy on the Malbec, a heartier choice than some others, but not what I would call intense or... *effronté.*"

She held the bottle up to the weak light offered by the window. "Forward? You think a wine can be brazen?"

"A wine can be utterly bellicose, enchanting, luminous, or gracious."

She passed the bottle back to him. "Are you flirting with me, Monsieur Fournier?" The question was laced with humor, always a fine quality in a lady.

"I would never presume to flirt when the topic was as serious as the choice of claret for Madame's dinner. If you sought to purchase a case of champagne, then, perhaps, I might be persuaded to flirt, but only within the bounds of good taste. I flirt outrageously when the older ladies are buying their cordials and am nearly somber when the topic is a young man's preferred Armagnac."

She *regarded* him, a somewhat unnerving experience when she was so heavily veiled. "You are teasing me." She put the claret back on the rack and passed him another choice.

"I am bantering," he said, studying the label. "You are a woman enduring a mourning ritual, and I think to myself, 'Who has more use for a little smile than the heavyhearted among us?' You have chosen a black wine, from Cahors. You English would call it cheeky, but the aroma is lovely and the color quite rich. Shall we sample a few of these vintages?"

She glanced at the window, which was like viewing a waterfall from the back. Torrents of cold rain coursed down the glass, and Xavier hoped that the lady hadn't far to travel when she left.

"I was told you did this—offered customers samples of your wines."

"The wines are their own best advertisements. I could rhapsodize at length, in several languages, but the proof is in the tasting. Shall we?"

He gestured toward the open door of his public office, a room used mostly to impress customers who sought to negotiate bulk sales. The appointments included a pretty inlaid escritoire rather than the massive oak desk preferred by the English, a pink Carrara marble fireplace to complement the burgundy velvet drapes and upholstery, and Savonnerie carpets.

If Xavier could not stand on French soil when discussing business, he could at least stand on French carpets.

"You will warm yourself by the fire, Madame, and I will pour. Please do have a seat."

She complied on a soft rustle of velvet, while Xavier pretended to study the wine rack along the inside wall. He knew precisely which wines he'd offer her, and he had a fairly good idea which one she'd choose—if the wine was for her.

And if the wine wasn't for her, and she was widowed, then for which lucky fellow did she purchase it, and would she be back when the time came to replenish her stock of cordials?

"We will start with these," Xavier said, selecting three more green bottles from the rack running the length of the inside wall and set them down next to the Cahors. "Ideally, the wine must breathe before sampling. Fortunately, we are in no hurry. Perhaps Madame would like to remove her bonnet?"

He wanted to remove Madame's bonnet, to see the face that went with the voice. For her to make this outing in such vile weather suggested she'd wanted the shop to herself, a reasonable objective for a widow, but then, where was her footman, her coach, her porter?

"I ought not," she said, slipping a hatpin free and sticking it through the strap of her reticule. "Veils are hot, though, and nobody warns one about that, not that there's anything one can do."

She lifted her bonnet off and passed it to Xavier, as if he were as much footman as proprietor of the entire establishment. That he wore the finest morning attire Bond Street had to offer and quite profitably traded exquisite wines throughout Europe did not, in English eyes, make him any less a shopkeeper.

Liberty, equality, and fraternity had a hard going on British soil, despite all of John Bull's bleating about his rights. Fortunately, Fournier also owned substantial acreage, most of it in France. London society grudgingly tolerated his gentlemanly pretensions as a result.

Fournier shook the bonnet gently before hanging it on a drying hook beneath the mantel. The label in the crown was from a fine shop indeed, and the brim had been finished with exquisite blackwork embroidery.

The elegant clothing prepared Xavier for the possibility that the lady herself was plain, which would have suited him quite well. Beautiful women were sometimes not all that interesting, after all. Like handsome men, pretty ladies could become so absorbed with their appearance that they failed to acquire other, more substantially attractive traits.

Humor, political acumen, literary sophistication, scientific expertise, musical skill... The list was long. Contemplating such feminine attributes left Xavier lonesome for France, even as the restored Bourbon monarchy tried to shove the whole nation back into the same wretched confines from whence the revolution had sprung.

"While the wine breathes, we must find a topic to discuss other than the weather," he said. "Would I offend Madame if I took a seat?"

"Of course not. Please do, Monsieur Fournier. I actually like rainy days."

"I will never understand the English," he said, taking the second of the two wing chairs before the fire. "Why on earth do rainy days appeal?"

As his guest gazed into the flames, Xavier got his first good look at her. Madame's features were unremarkable taken individually. An unprepossessing nose, particularly compared to Xavier's own aquiline beak. A lovely complexion—the dreary British climate giveth, occasionally. And a good, strong chin.

The lady's mouth was generous and curved at the moment in a faint, self-conscious smile. Her hair was somewhere between auburn and brown and done up in a simple braided bun at her nape.

"I am in thrall to good books," she said. "On rainy days, nobody comes calling, and I can order a tea tray, curl up with an old friend, and spend hours cast away in bliss. Snowy days are almost as lovely, but snow is so quiet, and the sound of rain comforts me."

Xavier had been speaking English almost exclusively for more than a decade. He still needed the space of a heartbeat to realize that when the lady referred to *curling up with an old friend* and spending hours *cast away in bliss*, she meant curling up with a treasured book.

His mental fumbling was not simply the result of a small linguistic confusion. The lady's eyes were also somewhat to blame. The impact of her gaze was extraordinary, both for the color—not blue, but rather, the majestic hue of the blooming iris—and for the directness of her regard.

Xavier was acquainted with only one family boasting eyes of that striking shade, and to the best of his knowledge, none of the Dornings had suffered a recent bereavement.

Who was she, and what was she about?

Veils were stuffy, and they made one's spectacles steam up, but Catherine appreciated the privacy afforded by thick black netting. Monsieur Fournier had been so charming, so... easy to be with, that the moment when he'd caught sight of her eyes brought more than the usual disappointment.

In the instant when a stranger first met her gaze, Catherine could discern who *knew* and who had yet to be disabused by the gossips regarding her situation.

Xavier Fournier clearly *knew*, but then, he was reputed to be a man of varied interests and wide connections. The émigrés had to be, if they intended to thrive in the London marketplace of products and influence.

"Shall I tell you about the wines?" he asked. "I am as effusive as a doting papa when it comes to my vintages. This verbosity is pointless. You will make up your mind based on your experience of the drink itself."

"One suspects you enjoy airing your opinions, monsieur, and I know next to nothing of fine wines. Why are all the clarets in green bottles, for example?"

Her observation pleased him, if the crinkling of his eyes was any indication. He was dark-haired and had a darker complexion than most Englishmen, and his eyes were a velvety brown. He was emphatically not a Saxon lord, a point in his favor.

"Most people don't notice the color of the bottles," he said. "Sunlight can affect the flavor of the clarets over time, just as it can wash out certain gems and fade many fabrics. The green glass protects the wine. Then too, some wines are not so lovely to look at in the bottle. Sediment, clouding, a color other than the customer expects for that vintage can all be unappealing. The tinted glass provides the wine a little privacy. One cannot begrudge a vintage that small boon, can one?"

He was reassuring Catherine in some regard about her own privacy. His perceptiveness both comforted and unnerved.

"So what have you chosen for me to sample?" Coming from another woman, the question could have been flirtatious. Catherine had learned of necessity how to ensure questions were simply questions and answers simply answers.

Monsieur Fournier launched into a little discourse about how to blend clarets, how each strain of grape had particular strengths, though any wine he offered would be well above reproach. One bottle was more affordable than the others because the product was more plentiful—the curse of a good harvest, *non?* Another—the Cahors that Catherine had chosen herself—was darker and carried more of a plum flavor from the Malbec grapes.

Fournier's native French gave the recitation a lilting cadence, decorated with the occasional charming cognate. The Cahors was too *audacieux* for delicate palates. *Le Merlot* occasionally too *arrogant.* A flourish of humility here and there—*comment dit-on ce mot en anglais?*—added a self-effacing quality to his patter, as if his opinions truly were an offering Catherine was free to accept or reject.

She let the mellifluous current of his voice wash over her as the rain washed down the latticed windows and created a barrier between the elegance of Fournier's office and the grit and coal smoke of the city beyond. Catherine knew exactly what she needed from Monsieur Fournier's wineshop, and the simple sound of his voice was part of it.

She also knew that Monsieur Fournier had no need to ask her how to translate this or that word into English, because despite his polite question—*how does one say this word in English?*—he always sailed right along, finding the exact right turn of phrase himself.

To a woman who loved books, such a skill merited notice.

A quarter hour later, Catherine noticed something else: She instinctively *liked* Xavier Fournier, which made no sense. He wasn't a lisping tulip of the *ton* or a strutting Corinthian, but he was still handsome, and that should have put her off.

He was nonetheless *interesting*.

Steak and potatoes affronted him. The new process for making a clear champagne fascinated him. English winters were a trial to his spirit. Unlike the typical lordling, Xavier Fournier did not resort to irony, understatement, and sarcasm to make his points. He was both subtle and forthright, blunt and deft.

Catherine grasped that beauty was easily mistaken for goodness in both men and women. While Fournier's looks warned her to keep a distance, everything else about him—the charm, the little personal confidences, the fine manners, the passion for his wine, for good food, for London newspapers—beckoned her closer.

Which would not do, though where was the harm in appreciating the man from a safe distance?

"Which one do you recommend?" she asked after he'd waxed effusive about a jocund—his word—Beaujolais that yet had surprising substance in the finish.

"We must taste," he said, getting to his feet. "And I thank you, Madame, for the opportunity to turn my afternoon in such an agreeable direction."

He poured them each four small servings, and Catherine observed the pleasant ritual of sampling wine, accompanied by another lovely little diatribe *à la Fournier*. Catherine enjoyed the wines all the more for Fournier's explications and found what she'd needed—what she'd hoped to find—in the "black wine" from Cahors.

She'd not tasted such wine in too long—dark as a ripe aubergine, with a brusque, substantial, fruity flavor. Not subtle and exactly what she'd longed for.

"The rain has not let up," Fournier said when Catherine had sampled all four varieties. "Shall I send you home in my coach, Madame?"

"I have not yet made a purchase."

"Nor must you. If none of the wines was to your liking, I can pour others, but I chose these based on my sense of your situation. One of them ought to be the best that I can offer. If these wines will not do, I can recommend Colonel Sir Orion Goddard's shop. He is best known for his champagne, but his other vintages are not to be underestimated."

Gracious of Fournier, to recommend a competitor, but that was part of his allure. Fournier was not petty. He was absolutely self-secure, and Catherine had almost forgotten there were such men.

"I will take the Cahors," she said, rising. "A case." She rattled off her old nanny's direction, for the wine must not be delivered to her own dwelling, lest the butler take offense.

The sole clue that Catherine had surprised her host came from a slightly raised eyebrow. Fournier rose and tugged a bell-pull twice.

"My coach will be under the porte cochere in less than a quarter hour. Before you go, Madame, I feel it incumbent upon me as a gentleman to ask you one further question."

"Please do ask," she said as Fournier retrieved her cloak from the back of the wing chair and draped it around her shoulders. Now he would inquire—so politely—if she was a cousin to the titled Dorning family, for surely that must explain the color of her eyes. Some people were bolder than that, asking which of the previous generation of Dorning menfolk had been her father—the earl, or his notoriously friendly younger brother? Perhaps the middle brother, who'd been as handsome as his siblings, but moodier?

Fournier took her bonnet down from the drying hook and ran a finger over the embroidery on the brim.

"Please do not think me forward, but I must know: Whom do you seek to poison, and what can I do to preserve you from the commission of hanging felonies?"

His gaze held only understanding, though handsome men who appeared kind were especially not to be trusted.

Catherine had taken only the smallest sips of wine, and yet, the drink abruptly sat uneasily. "I will walk," she said, taking her bonnet from Fournier's grasp. "Thank you for your time, and a case of the Cahors delivered by tomorrow noon would be appreciated."

"You do not need a case," he said, returning to the wine rack and taking down a dark green bottle. "You need only the one bottle and a hollow needle to inject the poison through the cork. The difficulty is that a competent butler will ensure the wine breathes, possibly as long as an hour. That is long enough that the poison can settle into the dregs. Unless you know your victim will consume the whole bottle down to the last drops, or a very small portion of poison will effect the desired result, a red wine does not promise your venture success."

Catherine made a production of placing her bonnet upon her head, adjusting the veil, and affixing her hatpin, but all the while, her composure was draining away.

She'd had no intention of poisoning anybody. She'd simply wanted a particular French wine for her own enjoyment, and here was Fournier so gently implying she was capable of murder.

"The other problem with adding drugs to wine," he went on, "is that some poisons work unpredictably when mixed with any sort of spirits. The result can be an *emétique*, to make one cast up the accounts, as the English say, and again, you have failure and, quite possibly, an angry victim determined on revenge. You must tread carefully, Madame."

Catherine was sick to her soul with treading carefully. "Do all wine merchants have such an impressive command of poisoning techniques?"

"I am not merely a wine merchant, just as you are not merely shopping for a decent claret." He wrapped the bottle in an oilskin bag —discreet of him—and passed it to her. "Let's fetch your umbrella, though sending you out into this downpour offends my gentlemanly soul."

"And accusing me of homicidal intentions does not?" A question that should have been aflame with ire came out merely curious.

"I have learned not to judge. I like you, and you need a friend."

All three statements were possibly true, more's the pity. Fournier accompanied Catherine back into the wineshop proper and retrieved her black umbrella from beside the door. He produced a card from his pocket.

"That is my private residence, and my staff is loyal. If you allow me the privilege, I will try to help."

What on earth was she to say to that? "Your kindness is both appreciated and misplaced. Thank you for the wine, and delivery by the end of the week will do if tomorrow does not suit."

He touched her arm, a presumption. "You want to know what gave you away. Not only are you not a good match for the Cahors, a confident specimen with no pretensions to subterfuge, but you would eschew the company of any man who finds that wine much to his taste. That wine is for young men enjoying a vigorous rural life on limited means, or for a hearty French farm wife indulging at the end of her day.

"Ergo," Fournier went on, "the wine is for an enemy, and you were most particular about examining the appearance of the products offered and the color of the bottle. The Cahors is the darkest and most robust of the wines you sampled and the one I knew you your-self would least prefer."

A backhanded consolation, that Fournier saw only the fine English lady in her mourning attire, not the Catherine Fairchild who'd been such a trial to her parents.

She tucked her umbrella under her arm and pulled on her gloves. "What an interesting imagination you have, monsieur. What sort of wine would I prefer?"

He smiled, the first true, open smile Catherine had seen from him, and the effect was devastating. The smile opened up a world of warmth and humor and created intimacy without speaking a word.

"Rosé, an underappreciated departure from the expected, delightfully agile and adaptable, far more complex than most wine drinkers will ever grasp. A carefully chosen rosé can be appropriate for nearly any occasion, but such vintages are seldom allowed to shine as they deserve."

Good God. He was dangerous. Any other descriptions of him—charming, witty, articulate, friendly, shrewd, attractive, handsome—were of no moment beside the fact that where Catherine was concerned, Xavier Fournier was dangerous.

She passed him back his bottle of wine and departed the shop without another word.

CHAPTER TWO

"You glance to the left before you begin an attack," Xavier said, tossing Sycamore Dorning a towel. "But for that clumsiness, your fencing skills show some improvement."

Dorning blotted the sweat from his face. "If the habit is so obvious, why didn't you offer that observation six months ago?"

"Six months ago, you were still trying to keep straight which foot is the left and which is the right. Your brother Ash has the natural instincts of a fencer, but you... The knives you love to play with have ruined you for finer pursuits."

Dorning used the towel on an impressively muscular chest. "My lady wife does not consider me ruined. She likes my swordsmanship just—"

Fournier brought up the foil in his left hand so the untipped point touched beneath Dorning's chin. "The Germans find facial scars attractive. Must we assay the fair Mrs. Dorning's opinion on the matter? She would disapprove of your bandying her preferences about in a venue such as this—as do I."

Dorning moved the blade aside with a cautious finger. "Point taken. My apologies. What has you in such a foul temper?"

Most days, Fournier enjoyed Sycamore Dorning's company. Dorning, a rarity among his kind, could admit when he was in error and apologize for the mistake. Other days...

Dorning was like a British mastiff, a great, gamboling beast of a fellow who had no tact and was unswervingly loyal to those he cared for. This loyalty was a fine quality in a man with eight legitimate siblings—all married—and a growing army of nieces and nephews.

But Dorning could also be a trial to the nerves. He swung with bewildering speed from astonishing perceptiveness to utter blundering, then back to perspicacity. Politics did not interest him, except in so far as the news of the day affected his fancy gaming hell, and his grasp of wine was knowledgeable for the same reason.

"Get dressed," Fournier said, "and I will walk you home." London was by no means as walkable as Paris, but the streets offered a kind of privacy that a busy fencing salon did not.

"If I instead suggest we pop over to the Aurora for a meal," Dorning replied, picking up a shirt of finest lawn, "will you deign to break bread with my clumsy self?"

Fournier considered him. "What has *you* in such a temper?" And so desperate for company, even an émigré in trade would do.

"I'm not in a temper. If I'm testy, it's because Jeanette is out at Richmond, in pitched battle with our paper hangers, and I must bide here in Town. The Season is getting under way, and Goddard demands my presence at The Coventry Club."

"One does not refuse the colonel's requests lightly." Dorning was married to Colonel Sir Orion Goddard's sister and likely refused Goddard's requests not at all. Goddard, manager at the club and married himself to the supreme authority in its kitchen, wielded an air of command that had little to do with his military experience.

"I will meet you out front in a quarter hour," Dorning said, snapping his towel at nothing in particular.

"Twenty minutes," Fournier replied. "One does not rush one's ablutions." Nor did one allow Sycamore Dorning to get in the habit of dictating terms. Xavier was waiting on the salon's steps when Dorning came jaunting forth twenty-five minutes later.

"Nothing like London on a pretty day," Dorning said, twirling a jade-handled walking stick that doubtless concealed a blade of some sort. "No place like it on earth."

For form's sake, Fournier parried that thrust. "And yet, even on fine spring days, the Londoner huddles in his dank pubs, swilling equally dank ale. No wonder the Saxon is so pale."

Dorning ambled along at Fournier's side, exuding panache no Englishman should be able to claim.

"Is business suffering?" Dorning asked gently. "Goddard praises your clarets to any who will listen, and his opinion is respected. I could put in a word with my brother."

In this instance, Dorning meant his oldest brother, Grey, Earl of Casriel, head of the family and soon to return to Town from Dorset.

"Thank you for that kind offer, but at the moment, I am of a mind to discuss your sisters with you."

Dorning touched a finger to his hat brim as a pair of dowagers bustled past. A footman followed them, as did a maid.

"I can introduce you to Kettering," Dorning said. "We refer to him as Lord Trysting at our peril. Worth and Jacaranda won't be underfoot in Town for another fortnight or so. Children apparently complicate the process of moving households. My sister Daisy can't be stirred from the shires for love nor money."

Fournier allowed a silence to build as they waited for a break in traffic at the street corner. This being the Great Metropolis, no such break occurred.

"I am acquainted with Lord Trysting and need no introduction to him. The topic of interest is *your sisters*, Dorning." A crossing sweeper in perhaps the tenth underfed year of his age ventured into the melee and brandished his broom in all directions. Dorning stepped off the walkway, and traffic halted.

Fournier flipped the child a coin and got a *"Mare-see, me-shure!"*

in response. Young Victor's French was not his most highly developed skill.

"What about my sisters interests you?" Dorning asked when they were again moving down the walkway.

"I am confident Lady Penweather and Lady Trysting are the most estimable of women, though I doubt they are contemplating murdering anybody at present. Your other sister has earned my notice."

Fournier had consulted that most convenient handbook for the peasantry, Debrett's. No female Dorning cousins were of the correct age to be his recent customer. Therefore, the lady was what the polite society carefully labeled a *legitimate by-blow*.

"My other sister?" Dorning replied, voice laced with puzzlement. "I have no—" His steps slowed.

He honestly did not think of Madame as his sister, which was both odd and infuriating. She had dressed in the first stare of mourning fashion—an intriguing contradiction in terms—spoken and carried herself as a fine lady, and been determined enough to venture onto fashionable streets without an escort.

She moved at least on the fringes of London Society, and Dorning, as an earl's brother, moved at its center. How could her own sibling forget her very existence?

"She is recently bereaved, I believe," Fournier said, "and she has need of her family."

"Why must the French be so given to drama?" Dorning replied, in the same tones he might have remarked the unfortunate direction of the breeze off the Thames. "Nobody in my family truly contemplates murder, not for long, and if they do, I am usually the cause of their frustrations. Catherine is... We have not openly acknowledged her because we have the sense such a gesture would be unwelcome."

Catherine. The name suited her. Proper, pretty, not as common as the ubiquitous Elizabeths, Annes, and Charlottes, but thoroughly respectable.

"Is she recently bereaved, or did she don weeds to protect her reputation?"

"Lost her mother a month ago. Lady Fairchild had apparently been ill for some time and had kept her situation from her daughter rather than seek treatment."

As if English physicians were worth consulting. "And Catherine's"—Xavier sorted through English vocabulary—"mother's husband?"

"Lord Fairchild predeceased his wife by a year or two."

That Dorning knew Catherine's situation suggested he wasn't entirely indifferent to her. "To lose both parents in close succession must be a considerable blow. Does the lady have other siblings?"

"Legitimate siblings?"

"One does not wish to offend needlessly, Dorning." Though one regretted being so merciful in the fencing salon.

"No legitimate siblings," Dorning said. "Cousins at some remove in Canada, and I know what you're thinking."

He could not possibly. "And that would be?"

"That we have neglected Catherine shamefully, except that's not how it works."

Fournier waited, because Dorning would surely explain how it worked, *it* being the self-serving and convoluted machinations of the British peerage.

"Jeanette and I will make a mourning call in a few weeks," Dorning said. "Casriel will do likewise shortly thereafter. We will do the pretty, but we will not intrude. Catherine has been left quite well fixed, much to the shock of the matchmakers. When her period of mourning is over, she will be received with exquisite good manners anywhere she pleases to go. The money will keep doors open, while openly acknowledging our connection to her just now would... It's complicated."

"'Complicated' being another word for 'stupid.' Catherine is grieving a double loss, assuming her mother's husband was kind to her. Now she will be besieged with the fawning scoundrels you call fortune hunters, as if penniless opportunists were intrepid denizens of the forest primeval. She has no one to safeguard her interests, and you keep your distance."

"We must keep our distance for a time, up to a point, but apparently, you are concerned for her."

Well, yes, and that was a problem. "A woman contemplating murder by poison is a woman in need of her family."

"Explain."

Fournier did as they navigated the wider and quieter streets on the fringes of Mayfair. "She did not take the wine with her, but she did not cancel her order either. If I pretend to have forgotten the transaction, she could easily walk into one of several other wineshops and purchase the same vintage." Fournier would have a discreet word with the clerks in those shops before the sun had set.

"You are making leaps, Fournier. Just because a woman—"

"Where does Catherine dwell?"

"Number seventeen, Houseman Square." Offered without hesitation, another indication that Dorning did, indeed, keep an eye on his sister.

"The address she gave me was on Delacourt Close. A fine lady does not typically dwell on a close, such as fill the eastern reaches of your noisome city. She would not give me her name, but she made the mistake of taking off her veil. That is the error of a smart woman for once not thinking clearly."

Dorning paused at the foot of the Aurora Club's steps. "Why would removing her veil indoors be a mistake?"

A fissure formed in the vast wall of patience Fournier had built while dwelling among the English.

"Because, *idiot*, her eyes give away her heritage to any person who has met a Dorning. All her life, she has been burdened in ways you cannot fathom, and now you keep your distance from her when she is most alone. I will never understand English honor."

Dorning glanced up and down the street, then ascended the steps. "Let's have lunch. A private dining room. I said the Dornings could not overtly take an interest in Catherine's situation, but we do very much care for her wellbeing."

Fournier climbed the steps, his sense of foreboding mounting as he approached the front door. "I have done my duty to the lady and informed her family that she is in difficulties. That is what my sense of honor requires of me." That was *all* his sense of honor required, and far beyond what pragmatic instincts advised.

"But you said she contemplated dire measures," Dorning replied as the door swung open from within. "If I doubled the claret order from The Coventry Club, would you consider having a closer look at her situation?"

"Do not insult me or the lady any more than you already have, *imbécile anglais*."

"I do so envy you that French accent." Dorning strolled through the door and nodded to the footman. "Makes every threat so much more convincing. Could have used that edge with my older brothers."

"Perhaps the lady sought to poison you. Somebody certainly should." Fournier had reviewed the entire encounter numerous times, and he could envisage no scenario by which Catherine Fairchild would have acquired a taste for the lowly Cahors.

Perhaps she was buying the wine for her lover, but what sort of lover put a lady up to such a purchase? And not once had Catherine *explicitly* contradicted Fournier's theory that she was buying a vintage that would disguise the taste of poison.

Dorning passed his hat and walking stick to the footman. "We'll need a private dining room, Jules, and warn the staff that Fournier is in a difficult mood. Only the very best vintages will do."

Jules, who hailed from Auvergne, bowed. "Very good, Mr. Dorning. You are in a difficult mood. You demand the best vintages be opened. I will warn the kitchen. The Iris Salon is available, if that would suit."

Dorning smiled. "*Vive le France*. The Iris Salon will do. Come along, Fournier, and let us continue our discussion."

Fournier did not want to continue the discussion. He did not want to provide Dorning a free lesson on the subtleties of good claret. He did not want to entangle himself in the troubles of a woman who was all but a stranger to him, and a stranger with at least seven English brothers better placed to take her situation in hand.

Dorning bounded up the steps and waited on the first landing. "She needs you," he said. "Nobody else can discreetly see to the matter."

And those were the exact words Fournier most especially did not want to hear. He took the steps slowly, as a man climbs to his doom, all the while mentally choosing among the most expensive bottles of claret ever to grace the club's cellars.

"Miss, you have a caller." Five clipped words were sufficient to convey that Deems was mortally offended by the arrival of company. Deems also managed to imply that such a great impropriety was Catherine's fault.

She set aside her Ovid and rose. "The condolence calls must begin sometime." She took the card from Deems's silver salver, expecting to see that some widow or gossip was leading the charge.

Xavier G. Fournier. The name was a shock and a pleasure. The card, like the man, was quietly elegant. Excellent stock, a coat of arms embossed on one side, and the name in swirling type. Purple ink, of all the vanities, probably a nod to his lovely clarets.

"Your caller is French," Deems said, as if this was further proof that the Fairchild household had fallen into ruin.

Catherine was within her rights to refuse callers for another few weeks, but if she sent Fournier away, he'd likely keep coming back. She doubted he was planning to join the list of her detractors, but neither would his errand be social.

"Show him to the family parlor, Deems."

Bushy white eyebrows rose to biblical heights. "The *family* parlor, miss?"

"The fire has not been lit in the formal parlor. I refuse to freeze for the sake of a few platitudes from one of Papa's Continental connections. Please have the kitchen send up a tray."

The late Lord Fairchild had accepted diplomatic postings from the Baltic to Italy to Canada, the most recent having been a brief stint in Paris. Fournier might well have crossed paths with Papa in Paris, and in any case, Deems responded to overt displays of authority provided the matter was petty. He bowed slightly and withdrew.

His bows to Catherine were never more than slight, and she well knew why. The housekeeper, out of loyalty to Mama's memory, had become Catherine's staunch ally, and thus the house was in a constant state of domestic skirmishing.

Catherine inspected her appearance in the mirror over the sideboard, and as always, eyes of the absolute wrong color gazed back at her. Every other feature was plain, as if to ensure nobody missed the peculiarity of her eyes.

She made her way to the family parlor, tarrying in the doorway to study her guest. Fournier's back was to her, the line of his burgundy morning coat showing off an excellent pair of shoulders and tapering to a lean waist.

"You might as well join me," he said without turning. "I do not bite, Miss Fairchild." His tone was humorous and patient, and Catherine should not be so pleased simply to hear that accented voice.

"But you do presume. This is a house of mourning, monsieur."

He turned and bowed. "All the more reason why friends should come along to offer comfort and support. Good day, Miss Fairchild, and my condolences on your losses."

He knew her name, he knew where she lived, and he knew of her specific bereavements. Fast work, considering he'd met Catherine a mere twenty-four hours ago.

"Thank you," she said, offering a curtsey and advancing into the room. "I've sent for a tray and can offer you tea, but you really need not have called."

"Do you mean I *should* not have called? In the opinion of polite society, you must be left in solitude to wrestle with your grief for weeks. Is grief like a criminal offense, then, such that the more severe the loss, the longer the sentence? If the French adopted these mourning eccentricities, the entire nation would be hung in crepe and shut up like anchorites for another twenty years."

Catherine gestured to the sofa. "You are diverting, and for that, I thank you. I was never one for swanning about in Society to begin with and certainly not without my mother. I am not bad *ton*, but I am questionable. The gossips labeled me Miss Dubious, owing to my antecedents, my bookish inclinations, and my perceived lack of settlements. Please do have a seat."

Fournier waited until Catherine had taken the wing chair before the fire—Mama's favorite. If Catherine closed her eyes, she could imagine a whiff of Mama's signature perfume wafting from the upholstery. Heady damasks with a hint of spice.

Mama, I miss you so.

Fournier took the end of the sofa closest to Catherine's seat. "How are you, Miss Fairchild? We have already established that I am presuming, so I might as well live up to my reputation."

"Thank you for asking. One manages."

His expression changed, gaze narrowing. "The weather is much improved over yesterday, is it not? Such a downpour, but a good rain does reduce the dust."

"And we need rain if the flowers are to come along." Catherine's reply was automatic, the result of any number of evenings spent sipping tepid punch with the wallflowers and chaperones. She'd no sooner spoken, though, than the underfootman arrived, bearing the tea tray.

"Thank you, Vincent. That will be all."

Fournier rose and closed the door. "Shall I pour out, or will you enjoy that office?"

"Why did you close the door?"

"To keep the heat in, of course. In mourning, we are more prone to illness, and as a gentleman, I must place concern for your health over the dictates of strictest propriety."

"You are not merely presuming, you are audacious."

"Thank you. When I asked how you were going on, you looked first at the open door, and then you served me a polite fiction. That tells me you do not trust your staff. I grow increasingly alarmed on your behalf, Miss Fairchild."

Catherine gestured to the tray. "Please do pour, because I gather you do not trust me to prepare your tea to your liking. I like mine with milk and honey."

Fournier resumed his seat and navigated the tea tray as deftly as any duchess would have. "Your tea." He held out the cup and saucer. "I come as an emissary from your Dorning relations, who believe that you would want them to exercise discretion rather than parade themselves to your door for all of Mayfair to see."

He fixed himself plain tea, took a sip, and set down his cup and saucer. "The kitchen has not reused the tea leaves, but they are skimping. What is afoot here, Miss Fairchild? Sycamore Dorning claims that you are an heiress, and impecunious bachelors will soon serenade you beneath the waxing moon."

"When did he tell you that?"

"Yesterday at lunch. Your family is concerned for you, but they also fear adding to your burdens. I come to assure you of their support."

"They are..." Catherine set down her tea carefully. "Good people. Mama always said the Dornings were good people." She'd said it quietly, but with unwavering conviction.

"I am not good people," Fournier countered, "but I can see that your situation is difficult. Do even your domestics hold your patrimony against you?"

Catherine was reminded that Fournier was dangerous. If he could leap from weak tea to Deems's snobbery, he was the social equivalent of Wellington's legendary sharpshooters. No wonder his business prospered.

"The tea merely needed more time to steep," Catherine said, though if Cook was off to market, then Deems had overseen the preparation of the tray.

"Miss Fairchild, I am French." Said patiently.

"One grasped as much."

"I was a small boy during the Terror, and fortunately not in Paris, but I am nearly impossible to shock. If you need to sack your butler, or pension *le vieil âne*, then you send for your solicitors, arrange the legalities, hold a summary court-martial, and be done with it."

Pension *the old donkey*. Such plain speaking ought to be offensive rather than comforting. To Catherine's horror, an ache started in her throat.

"The effort involved to sack Deems is beyond me at present. I'm accustomed to his little games."

"But your parents are no longer on hand to keep him in check, and he is nasty to the woman now paying his salary. That suggests an untenable degree of arrogance, even for an English butler. Shall I sack him for you?"

Catherine was tempted. She was so tempted. "I could have the solicitors do it."

The idea of a household without Deems lurking in the hallways... going through Papa's things, standing by when the lawyers came around...

"You are not by nature weak or retiring," Fournier said, holding out the plate of shortbread to her. "You are, in fact, quite formidable. Why do you hesitate?"

Because I am afraid. Because the gossips don't know the half of it. Because I am weary and sad and uncertain.

Fournier clearly expected an answer. "Laziness?" Catherine suggested. The shortbread was good—fresh and sweet.

"Battle fatigue," Fournier replied, "is not laziness. While I am sitting here, jot a note to the solicitors, and I will see it delivered."

He was giving her an order, or possibly encouragement. Catherine took her tea to the escritoire, thought for a moment, then penned a quick epistle. That she'd pension the butler upon Lady Fairchild's death was almost to be expected, viewed from a certain perspective. Why hadn't she thought of that?

"Was it this butler whom you sought to poison?" Fournier asked.

The question was clever. Answering in the negative implied that Catherine had intended to poison somebody else.

"Your imagination is prodigious, monsieur. Will you take a message back to the Dornings for me?"

"Does the butler watch you so closely you cannot even write to your own siblings?"

The ache grew sharp. "I do not *know* the Dornings. I would rather trust to your good offices than try to put words on paper. Please thank Sycamore for his concern and convey to him that I will be grateful to receive condolence calls a few weeks hence."

Fournier considered her from his end of the sofa, while Catherine remained at the escritoire. "I will tell Dorning that you are exhausted, that you have no allies worth the name, that after years of polite society's ill-treatment, you have been besieged in your very home by judgment and disrespect. I will tell him he is a failure as a brother and a gentleman, and I will ensure his wife hears my words. Jeanette Dorning is half French, and she will not tolerate these excesses of English delicacy."

Fournier meant well, but then, Mama had meant well when she'd gone walking with the late Earl of Casriel, to hear her tell it.

And Fournier's good intentions could end in a disaster to equal the one Mama had caused.

"The highest praise my father—Lord Fairchild—gave me was, 'You'll do, Catherine. You'll do.' He was fond of me, and I of him, though I did not realize it until his most recent return from Paris. Papa had seen enough of the world to doubt the myth of English superiority, and his love for Mama and me was real."

"But?"

"But he was an old-school aristocrat nonetheless. When after years of marriage, he still had no heir, he all but encouraged Mama to stray. The problem is the title."

Fournier made a circular motion with his wrist.

"The baronies are the oldest titles," Catherine went on, relieved to have somebody to explain this to. "So old that they can sometimes be preserved through the female line, depending on how the letters patent were written and what plagues had passed through lately. Papa needed any child, any child at all, to prevent the title from reverting to the crown. Polite society was kept in ignorance of that fact." As Catherine had been kept in ignorance.

"And the significance of this?"

"Polite society was also not informed that I was my uncle Erasmus's heir. I did not know, and I suspect my parents did not either. I am thus wealthy, and my offspring will claim a title, despite my illegitimacy. This is rather more than the gossips are willing to forgive."

Fournier's brows drew down. "I am technically a *comte*. Should I expect my butler to take me into immediate dislike when I disclose that fact?"

"Why don't you disclose it?"

"Because I am no great believer in privileges that attach through an accident of birth. Mind you, I keep my radical leanings quiet when I'm trying to convince the lordlings to purchase my claret."

"And I try not to annoy the very Society to whom I am a walking affront."

Catherine was being more honest about her situation than she'd intended to be, and she sensed her guest was appeased by her explanations. She'd explained much, though certainly not all.

Fournier rose. "Have you considered changing societies? Many a Frenchman has found a good life here among the English. The same can be said in reverse."

Did he include himself among those contented Frenchmen? "I have journeyed extensively on the Continent with my parents," Catherine said. "I may travel again, though one is to serve out one's mourning at home." When that chore had been tended to, traveling on the Continent might be a possibility.

"Go to France," Fournier said, his gaze bleak. "You can live well for a song in the provinces, and aristos are all the rage again. I am certain I could find you a château to rent where the butler would not judge you for decisions your parents made before you were born."

"He would judge me for being English."

"Not as much as you might think. Most of my countrymen grew sick to death of Bonaparte's bellicose version of liberty and his imperial variety of equality. Will you write to the Dornings?"

"I want to."

Fournier came around to the desk and offered his hand. Catherine took it, because she thought his intention was to bow his farewell. Instead, he drew her to her feet and away from the window.

After taking tea, neither he nor Catherine had donned gloves, and the warmth of his grip was a shock. A pleasant, comforting shock.

"You are managing as you always have," he said, "on your own, but you fail to see that solitary maneuvers are no longer the best approach to the battle. If you cannot approach your family just yet, then allow me to serve as an ally. Even a house of mourning must keep its wine cellar stocked. Send to me if there is need, or if you are simply in want of company. Order some pear cordial. I have no use for your money and no regard for an English title."

You can trust me. He did not speak the words, which was kind of him, but he did hold Catherine's hand between both of his, enveloping her in the warmth of his touch.

"Say yes, Catherine," he went on, still holding her hand. "Say, 'Yes, Fournier, I will send for you, because I know you will make a pest of yourself if I do not.'"

Catherine. He used her name, he touched her. "Yes," she said when her considerable stores of common sense shouted *no*. "Yes, I will send for you, if I must send for anybody."

He bowed. "I adore a stubborn woman." He took her missive from the desk blotter and tucked it into a pocket. "I will see myself out and convey your message to the solicitors. You will be amazed at how much one act of authority on your part will change your household. Hire a young Frenchman to be your butler, and you will never regret it."

Not a bad idea. "Away with you," Catherine said, waving toward the door. "And, Fournier?"

"Mademoiselle?"

"Thank you for calling."

Her concession, for that's what it was, earned her another of those warm, sweet smiles. "The pleasure is mine."

He closed the door quietly in his wake, and Catherine returned to her cooling tea at the escritoire. A moment later, she heard the front door close, then caught sight of Fournier striding along the walkway.

He'd alluded to a childhood in revolutionary France and being hard to shock. He was also nearly impossible to deceive, and yet... He had touched her, he had listened to her, and—this should have alarmed her—he had *understood* her.

Xavier Fournier was a threat to her wellbeing, and also a surprising comfort. He cut an impressive figure, a touch more flamboyant than the average English gentleman, even in his manner of tossing a coin to the crossing sweeper.

His visit had done her good, though she would not be sending for him. Still... She was curious. How had that provincial boy made the journey from a country racked by violence to the genteel surrounds of London's best neighborhoods?

And along the way, who had comforted Xavier Fournier?

CHAPTER THREE

"Mind you don't get obstreperous, Fournier." Sycamore Dorning peered up at the staid façade of Belcher and Sons. A discreet brass plaque near the door was the only hint that the premises housed a solicitors' office. "Lawyers gossip, despite their much-vaunted discretion."

"I am counting on them gossiping, which is why you have accompanied me. The point of the errand is not only to see Miss Fairchild's execrable butler sacked, but also to send a message to the lawyers. She has allies."

"She certainly has a champion in you," Dorning muttered. "One hears that you take an interest in the occasional impecunious émigré, but why her, Fournier?"

Because Dorning himself had asked it of him? "I am nobody's champion. I am merely seeing a note delivered." And yet, Dorning, with his usual ability to sniff currents in the wind, had sensed a truth. Catherine Fairchild's situation had piqued Xavier's protective instincts, and that was a very bad thing indeed.

"A note that will result in a respected retainer being turned out on his ear. Why did you take old Deems into such dislike?"

To appearances, they were two gentlemen stopping to pass the time on an overcast spring day. The sky had that undecided look, as if making up its mind whether to rain in the next fifteen minutes or this afternoon, or both—this was London—but rain, it would.

Xavier, however, was using the moment to assess the surrounds. No potted heartsease on the stoop, no daffodils blooming in the small patch beneath the lamppost. The brass plate was shiny, the door freshly painted an uninspired dark green. The bricks of the façade could use a new coat of whitewash. The shutters were overdue for blacking. The railing along the steps was spindly and also in want of paint.

Not shabby, exactly, but... stingy. Penny-pinching. Was that a good quality or a bad quality in a wealthy young lady's attorneys?

"Old Deems, as you call him, is disrespectful toward his employer. He brought weak tea up from the kitchen and tried to keep me from seeing Miss Fairchild. She was loath to close the parlor door on a chilly day, a simple act of pragmatism that should not earn the censure of a lady's staff. She cannot trust her butler, and he all but manages the household."

Dorning made a face. "How do you know she does not trust him?"

An older woman, companion in tow, exited the premises. She was well dressed—brown velvet carriage dress, fashionable bonnet, embroidered lace parasol despite the gloomy day. Her companion was also well attired, if modestly so, and the companion's boots were either new or had new heels.

Belcher had some wellborn clients, then, though attorneys would discreetly call on clients who were true aristocrats. Across the street, Lord Fortescue Armbruster was chatting up some dandified sprig, and the passing traffic included more than a few crested carriages.

"What is a butler's first duty, Dorning?"

Dorning tipped his hat to the ladies as they passed. "In the old-fashioned sense, a butler handles the bottles. He decides when to decant wine purchased in casks, if his employer doesn't express an opinion. He oversees the cellars and the drinks pantry and chooses which bottles to send up based on the menus devised by the lady of the house. In these modern times, he also manages the male staff and can serve as house steward in smaller establishments."

"And yet," Xavier said, advancing to the door, "Miss Fairchild came to buy her own wine, without her butler, without a footman who answers to that butler, and without troubling the coachman or grooms who might receive their wages from that butler. She did not consult that butler regarding the selection of a hearty red meant to accompany a beef dinner."

Dorning paused outside the door. The knocker was small, a brass lion with a ring in its mouth, though one did not knock at a commercial establishment.

"If an English butler knows one class of wines in particular," Dorning said, "it's the clarets that go well with good British beef. I concede you might have a point."

"Such flattery from one I so highly esteem will give me *palpitations du coeur*."

"You speak Frog when you want to avoid honest feelings," Dorning said, hand on the door latch. "Rather like I signal an intent to attack by looking left." He sailed over the threshold on that observation and did what Xavier had brought him along to do and what he did so well—played the charming lordling while setting all about him aflutter.

Within five minutes, clerks had taken hats, coats, and walking sticks, despite the lack of an appointment. Xavier and his escort were shown to a fussy little parlor overstuffed with old tomes and a few disintegrating editions of *La Belle Assemblée*. A tea tray arrived a few moments later, followed by no less personage than Frampton Belcher, senior partner, who offered bows all around.

Belcher's pale blue eyes held speculation where Xavier was concerned. His manner through the introductions was that blend of bluff good cheer, deference, and self-importance that characterized successful shopkeepers.

And successful swindlers. The luxurious appointments in Belcher's private office suggested he might be a bit of both.

"Our call is an occasion for some delicacy," Dorning said, assuming a wing chair before it had been offered. "We bring you tidings from Miss Catherine Fairchild."

Dorning had chosen the grouping before the hearth—which held only a dying gesture in the direction of a fire—rather than allow Belcher the advantage of sitting behind his desk. Belcher thus had no choice but to gesture Xavier into a chair before assuming one himself.

"Miss Fairchild's bereavement is much to be pitied," Belcher said. "Her parents loved her dearly."

Platitudes that did not even admit Miss Fairchild was a client. Dorning withdrew her note from his breast pocket and passed it over to Belcher.

"We come as her emissaries," Dorning said. "You are to establish a pension for her butler, Deems, payable directly to him at the address of his choosing for the rest of his natural days, effective immediately. Miss Fairchild has chosen the Wentworth bank for this transaction and asks you to have an appropriate principal sum moved for that purpose."

Belcher's expression did not change, but his gaze narrowed as he read Miss Fairchild's missive. "This will take some time. I must meet with Miss Fairchild, authenticate her direction, consult with her present bankers..."

Dorning affected puzzlement. "You do not recognize your client's signature, Mr. Belcher? In recent months, you have had to handle not one but two estates on the family's behalf, and even I know that requires a great deal of signed paperwork from the beneficiary. Then too, Miss Fairchild inherited significant sums from her uncle, and that would also necessitate that you become familiar with her signature— or do I mistake the matter?"

Calculation, or recalculation, filled the ensuing silence.

"I recognize this as her signature," Belcher said, visually dismissing Xavier as the lackey brought along to serve as a witness. "I do not encourage my clients to act in haste following a bereavement, Mr. Dorning. One's judgment at such a time—"

"Miss Fairchild's guidance is quite clear," Dorning said. "Deems has served long and loyally and has earned his recompense. With the death of Lord Fairchild, the butler should all but expect to be granted retirement. That you have not suggested pensioning him surprises me. Good help becomes much more difficult to hire as the Season advances."

Xavier had had to point that out to Dorning, who probably thought trustworthy butlers sprang from the head of Zeus on command.

"I will send to the agencies," Belcher said on a sigh. "When we have a replacement in hand who can meet the standard Deems has—"

"Deems will be given the happy news tomorrow morning," Dorning said, rising, "and he will be free to quit the metropolis by sundown. You will deal with the bankers this afternoon, and Miss Fairchild has already chosen Deems's replacement. Thank you for giving this matter your utmost attention, Belcher. I will be sure to remark your attentiveness when next I am in conversation with my brothers. Miss Fairchild is available should the bankers need any signatures from her, though of course they will have to call on her privately, given the circumstances."

Dorning beamed lordly benevolence at the solicitor and gave Xavier a moment to bow as well. Xavier adopted the demeanor of a well-mannered aide-de-camp embarrassed by his superior officer's high-handedness and left the interview without having uttered a single word.

"That went well," Dorning said. "You are correct, though, that something doesn't smell right. Why would Belcher drag his feet implementing a predictable decision on Catherine's part when she's in a position to sack *him*?"

That had not occurred to Xavier. "With two estates to settle, she'd sack her solicitors?"

Dorning rested his walking stick against his shoulder. "Lady Fairchild's late brother is the source of most of Catherine's wealth. Using her maternal family's solicitors for the estate matters makes more sense than sticking with Lord Fairchild's firm."

"Because Catherine is illegitimate?" Xavier asked.

"Because *the money* comes from the maternal side of the family," Dorning said. "Those solicitors are already familiar with the investments, the real property, the contractual obligations. Belcher has no grasp of those factors, and why should Catherine pay for his education?"

"She should not. Do you know which firm her uncle used?"

"I can find out, or you could simply ask her."

On the far walkway, Lord Fortescue parted from his companion and dodged vehicles to cross the street. He nodded to Dorning, passed an indifferent glance over Xavier, and let himself into Belcher's office.

"You don't care for Lord Fortescue?" Dorning asked.

"He buys good brandy and doesn't pay for it," Xavier said as a breeze scented with horse droppings wafted by. "Loses the invoices, swears he sent along payment, then orders more. I do not do business with him, and I warned Goddard not to do business with him. By mutual agreement, the colonel and I are both out of whatever vintage Lord Fortescue needs."

"Don't be too hard on the fellow," Dorning said. "We younger sons don't have it easy. For all that Armbruster's a dashing blade turned out in the first stare now, his nickname at school was Lord Fartescue. Lord Fart for short."

The English did have their endearing qualities. "What was your nickname?"

Dorning swung his walking stick. "Dimwitted Dorning. Don't tell Jeanette. I was never much of one for the books. You'll be at Angelo's on Tuesday?"

"Depend upon it, and by the time I am done with you, you will be able to best all six of your brothers at once."

"I already can," Dorning said, assaying a roguish smile, "with my rapier wit and my signature charm. If I could beat Ash with foils from time to time, I'd be forever in your debt."

Xavier bowed. "Consider it done, and my thanks for your assistance today."

"You will explain the situation to Catherine?"

"Most assuredly."

"Until Tuesday, then." Dorning saluted with his walking stick as he would have with a foil and strode off.

Xavier turned his steps in the opposite direction. *Lord Fart.* He would pass that appellation on to Goddard, who had a former soldier's fine, if irreverent, sense of humor.

Though why would a lordling who did not pay the trades number among Belcher's callers? Xavier let that question drift to the back of his mind as he spied a footman out walking some nearby household's pet canine.

A fine, sizable beast with a silky coat and waving tail. One of the Dorning brothers raised and trained dogs, then sold them for exorbitant sums to dandies and Corinthians, also to lonely dowagers and spinsters.

Xavier liked dogs, but then, he liked cats and horses too.

He also, somewhat to his dismay, liked Catherine Fairchild. On that thought, he crossed the street and took himself in the direction of Soho, where he was certain to find decent French cuisine and the music of his native language spoken in all its delightful variety.

"You have a caller." Deems held the card tray out to Catherine, though his air of injured dignity spoke more articulately than the violet lettering on the linen stock. "I again reminded Monsieur that this is a house of mourning and further indicated that the hour is inappropriate for a condolence call. His reply was less than well-mannered."

Good for Monsieur. "You will please show him in."

Deems drew himself up, then left Catherine's private parlor with a disparaging glance at the window she'd opened.

Le vieil âne. She'd found Fournier's characterization of Deems fortifying. Monsieur's presence in her parlor was a tonic of a different magnitude.

"If you please," he said to Deems, "a tea tray is in order. You will be sure the kitchen uses a proper quantity of leaves this time and sends along a few sandwiches. The noon hour approaches, and Miss Fairchild's appetite must not be neglected."

Deems pokered up again. "Anything else, *miss?*"

"Thank you, no."

The look Deems gave Fournier should have withered the ferns potted beneath the window. The butler withdrew on a single shallow bow aimed in Catherine's direction.

"He was never this bad when my parents were alive," she said, rising and offering Fournier her hand. "Papa said Deems lent the household consequence, so Mama and I put up with him."

Catherine wasn't wearing gloves, and too late, she realized Fournier wasn't either. Such a warm grasp he had.

"You have not yet given Deems the happy news of his impending retirement. Wise of you. The element of surprise should never be surrendered lightly. I found this among the post at the front door."

He passed over a sealed missive, no return address.

"You snoop through my mail now?"

"Somebody does, else why leave those letters lying on the sideboard hours after they arrive? This is from Mr. Belcher, I believe."

Catherine looked more closely at the letter. "How can you tell?"

"That is a clerk's fine hand on the direction. The paper is good quality, but not too good, and also clean, meaning it was delivered by messenger from somewhere in London. No franking, no postage due. Besides,"—one corner of his mouth kicked up—"I prevailed upon Mr. Sycamore Dorning to accompany me when I delivered your note to Belcher's offices yesterday."

Catherine resumed her seat. "Involving the Dornings was a very great presumption on your part, monsieur." How did she feel about that? She knew Sycamore Dorning in passing, knew he was protective of his wife and family and that he ran a gaming hell doing business as a fancy supper club.

What did it say about Catherine's life that her half-brother dwelled a few streets away, and her knowledge of him was limited to a handful of sentences?

"May I?" Fournier gestured to the wing chair.

"Please do have a seat."

"I did not presume so much as I exercised strategic deference to a man in a better position to gain Belcher's attention. Dorning issued Belcher's orders in a manner Belcher understood. That little letter should confirm that a pension account has been set up for Deems at the Wentworth bank, payments to be sent wherever Deems pleases. You have only to explain his good fortune to him, and he's off to enjoy a well-earned reward."

"And what am I to do for a butler until I can hire one from the agencies?"

"Do you need a butler?"

Not a question Catherine would have thought to ask. Many households made do without, particularly households having few social obligations.

"I have two footmen, an underfootman, a potboy, a gardener who doubles as our man-of-all-work, plus a groom, undergroom, and coachman. That is eight male staff who must look to somebody to settle their squabbles and hand out their pay packets. Somebody must count the silver and inventory the wine. Somebody must ensure the footmen apply themselves to their tasks rather than to dicing away the afternoon at The Boar's Bride."

"And you," Monsieur said, "are itching to be that somebody."

Catherine looked about the parlor, the one room in the house where she'd insisted on imposing her will. No crepe covered the mirrors, no black silk bands adorned the silhouettes of Mama and

Papa hanging over the sideboard. The clock ticked along rather than remain frozen at the hour of anybody's death, and a vase of daffodils graced the quarter shelves.

"When we lived on the Continent," she said, "I grew accustomed to organizing my father's household. A diplomat entertains a great deal, and we had to rely on what local staff were willing to work for an Englishman. Mama was sick for some time before she admitted anything was wrong—probably for years, now that I think back on it—and I took over her duties to the extent that I could."

A tap sounded on the door.

"Come in," Catherine called. The tea tray had been entrusted to Harry, the first footman. He was young, blond, and on the tall side. A credit to his livery, as Mama had said. He set the tray before Catherine without even looking at Fournier, though Fournier was doubtless taking in every detail of Harry's person.

"Thank you, Harry, that will be all."

He bowed and withdrew.

"That one is in love with you," Fournier said.

"You shall cease making shocking declarations for the sheer deviltry of it. Harry can't be but eighteen years old. He falls in love on the hour, to hear my housekeeper tell it."

"Then your hour has come, and you might as well enjoy it. Shall I pour?"

"Please." Enjoy a footman's infatuation? Catherine was beyond such folly, though she did enjoy Fournier's audacity. While he navigated the tea tray with careless grace, Catherine read Belcher's letter.

"Sycamore made an impression," she said, putting the letter aside. "I am reminded that in future I need only send along a note, and my devoted solicitors will deem it their greatest privilege to see to my needs."

"Unctuous words," Fournier replied. "How much honey do you prefer?

"Just a drop to smooth out the bitterness."

He fixed her tea in silence and passed over the cup and saucer.

Another brush of warmth, accompanied by a glance that took far too much notice of Catherine's word choice.

"Are you bitter, Miss Fairchild? A double loss such as you've suffered could have that result."

Oh yes, she was bitter, but her parents' deaths had nothing to do with her grim outlook. She took a sip of her tea—good and strong—and thought about her reply. Fournier had a nose for falsehoods, so a version of the truth would have to serve.

Then too, she did not want to lie to him. She lied enough in the course of a normal day as it was.

"I took too long to realize Mama was ill. Papa knew, but he respected Mama's wishes to say nothing. He was somewhat older than she and had lived a vigorous life. His death took me quite aback. I had assumed..."

Catherine took another sip of tea, the only dilatory tactic at hand. "Yes?"

"Aren't you having any tea, monsieur?"

He poured a second cup, the steam curling up through the midday sunshine. "You assumed you had a secure place as your Papa's unpaid secretary, from which you could make a graceful transition into spinsterhood, *non*? Your mother apparently endorsed that plan, and I ask myself why. You are well educated, likely fluent in several languages. You have a fine grasp of world affairs. You are well-read and sensible. You are lovely—also wealthy now—and yet, your mother held out no wish for you to marry well. This puzzles me."

Catherine set down her tea cup rather than fling it at Monsieur's handsome, *puzzled* head. "I am not lovely. I am too tall and too"—she waved her hand over her person—"not-willowy, and my eyes are the wrong color. I do not wish to take a husband, monsieur. If your interest in my situation is motivated by matrimonial ambitions, you may leave now."

Fournier did a better job of dithering over a sip of tea than Catherine had. She watched while he silently rearranged arguments, chose tactics, and formed a battle plan all in the time it took him to drink, study the flowers on the porcelain saucer, and set his cup aside.

"France has been a mess for decades," he said. "Before the revolution, for most of Louis's reign, we were in a state of upheaval. Bad harvests, corrupt government, a king who turned up practical, to the frustration of his nobles, and fanciful, to the frustration of his subjects. Then the Reign of Terror, then the first White Terror. Bonaparte's greatest attribute was that he drew us out of chaos for a time, though now chaos has descended again."

"That chaos touched you." It had to have, and in a personal way. The French ultraroyalists were determined to wipe out any legacy of the revolution and the empire, but even they could not turn the clock back thirty years for an entire country.

Fournier rose and went to the window, standing so that he could see into the garden while Catherine could yet study his face.

"Napoleon understood that the wineries had value," Fournier said, "so my family fared better than most. We did what we could, but it was never enough, and sometimes... *On a des regrets.*"

One has regrets.

Yes, one did, and those regrets could make a woman churlish and ungracious.

"Finish your tea," Catherine said. "Have a sandwich, or the kitchen will mutter about presuming Frenchmen and food going to waste."

He lingered by the window, probably for form's sake. One did not tell Xavier Fournier what to do, a quality Catherine both understood and approved of.

"You should trust me," he said, resuming his seat. "Jousting with you is enjoyable, and I do respect your caution, mademoiselle. Nonetheless, you may be assured that, like you, I have no interest in matrimony. Like you, I have sufficient means that I look askance at anybody who seeks to curry my favor. Like you, I cannot tolerate the company of fools. I have nothing to gain by taking an interest in your situation, and besides,"—he passed Catherine a plate and held out the tray of sandwiches—"the Dornings would ruin me were I to serve you a bad turn."

Catherine chose two sandwiches of watercress, butter, and soft cheese. Now that food was before her, she was hungry.

"They cannot call on me, but they can ruin you?"

"Most assuredly. Sycamore Dorning is married to the sister of one Colonel Orion Goddard. Goddard runs Dorning's fancy club, and he also owns vineyards. Goddard is assisting me to learn the new technique for making champagne. His champagne sparkles, mine has bubbles. My English is not adequate to describe the difference, but his champagne is far superior to the eye, if not the palate. Should Goddard take me into dislike, I am finished as a London wine merchant. His clarets cannot compare to mine, but he is an English war hero connected by his sister's marriage to a large and titled family. I am merely a homesick Frenchman."

Catherine ate her sandwiches and considered that speech, which appeared to adhere to relevant facts.

"Are you truly homesick?"

He topped up her tea. "In the manner you miss your mother, I suppose. Her passing leaves a terrible void, but you would never have wished to prolong her suffering. I miss France, but I do my part here, building a London business that helps me rebuild what was lost in France."

An interesting analogy. "Except that you can travel to France anytime you please." Or could he? Royalists, republicans, and revolutionaries had each taken turns in and out of power in France, meaning everybody was somebody's enemy.

Fournier rose. "Enough gloomy talk, mademoiselle. I brought along somebody I would like you to meet. He awaits us in the mews, and surely you trust me enough to stroll with me in your own garden on such a pretty day?"

Catherine had learned not to trust charming men who professed to offer friendship. Still, Fournier had spoken honestly—the Dornings *could* ruin him—and she was sick to her soul of her own house.

"Let me fetch a cloak and bonnet," she said. "And you have my thanks for resolving the situation with Deems."

"Thank him profusely for years of loyal service, pass him a bank draft, and tell him a room has been reserved for him at your expense at Whitaker's Hotel."

"Has it?"

"Of course, though I doubt he will tarry long in London. I will await you in the foyer, Miss Fairchild." He bowed politely, while Catherine took another sandwich from the tray and used the back stairs to get up to her room. She did not trust Fournier, but she liked him.

She hadn't ever thought to like an unmarried adult male again. How odd that it should be a somewhat arrogant, homesick Frenchman who challenged her assumption.

CHAPTER FOUR

A man who would not see thirty again, who hadn't seen thirty for some time, had no business allowing a female to knock him off-balance. Fournier lectured himself on this topic as he waited for Miss Fairchild to descend from her bonnet-fetching expedition. He lectured himself at greater length as he escorted her into a garden with prodigiously high walls—seven feet at least.

Fournier approved of high walls. Better for privacy and for safety.

Though privacy and safety could become so much dreariness. Catherine Fairchild was the opposite of dreary. She was quick, forthright, and smarter than she wanted the world to know.

A conundrum, in other words. "The fellow I'd like you to meet is at the gate," Fournier said. "Waiting in the alley."

Miss Fairchild slanted him a look. "You would not try to kidnap me, would you?"

"Is that hope I hear in your voice, mademoiselle?"

"Somebody did try, during the Congress of Vienna. Holding the wives and daughters of diplomats for ransom became a sort of cottage industry in certain quarters. I believe all were returned unharmed, but rumors abounded regarding the perpetrators' motives."

"Miss Fairchild, I must compliment you on your highly original version of small talk. How were your kidnappers foiled?"

She paused to consider a statue of some heroically muscled Greek fellow preparing to hurl a discus.

"How did they stay on?" she murmured, gaze upon the statue's crotch.

Fournier took a moment to realize that the lady referred not to granite testicles, but to the cluster of fig leaves obscuring the same from view.

"They didn't. The Greeks competed naked, as I understand it. Those fig leaves are held fast by the glue of British prudery. Tell me of your kidnappers."

She patted the statue's *hip* and resumed walking. "My kidnappers were amateurs. I kicked one in his... fig leaves and brandished my peashooter at the other. Vienna is quite brisk in wintertime, so I carried a muff, an ideal place to conceal weapons. My footman did not do the expected thing and disappear at the first sign of trouble, though the kidnappers did."

She offered this recitation as if she were remarking the progress of the hyacinths blooming along the south-facing wall.

Hyacinths one shade paler than her eyes. "Those amateurs have probably been thanking *le bon Dieu* for their narrow escape ever since. I am not in the business of kidnapping fair demoiselles, fortunately for me and my fig leaves. If you would please wait here?"

Fournier was also not in the habit of becoming infatuated, not with young ladies. He'd allowed himself to fall for an exquisite Beaujolais nouveau two years ago. A superlative Merlot could still turn his figurative head, but he hoped a woman would never again have that honor.

The feelings that presaged such folly were all too obvious. A lightness of spirit when in the lady's presence. A tendency to consider her situation when absent from her. A curiosity about her that bore much of eagerness and not enough of caution. Attentiveness above and beyond the natural vigilance of any alert mind.

Joy limned with anxiety. Speculations about the future that had no basis in reality.

Catherine Fairchild could inspire much foolishness if Xavier were not careful.

She waited for him on the walkway as he'd asked her to, her black weeds a stark contrast to a garden bathed in spring sunshine. As much as mourning attire set her apart, her experience as a diplomat's daughter apparently did as well.

As did her eyes, so watchful and lovely.

Fournier opened the gate. "Caesar, come."

A stately mastiff trotted into the garden. He sniffed delicately at Miss Fairchild's hand, then sat on his haunches by her side.

"He'll lean upon you if you allow it," Fournier said. "The beast exudes such dignity as his species claims, then shows himself to be a shameless flirt."

Miss Fairchild stroked the dog's head. "He's majestic. His name is Caesar?"

Soulful dark eyes turned on Miss Fairchild as she spoke the dog's name.

"He's a wretched beggar, not an emperor," Fournier replied, closing the gate. "Caesar belongs to a friend, so please don't think I'm responsible for giving the beast airs above his station. My friend is preparing to travel with her spouse now that the weather is moderating. I thought you could use some company, and Caesar will mope for having been left behind."

He'd mope for about fifteen minutes, before his pathetic-puppy routine earned him a juicy bone from the cook, a nibble of ham from the footmen, a game of fetch-the-stick with the grooms, and a protracted brushing out from the gardener.

"Being left behind is awful," Miss Fairchild said. "How long can he stay?"

She pulled gently on the dog's silky ear, and Fournier had to look away. "Their Graces will be traveling until summer, though you could also send to Willow Dorning for your own dog."

The disgraceful cur was leaning now, his great bulk comfortably wedged against Miss Fairchild's leg as he doubtless got dog hair all over her skirts.

"This is a *ducal* pet?" She switched to the other ear.

"Right now, he is a lonely beast, abandoned to the indifferent attentions of a staff who were relieved to see the back of him."

The Duchess of Quimbey's housekeeper had harangued Fournier for a quarter hour about dear Cee-Cee's moods and crotchets. The butler's lecture had been even longer.

"I haven't a leash," Miss Fairchild said.

"You won't need one. He's that well trained. You tell him to sit, and he will sit until midsummer. You tell him to stay, he will still be where you left him until Michaelmas. He can guard, hold, fetch, and he knows the usual parlor tricks."

"What is the command for..." Her hand slowed. "Deterring an intruder?"

"'Attack,' though the dog will also make a lot of noise if you tell him to bark."

Caesar cocked his head and gave a soft woof.

"Good boy," Miss Fairchild murmured. "I've always wanted a dog. We never knew when Papa would have a new posting, or where that posting would be, so a pet wasn't possible. I can't imagine Caesar would enjoy the climate in Cairo very much."

Caesar's gaze had gone from adoring to besotted, while Fournier was jealous of a damned dog.

"He's enjoying your company already," Fournier said, "and thus I have accomplished what I set out to do. You will sack Deems today?"

"After the kitchen serves lunch, I will inform Deems of his good fortune and thank him for all his years of loyal service."

"And tell him that he has lodgings elsewhere for the nonce." That part mattered very much. If one wanted a villain to flee the scene, one had to provide him an escape route.

"You were very considerate, monsieur, to arrange for me to borrow Caesar. I would never have thought... That is..." Miss

Fairchild used the back of her hand to swipe at her cheek. "Caesar and I will get on famously. You have my thanks."

The other side of all those stupid, infatuated feelings reared its inane head: a horror of seeing the lady displeased or discommoded, an inability to ignore her suffering.

"I must apologize," Fournier said, passing over his handkerchief. "I did not mean to upset you."

"You have not upset me." She touched his linen to the corners of her eyes. "I am simply not at my best. A bereavement brings many adjustments, and I never anticipated one result might be to introduce me to a new friend."

She meant the dog. Fournier was almost certain she meant the dog.

"When my wife died, I was lost," Fournier said. "Gabriella was my everything. I have been years putting myself back together, but what choice does one have?"

"You were married?"

"I don't generally speak of it." He *never* spoke of it. Goddard probably knew, but Goddard was blessedly discreet. "In the last years of my marriage, my wife remained in France, while I spent most of my time in London. Thanks to the decimation of the French fleet at Trafalgar, Napoleon's blockade was not as formidable as it might have been, but I still wish..."

That he'd never agreed to leave Gabriella in France, tending to the vineyards and hoping the château would still be standing after the next wave of violence.

That he'd not waited so long to send Gabriella to her cousins.

That he'd had the wisdom to withstand the selfish impulse that had seen him married to her in the first place.

"I'm sorry," Miss Fairchild said, touching his shoulder. "You seem so self-possessed, the equal of any situation, and yet, I know such savoir faire is usually earned at a high price." She folded Fournier's handkerchief into eighths and tucked it into her pocket. "I hope she appreciated you."

"She did." Gabriella had appreciated more being lady of a fine château and then de facto supervisor of the winemaking. Even her boldness and confidence had appealed to him, at first.

"You have savoir faire too," Fournier said, knowing the change of subject was clumsy. "But that puts you out of the common mode in the society where you dwell. I think you might be happier on the Continent."

He would love to show her his home, love to walk with her in the cool of the morning as the mist rose from the river and the sun shone golden on the vineyards. That he could experience such longings nearly in the same breath as he mentioned Gabriella was astonishing.

Where guilt should have been, Fournier instead felt a measure of relief. Gabby had been gone for years, and she would not have wanted him to wallow. Then too, there was little of desire in these longings, just enough desire to confirm that Fournier's animal spirits had not expired along with his wife.

"I did enjoy my time abroad," Miss Fairchild said, "and I will enjoy getting to know Caesar. I am in your debt, monsieur."

"Friends do not keep a tally of kindnesses, Miss Fairchild, and it is Caesar who is in my debt—and yours." A fine little exit line, so Fournier bowed. "I will be on my way. Send to me if you have need, and thank you for extending your hospitality to Caesar. If he becomes troublesome, I will escort him back to his home."

She walked with Fournier to the gate, the dog panting at her side. "And if I merely want to see a friendly face? If I long to stroll my garden while recounting attempted kidnappings and admiring nearly naked statues? Must I have *need* of you to gain your notice?"

She had his notice, and that was not a good thing. "One does not want to intrude."

"You excel at intruding. You are rather like Sycamore Dorning in that regard."

Fournier paused at the gate and mustered his reserves of charm. "I am tall and dark-haired, but that is where my resemblance to your brother ends. To suggest otherwise will provoke me to strutting and dramatic proclamations, which will only prove your point. Take good care of Caesar, and he will take care of you. I wish you good day."

He bowed over her hand, her fingers cool in his grasp.

"Will you call again?" she asked, keeping a grip on him. "Without a butler, I will be forced to purchase my own wine. You might as well agree to pay the occasional call, monsieur, lest I ambush you among your Merlots."

She had already ambushed him—among the Merlots, over the tea service, and all over again before the discus thrower.

Fournier was reminded that she'd chosen the Cahors for reasons he still did not understand, that she'd been loath to sack a butler who far overstepped his authority. Formidable Catherine Fairchild might be, but she was also without allies.

"I will call again," he said, "and we will tour your wine cellar, and there will be no need for you to lurk among my Merlots."

He bowed again and let himself out through the gate before he did something truly stupid, like kissing her in her own back garden, where any servant could witness him being once again lured into utmost folly.

"And who is this fine fellow?" Mrs. Trask extended a hand to Caesar. "He has the look of a lad who'd enjoy Cook's soupbones."

Harry followed Mrs. Trask into the library, a tea tray in his hands, wariness in his eyes.

"Caesar is on loan to me while his owners travel," Catherine said. "Thank you, Harry. Tray on the desk, please. You may leave the door open, and if you'd welcome any callers, I'd appreciate it."

Catherine wanted this exchange with Mrs. Trask to be overheard, and leaving the door open would accomplish that end. Deems had left the library on a frigid bow not a quarter hour past and had gone directly to his quarters, where he was doubtless packing his effects.

Harry set down the tray, bowed, and sent Caesar another dubious glance.

"Caesar is very well trained," Catherine said, "and I'm sure Nevin will be happy to take him for the occasional outing." Particularly if Nevin, the undergroom, could use walking the dog as a pretext to stop by the corner pub.

"My Nevvie likes dogs," Mrs. Trask said, slipping into the chair facing the desk. "He and yon canine will manage splendidly."

Harry withdrew rather than argue with Mrs. Trask. She was Nevin's aunt, and he was the apple of her eye, much to the frustration of those who had to work with him. Nevin was cheerful, good with the horses, and willing to work as long as somebody stood over him the whole while and kept him from wandering away from the job.

"I know what you're thinking," Mrs. Trask said, laying a ledger on the desk. "Nevin's a slacker. He's not, but he's imaginative and has wanted for guidance. Puts me in mind of his mother. A featherbrain when she was young. You're very good to keep him on when I know you won't be using the carriage much for some time."

"He's young," Catherine said. "He has time to settle to his duties. Let's have a look at the accounts, shall we?"

Catherine's mother, during her husband's frequent protracted absences, had instituted this practice of reviewing accounts, as well as menus, with the housekeeper over a cup of tea. Catherine had endured the same exercise with Deems on a monthly basis—no tea— and found the undertaking more grueling than an archbishop's annual sermon on temperance.

Every expense, explained to the penny, every month.

Mrs. Trask, by contrast, passed over her ledger book and left it to Catherine to raise questions. They shared a tea tray and chatted about menus and the household staff in general.

"I've retired Deems," Catherine said when the accounts had been dealt with. "He's earned his pension and then some, and I'm sure my parents would want him to have some time with family after all his years of service."

He'd not actually been with the Fairchilds that long—only since their return from Vienna—but he was old enough to be put out to pasture.

"Deems is a pensioner now?" Mrs. Trask looked neither pleased nor dismayed, but then, she was Scottish and practical to her sturdy bones. She was also a handsome woman, her red hair fading to ivory at her temples and her smile often in evidence. "He'll find another job, that one. Idleness is the devil's workshop. If he said it once, he said it twelve times a day."

"And yet," Catherine replied, "even the Deity idled away at least one whole day out of seven. A theological puzzle, I suppose."

They shared a smile, and all over again, Catherine felt the relief of having ousted Deems from her household. He'd truly been a blight, making all the burdens of mourning doubly oppressive.

"Will you hire another butler?" Mrs. Trask asked. "Harry would love to step into Deems's role, but our Harry was never permitted to assist Deems with the inventories and decanting and accounts. Harry would have a lot to learn."

And without a butler on hand, Mrs. Trask would become the undisputed senior domestic.

"We will have few callers for at least the next month," Catherine said, "and I'm sure our stores of wine will be adequate for the present. I haven't sent to the agencies just yet, but I likely will soon."

"Life goes on," Mrs. Trask said, finishing her tea. "We'll manage, as we always do, miss. That Frenchie who was here this morning sells wine. Makes it too. He's the one who brought the dog around, isn't he?"

No point denying what Mrs. Trask had likely seen with her own eyes. "Monsieur Fournier did ask me to look after Caesar for a time. You should know that Monsieur is a particular friend to my extended family. The staff is to show him every courtesy."

Catherine had no extended family in London, other than the Dornings.

"I've always liked dogs," Mrs. Trask said. "I like dogs better than I like most people, to tell you the truth. Should we anticipate any other changes to the staff, miss?"

A reasonable, if bold, question, but then, Mrs. Trask's forthright nature was part of her charm. No disapproving glances. No sermons about the price of candles. No subtle innuendo about stray dogs or handsome Frenchmen.

"You may assure the others their posts are secure," Catherine said. "I am grateful to have familiar faces around me as I grieve my mother's passing."

"You are very like her ladyship," Mrs. Trask said, organizing the dishes on the tea tray. "She wasn't one to suffer fools, but she was kind. The best sort to work for. I'll take these menus down to Cook, shall I?"

"Please do, and if Deems needs assistance with his effects, we will offer him that aid."

"Of course, miss." Mrs. Trask rose. "To be completely honest, Deems wasn't the most..."

"We will miss him," Catherine said, rather than encourage unkind talk. "He was conscientious in the extreme and competent in every regard. I have written him a character to that effect in case he wishes to pursue further employment, but my mother made it plain he had earned a pension."

Mama hadn't done any such thing. She'd left dealing with Deems to Catherine, claiming that Deems had a furtive air. Mama of all people would understand why Catherine had heeded Fournier's advice.

Mrs. Trask lifted the tea tray and rested it against her hip. "Perhaps the Frenchman can find you a new butler. French butlers are all the rage, and I'm told they abound on the staffs of the gentlemen's clubs too."

"Monsieur is merely a friend, Mrs. Trask. He is no stranger to grief himself and is truly a family connection."

Xavier Fournier was no stranger to deception either. He'd clearly lost the love of his life when his wife had died, and yet, to all appearances, he was the nearest thing to a bon vivant. Catherine was certain he hadn't meant to allude to his own bereavement, but she liked him better for having made that admission.

Trusted him a little more too, drat the man.

Mrs. Trask departed, taking the tray with her, and Catherine closed the library door. A fussier housekeeper would have left the tray for the maids or footmen, but by degrees and inches, Catherine was coming to realize that the house was no longer that of Lord Fairchild, diplomat and discreet international negotiator. Nobody need be fussy about much of anything, especially now that Deems had been given the sack.

Nor was the household that of his lordship's gracious, quiet widow.

The household was *Catherine's*, and if she chose to admit friends on the occasional social call, she had that right. Nobody could object to a near spinster taking tea with a family friend, could they?

"I'm lying to myself."

At Catherine's words, Caesar looked up from his place on the carpet.

"The simple truth is, I like Fournier. He is hard to shock, he doesn't judge, and his flirtation is the kind that need not be taken as flirtation at all." More like gentle teasing.

Caesar's expression went from inquisitive to vaguely worried.

"I know," Catherine said. "Friendship with him must go nowhere, but can't I enjoy his company in the odd moment? You are only on loan to me, and already, I am attached."

Had Fournier known how lonely Catherine had become? How hard she'd had to fight the temptation to hug the dog?

"I have correspondence to see to," she said. "More perishing letters of condolence no doubt." A diplomat's widow knew everybody, apparently. Some of the letters had come from Canada, Saint Petersburg, Greece... A few had come from royal courts.

"Perhaps I should go to Greece," Catherine said, retrieving the stack of mail from the tray at the corner of the desk. "Except I won't go to Greece, or anywhere else. I won't cause talk, as much as I am sick to death of pretending."

She sorted through the post, about half the missives bearing the black border indicating a card of condolence. The flood was ebbing, which was fortunate. Acknowledgments were a chore Catherine had to force herself to complete. She had sorted to the end of the stack— bills to the left, letters to the right—when she reached the limit of her willingness to deal in gracious, empty gestures.

"Come," she said to Caesar, putting both stacks aside. "I will introduce you to Nevin. As long as you don't mind stopping by The Boar's Bride on every outing, you will be walked as much as you please."

She made her way back to the garden, and rather than take Caesar to the mews, she tossed a stick for him and wished for the ten thousandth time that she had not been such a foolish young woman. What would Xavier Fournier think of her if he learned of her past?

She did not voice that question even to Caesar, even in the relative privacy of the walled garden.

"Nothing good could come of airing old linen," Catherine murmured, and yet, she looked forward to Monsieur's next call. Foolish of her, but she had the sense that as much as she longed for friendship and affection, Fournier did as well. She had little enough of either to offer him, though the truth was, she felt safer when he was on hand.

"I have it from no less authority than Mrs. Sycamore Dorning that you need to get out." Fournier injected an apologetic note into his statement. "I must agree with her." Miss Fairchild looked a trifle wan compared to when he'd seen her earlier in the week.

Not tired, exactly, but daunted. Her smile was gently forced, she relinquished Fournier's hand at the earliest instant, and she was wearing the same dress she'd had on three days ago.

Less work for the staff, to simply don the wrinkled attire. Fournier had told himself the same thing after he'd lost Gabriella. The British practice of condolence calls starting three months after a bereavement was probably an attempt to foil that self-indulgence.

"You need not check up on me," Miss Fairchild said. "I gave Deems his congé, and he went more or less without a fuss."

Deems was kicking his heels at Whitaker's Hotel. He'd had no callers and sent no mail. Until the man was ensconced in the household of some sister or cousin in the shires, Fournier would keep an eye on him.

"And has the household descended into chaos?" Fournier asked. "You are answering your own door, which even I can assure you is not the done thing."

"I was retrieving the post from the sideboard," Miss Fairchild replied a little too brightly, "and you seem to enjoy paying calls well before proper visiting hours."

A considerable pile of letters did indeed sit in a tidy stack on the sideboard, perhaps several days' worth. "The mail will have to wait, Miss Fairchild. I have been tasked with escorting you to Richmond."

Miss Fairchild's extraordinary eyes lit with some fleeting reaction. Confusion? Distrust? The emotion was gone too quickly to be accurately labeled, but Fournier's invitation was clearly unwelcome. How well he knew that resentment, that stubborn unwillingness to depart from safe, sad spaces and numbing routines.

"I am in mourning," Miss Fairchild retorted. "One does not go picnicking in the countryside when one is in mourning."

"If one did picnic in the countryside at such a sad time, one might find one's grief more bearable. As it happens, I do not offer you a picnic. I offer you greetings from Mrs. Dorning, née Jeanette Goddard, former Marchioness of Tavistock, who has some experience with bereavement."

He passed over a sealed missive. Miss Fairchild accepted it, though again, that hint of wariness imbued her actions.

"Come," she said, turning on her heel. "I can ring for a tray, and if

Mrs. Dorning's epistle merits a reply, you can convey it to her for me."

"My sainted mother would be so proud," Fournier observed. "I am an English post boy now. The realization of my life's ambitions is a dizzying achievement. I maintain my dignity in the face of this overwhelming joy as best I can. I beg for your understanding should I begin spontaneous saltation and whoopering, if that is the English word."

"You know it is not." Miss Fairchild pushed open the door to her parlor. She was smiling, so Fournier ceased his nonsense. "Sit if you like, sir. Shall I order tea?"

"We have no time for tea. We have an appointment to keep with your sister-by-marriage. Mrs. Dorning was quite clear that I am not to allow you to decline her summons. I told the lady that 'allowing' doesn't come into it, as you are very much your own person, but her ladyship—one still thinks of her as such—is formidable. Married to *cet homme*, she has to be."

"*That man* apparently did not know I was his sister until recently. Of all the Dornings, Sycamore is the one I can least expect to take an interest in my situation."

"He is the most exuberantly fierce of the lot. The others are formidable in different ways, as are their spouses, though I have not met the youngest sister or the Dorset farmer." Goddard had provided many of those introductions, at social events, hacking in the park, or in business contexts.

For a man who professed to be a gruff old soldier, Goddard could exercise surprising tact, but then, he was half French.

Miss Fairchild slit the seal and scanned the note's contents. "Mrs. Dorning says a marquess's widow knows all too well the pitfalls and temptations of early mourning. I am permitted to call on family, and she is my family. The day is lovely, ergo, to her Richmond abode I must go. I barely recall meeting this woman at some house party or other..."

"Well, there you have it," Fournier said, prepared to take the gloves off if necessary. "Sycamore Dorning's bad influence has inspired his wife to friendliness, and her a former marchioness. You would think the erstwhile Lady Tavistock would know better. I've met her step-son. The present marquess is young, but he knows an excellent Merlot from a presuming one. This is the hallmark of a true gentleman, and Mrs. Dorning was largely responsible for his upbringing. More evidence of her waywardness, for, as is known to all, English marquesses should be wretched bounders."

From all reports, Jeanette Dorning's first husband had been exactly that.

"I might have crossed paths with the current marquess in Paris," Miss Fairchild said, "but I am barely acquainted with Sycamore, and a drive to Richmond will take *two hours*."

"Then the sooner you change into a carriage dress, the sooner we can get you out of this stinking metropolis and into greener surrounds. Come, Miss Fairchild, the day is fine, my company is irresistibly charming, and you need to change your dress."

She smoothed a hand over her skirts. "Mama liked this dress."

"You wear aubergine quite well." The color brought out her eyes, an observation Fournier kept to himself. "I assure you my traveling coach is unremarkable. No crests, no bright red wheels, no liveried attendants. And you wear that dress day after day rather than add to the burden of the laundresses, or so you tell yourself."

He approached her, holding her gaze by force of will. "You take a tray rather than sit down to a proper meal on the same pretext. You ignore the post because every note of condolence is more proof of your loss. You promise yourself you will sort through your mother's things, but you simply sit among them, your mind blank, your heart aching. You sniff at her scent bottles, you might even go so far as to wrap yourself in her favorite shawl, but nothing and no one can bring her back. You fear if you begin to cry, you will never stop."

He had hoped to provoke his hostess into a display of temper, however ladylike. She merely regarded him, her calm unnerving.

"I have cried more than you or anyone else will ever know. Wait here."

Fournier bowed rather than retort. Miss Fairchild had given him an order, and considering how far he had pushed her, he owed it to her to wait as faithfully as would a slobbering hound longing for the merest touch of her hand.

CHAPTER FIVE

Catherine debated taking Caesar with her to Richmond, but when she came down to rejoin Monsieur Fournier, Harry told her that the dog was out with Nevin.

"Third time today," Harry said as Catherine collected a black cloak, black parasol, and a bonnet heavily veiled in black tulle. "In some households, walking a dog is an underfootman's job."

"That is a good suggestion, Harry," Catherine said, pulling on black gloves. "Let's divide the task between Nevin and Vincent, shall we? Vincent can look after Caesar until midafternoon, then Nevin can take over after most of the work in the stable is done. Caesar can have a ramble in the garden for his last outing of the night."

Harry gained two inches of height. "I'll explain the schedule to Nevin, miss, and to Vincent."

"Thank you, Harry, and please tell Cook not to expect me for supper. I'm off to visit family and will be gone for most of the day."

Harry had the requisite height and good looks expected of all footmen. He was also sensible, as the oldest of seven siblings had to be. He had not yet acquired the faultless discretion of a London domestic servant.

"But I thought... That is..."

"Come, Harry," Catherine said. "I do have family. Every person in this household knows it, and in the circumstances, that family has decided to be kind to me. Take the unplanned half day and enjoy it."

Harry smiled. "You sound like Mrs. Trask."

"I will consider that a compliment." Albeit an unusual one. Catherine draped her cloak over her arm and found Monsieur Fournier in the parlor, on his knees and peering at the underside of the desk's kneehole.

"French," he said, easing to his feet, "as I thought. The inlay is too lyrical to be English, the brass fixtures too ornate." He took Catherine's bonnet and parasol and set them on the sofa, then appropriated her cloak and swirled it about her. He completed that courtesy—or presumption—by smoothing the fabric over her shoulders in a light stroke of both hands. "This garment is not French. It does not murmur of a lady's grace with each step. It turns her into a peevish nun."

"I did not dye my favorite clothing black," Catherine said. "Bad of me, I suppose, but mourning does not last forever, and many of my best dresses are French. They cannot be undyed, and I cannot have them remade here in London."

Fournier came around to do up the cloak's frogs. "Mrs. Dorning informs me that first mourning for a parent is to last only a month, though second mourning is observed for six months. This strikes me as ridiculous. Is a woman to mourn a man to whom she has been married only a few years twelve times longer than she does the parents who gave her life, raised her, and loved her all of her days? Apparently so. I will never understand the English."

He understood them very well, probably better than Catherine did. "You will bring me home before dark?" She hated the nervous note in her question.

"Unless you decide to bide for a day or two with your family. In that case, I will see your household informed of your decision and commend your good sense for quitting Town. When you summon me, I will retrieve you from your respite if Dorning himself cannot return you to Town."

"Will it be a respite?" And why was she dithering over a simple excursion to the country? This call would involve sipping two cups of tea with Jeanette Dorning, admiring her garden, thanking her for her kindness, and tooling back to London. Fournier would be half amusing and half vexing for the duration, which was somehow exactly what Catherine needed him to be.

"I do not know Mrs. Dorning well," he said. "Her spouse clearly adores her—one of his few endearing features—and she has been through much at the hands of her first husband and his ilk. Society was unkind to her, the much younger wife of an arrogant nobleman, but she, being half French, ignored Society at the earliest opportunity. I suggest you do likewise."

"I try, monsieur. Shall we be off?"

He took her parasol and bonnet from the sofa, apparently content to carry them. "My carriage awaits in the alley, the better to protect your privacy. You must not be anxious, Miss Fairchild."

Catherine was not anxious so much as she was afraid, which made little sense. This call was also an acknowledgment of Mama's passing. Another acknowledgment.

"You tell me not to worry, when I hardly know Jeanette Dorning, she's a former marchioness, and I'm leaving London in a closed carriage with a man I barely know—and arguably bending the rules of mourning to do it."

Fournier accompanied her into the garden, and for a moment, the sunshine was blinding. Catherine was tempted to don her bonnet and parasol—seeing the world through a dark veil had become that much of a habit—but Fournier was right. The time for deepest mourning had passed, at least according to the rules.

"I thought you were a widow when I first saw you in my shop," he said, surveying the garden. "You are not a widow, but you had the same air. Widows are wary, Miss Fairchild. Life has delivered them a blow, and no matter a person's intelligence, confidence, or worldly means, the pain of that blow never entirely fades. The loss is deep and permanent and seems damnably unfair."

He escorted her down the steps, and Catherine again had the sense he'd said more than he'd meant to.

"You speak from experience."

"To my great sorrow, I do, but our objective today is to enjoy the fresh air and introduce you to Mrs. Dorning. What did she say in her note to inspire you to leave Town with me?"

"She said I wasn't to be cowed by polite society, or by the Dornings. An heiress must begin as she intends to go on, and anybody who'd begrudge me some fresh air and congenial company was of no moment."

"Half French. The pragmatism and independence of spirit shine through, despite the English preoccupation with protocol."

Mrs. Dorning had also said that Xavier Fournier was an old-fashioned gentleman, to be trusted in every particular. He was much respected by her husband and brother and by Jeanette herself.

Catherine respected Fournier, too, else she would not have let him hand her into his traveling coach, a sizable conveyance noteworthy for its outward plainness and inward luxury. He took the place beside her.

"I do not deal comfortably sitting with my back to the horses on these execrable English roads, if you will forgive my presumption."

Catherine was not about to admit that she liked having Monsieur sit beside her. "Compared to the French equivalents, English roads are awful."

Fournier deposited her parasol and bonnet on the opposite bench, along with his hat and walking stick. The coach rolled forward, and Catherine was seized by the impulse to leap to the cobbles and run back into the garden.

Fournier drew down the shades. "Nap if you like. We will be forever getting through the London tolls, but once we cross the river, the scenery will improve. We have food and drink, and should you take a chill, the lap robes are under the bench."

"I'm fine," Catherine said, though she wasn't.

"Of course you are." Fournier looped an arm around her shoulders. "I make a good pillow. Close your eyes, mademoiselle. You are safe, and you need your rest."

He followed up that shocking presumption with a little half hug, and some of Catherine's nervousness eased. Fournier did this—presumed, fussed, slighted the rules. She liked that about him, and his warmth was a profound comfort.

Catherine closed her eyes, turned her cheek against the fine wool of Fournier's coat, and felt slumber beckon. Caution railed at her from the tired depths of her mind. She was in a closed coach with a man she barely knew, et cetera and so forth, and all but snuggled into his embrace. Had Fortescue Armbruster taught her nothing?

He had taught her much, unfortunately, but she was no longer an infatuated girl, and Xavier Fournier was not a lying schemer. He was honest, blunt to a fault, and a very comfortable pillow.

When Catherine woke, she was wrapped in the circle of Fournier's arms, his chest rising and falling in a slow rhythm beneath her cheek. She kept her eyes closed and her breathing even halfway to Richmond, because she was that loath to part with his embrace.

"The ladies seem to be getting on at a great rate," Colonel Orion Goddard observed, as his boots crunched the crushed white shells of the walkway. "Miss Fairchild apparently has some menus from her time at the Congress of Vienna. My Ann will not rest until she gets her hands on copies."

Fournier should have known that Mrs. Dorning would have included Goddard and his wife in her plans for the day.

"Your wife is the only English cook I know who can prepare French cuisine so it tastes French," Fournier said. "How long can three women spend over a teapot?"

"Eternities," Sycamore Dorning replied, turning down a shorter path that led to an enormous glass house. "Jeanette claims if we want to bring London to a screeching halt, we need not close down the gin palaces. Simply cut off the supply of tea." He opened the door and led his guests into the glass house, where tables of potted greenery stretched from wall to wall.

The air was warm, humid, and redolent of dirt—a good smell to a man longing for his vineyards.

"You don't think brandy figures in London's smooth functioning?" Goddard retorted. "Fine wine, beer, ale?"

"He does not," Fournier said, counting six gardeners, all busy at their work. "Dorning's universe is defined by his wife's wellbeing. All the brandy in the world would not put him to rights if his darling lady grew fretful."

Dorning slanted him a look. "Did somebody best you at foils, Fournier?"

"Angelo might," Fournier replied, "if I'm having a slow day, though his age is showing too. What all do you grow here, Dorning?"

The gentlemen had left the ladies to their scandal broth, ostensibly so their host could provide a tour of his crop garden facilities. Watching beans grow had to be the least interesting excuse for allowing women some privacy, but Fournier had craved movement—and some distance from Miss Fairchild.

"We're still sorting out what we should grow," Dorning said. "My family has a thriving business selling scents and botanicals, but our holdings in Dorset lack proximity to London and have only one modest conservatory to serve as our propagation house. I'm inclined toward flowers, Jeanette argues for medicinals, and Ann Goddard demands culinary herbs, spices, and vegetables."

"Vintners face a similar dilemma," Fournier said, brushing his fingers over a potted bush of rosemary. "Which grapes to plant on which terrace, how much of each variety, when to harvest each kind... One guesses and God laughs, but some good wine is made every year."

"You must miss your home, Fournier," Dorning said, while Goddard characteristically remained silent.

A gardener approached, an older fellow wearing the leather apron of his trade.

"What is it, Morton?" Dorning asked.

"Sorry to intrude, sir, but if you could have a look at the cold frames, you'd save us a lot of arguing. I say they must not be too deep, or we'll waste the manure, while Higgins wants us buried in horseshite."

"Can't have that here in Richmond as well as in Mayfair." Dorning saluted his guests with two fingers and loped away between tables of potted spices.

"And he's off," Goddard muttered. "His energy alone tires me, but then, he's young and in love."

"And you aren't?"

"I'm old and in love," Goddard said, though he was of an age with Fournier. "How's business?"

They frequently compared notes regarding the wine trade, an enjoyable exercise in cadging information from a competitor and honestly commiserating with a colleague.

"Business is brisk, as one expects this time of year. What do you know of Miss Fairchild?"

Goddard ambled along the rosemary bushes. "Her late father was a diplomat by trade, probably a spy, seemed a decent sort. Went where he was told to go, didn't put on airs. Most of the diplomatic types are canny people—the men, the women, their children, and employees. Miss Fairchild was the dutiful daughter, not too pretty, not too outspoken, when anybody was looking."

"Was she also a spy?"

"I doubt Lord Fairchild would have stood for that. Nor would Lady Fairchild, though I am confident Miss Fairchild has the requisite ingenuity. She is half Dorning, after all. Why the concern?"

"The lady is wary." Perhaps even afraid? "Her butler was tyrannizing the household, her solicitors are arrogant, and she is new to her wealth." More than that, Fournier could not say, because he was probably in thrall to overly active instincts.

"Loss of a parent, particularly the second parent, is an adjustment," Goddard said. "The acquisition of unexpected wealth is an adjustment. Even unexpected happiness is an adjustment."

Goddard had switched to French, either out of consideration for Fournier's natural inclinations, or because they approached an under-gardener apparently working on grafts. The young fellow touched the brim of his cap and went back to his slicing and tying.

"Miss Fairchild's mother had been ill for some time," Fournier said. "Her father was elderly. She was an only child. She was bound to inherit some wealth and bound to lose her parents. I would expect her to be sad, but why have the diplomatic ladies not flocked to her side? Where is her priest? Why did the Dornings not even look in on her?"

"I'm sure you will share your theory."

"I cannot speak for the Dornings, but I suspect Miss Fairchild has trained all of creation to assume she is self-sufficient. She does not make friends easily, though she makes flawless conversation. She doubtless dances exquisitely, but does an even more creditable job sitting among the wallflowers and listening to dowagers trade recipes for their tisanes. This is a woman who has learned to hide in plain sight."

And Fournier knew exactly how it felt to wear a disguise the live-long day, to go about as a jovial and harmless French shopkeeper while ignoring a childhood and youth steeped in violence and tragedy.

Goddard paused before a vine twining around a wire frame to snap off a green bean and pop it into his mouth. "The taste of summer, but not exactly. Perhaps the taste of longing for summer."

"Does Mrs. Goddard know she married a romantic?"

"Mrs. Goddard *is* a romantic. Tell no one."

Before the colonel's marriage, he'd been a stranger to whimsy. Now he smiled occasionally, and when his gaze rested on his wife, he was a man besotted. His champagne would likely reach new heights of glory, because vintners were human, and their products could reflect their fates.

"Back to Miss Fairchild, Colonel. Could she have come across secrets in the course of her father's diplomatic work?"

"Of course, but why not simply ask her, Fournier? When you wish to be, you are as blunt as Dorning on his most determined day. If Miss Fairchild trusts you to escort her from Town, she must have your confidence to some extent."

The ride out from London had been a revelation. Fournier had lied, of course. He cared not whether he sat on the forward- or backward-facing seats, rode on the box, lounged on the coach roof, or clung to the boot. Coach travel was coach travel. One endured until one reached the desired destination.

But he'd wanted to sit beside Catherine Fairchild, to bask in her proximity, to offer her closeness to another human being. He had not planned to put his arm around her, but the gesture had felt like the sort of presuming, not-quite-rude gesture Monsieur Xavier Fournier would make, and the lady had allowed his forward version of friendship.

She had rested against him, sleeping for a time—he was sure of that—and then awakening and pretending to sleep yet more.

"I could ask her," Fournier said, "but one does not want to overstep." Not with Catherine Fairchild.

"One does not know what the hell to do when an absolutely unexpected woman knocks one arse over teakettle. I did wonder about you, Fournier."

"Are you being vulgar, Goddard?"

"I assumed you had a family in France, perhaps an irregular union. Some widowers vow not to remarry. If you'd made your late wife such a promise, you would keep it."

"Gabriella was practical. She would never have demanded that of me." Nor, to be honest, would she have deserved such pointless devotion.

"Miss Fairchild is practical too," Goddard said, "but you don't want to put her off by being overtly protective, so you lurk in glass houses, interrogating her family connections."

Fournier could dissemble, gather up a few fig leaves of dignity and discretion, but Goddard was nearly a friend and he was absolutely trustworthy.

"I was insufficiently protective of my wife. Gabriella is dead because I trusted too much to her confidence. She ran the château while I managed affairs in London. That was her scheme for getting through the war, and I acceded to it. I waited too late to send her to safety, and by then... she had lost the knack of listening to me, not that she'd ever been very good at it."

Goddard munched another green bean. "I thought your wife died of influenza."

"That's what everybody thinks who even knows I had a wife."

Goddard waited, but Fournier had already disclosed more than he'd intended. "Suffice it to say, I am concerned for Miss Fairchild. If I am too insistent about my worries, she will give me my congé. If I am too deferential, I will be useless to her."

Goddard plucked another bean and resumed ambling between the rows of tables. "Are you building dungeons in Spain, Fournier? What is the worst that could happen to her? She can hire all the burly footmen she pleases, bar her windows, entrust her wealth to three different banks, arm her grooms."

The question was helpful, because it clarified Fournier's thinking. "Whatever concerns her, it has nothing to do with her wealth. I expect she'd rather not have inherited from her uncle and will end up giving much of that money away."

"And your revolutionary principles admire her for that."

"My human heart admires her for that. Children starve daily in London, or die for want of a blanket, as you well know." Goddard looked after a small army of children who were otherwise at large on London streets, and they, in their way, looked after him.

"If you think somebody wishes Miss Fairchild harm," Goddard

said, "I will put the word out among my eyes and ears to keep watch. I can ask MacKay to do the same with his streetwalkers and send word to Powell's connections among the old soldiers."

MacKay and Powell were cousins to Goddard, also former soldiers with pronounced charitable interests. Fournier knew them casually, having played cards with them at the club, filled their wine cellars, and occasionally socialized with them.

"Thank you."

He emerged from the glass house into spring sunshine. Goddard pulled an eye patch from his pocket and tied it around his head.

"The hardest thing about all the years I was in disgrace," he said, "was keeping my distance from my sister. Jeanette thought I did not care, that I wanted nothing to do with her, when it was my fault she'd married that devil Tavistock."

"Your fault?"

"Her marriage settlements included buying a commission for me in addition to paying off our father's debts. She thought Tavistock was being generous when he was, in fact, making sure Jeanette had no allies in London."

"And after the war, you were in disgrace," Xavier said slowly, putting pieces together, "so you kept your distance and allowed her to think the worst of you."

"Something like that. You have no reason to keep your distance from Miss Fairchild, do you?"

A thousand reasons. "Just the usual. I'm the wrong nationality, I claim no title, I am in trade, and she deserves better."

"No reason at all, then. Ask her what troubles her, and she might simply tell you if something was truly amiss."

No, she would not. She would smile, curtsey, and never speak to him again, which suggested the problem was damnably serious.

Goddard clapped him on the shoulder, and Fournier said nothing. He'd said too much already.

CHAPTER SIX

Lord Fortescue Armbruster paused inside the door of The Boar's Bride to give his eyes a moment to adjust to the gloom, and also to give the Bride's denizens a moment to gawk at him.

According to the matchmakers, he was more than an eligible, he was a fine catch. Perfect height, perfectly curling blond hair, perfectly arresting blue eyes, and a perfect physique. He also had a perfectly titled and wealthy marquess for a father.

This close to St. James's, the pub patrons were doubtless accustomed to fancy lordlings passing through humble establishments. The ale was cheaper in the unprepossessing taverns, the women friendlier, and privacy more assured than in fancier surrounds.

"A lady's pint for me," he said, sweeping off his hat and smiling at the plump, red-haired barmaid. She smiled back, though she couldn't have been more than fifteen.

"Aye, milord."

Armbruster's quarry was in the snug, and not alone. "What on earth is that?" his lordship asked, hanging his hat on a peg and sliding onto the bench opposite Nevin Thurlow.

"Mastiff," Thurlow said, smiling genially. "M' duties now include walkin' him from time to time until midafternoon, then one of the footmen takes over. Can't have a mere groom showin' off the beast for the carriage parade."

Thurlow was an undergroom, in point of fact, and not a very good one, if Armbruster's intelligence was accurate, and it nearly always was.

"Has Miss Fairchild taken a fancy to enormous canines?"

The dog was absorbed in watching the activity at the inn and ignoring Armbruster. A dull-witted beast, but handsome and vaguely familiar.

"Auntie says the dog is on loan to Miss Fairchild while its owners travel."

The barmaid brought over Armbruster's half-pint.

Thurlow's glass was predictably empty. "Another for my friend," Armbruster said, though allowing Thurlow to get drunk in the middle of the day would not do.

The barmaid smiled bashfully and trotted off.

"You lot," Thurlow said. "You crook your lordly finger, and the ladies all but lift their skirts for you."

"She's little more than a child." Besides, Armbruster had a fitting at the tailor's in less than an hour, and one did not keep a Bond Street tailor waiting for a mere passing tup, even if one had the coin for such an indulgence. Barmaids did not lift their skirts for free. "Tell me more about the dog."

"Don't know more about the dog. Auntie says he'll be good company for the young miss, and Miss Fairchild does seem to like him. Beast attaches hisself to Miss Fairchild if she's on hand, watches her like a lad in love watches his lady fair."

Armbruster knew how that felt. A wisp of gossip tugged at his memory. "One of the Dornings raises dogs. Fancy dogs. Teaches them to all but speak French. Won't sell them to just anybody. Is this one of Willow Dorning's dogs?"

Bad news, if so, the first, subtle indication that the Dornings intended to acknowledge their connection to Catherine, and that Catherine would allow them to.

"I don't know who owns the dog. I just know I can make an extra pass to wet my whistle when Caesar needs to lift his leg."

"Caesar?" The name rang a bell, a wealthy Mayfair sort of bell. "Find out what more you can about the dog's origins."

"His dam were a bitch," Thurlow said, "meaning no insult. His sire were a dog. What else is there to know?"

The barmaid brought over Thurlow's pint and set it down without sparing Thurlow a glance. He wasn't a bad-looking young fellow, and his smile was pleasant, but he was clearly nothing more than a stable lad slacking at midday.

"Whose dog is he? Who brought him to Miss Fairchild, or did she ask somebody to lend him to her? I pay you handsomely to ensure that I know everything that goes on in Miss Fairchild's household." Armbruster paid others handsomely for the same purpose, but Thurlow need not know that.

"You barely spare me coin for an occasional pint, and as for where the dog came from, the Frenchie brought 'im around."

"London is host to thousands of Frenchmen."

"This one sells wine."

"That hardly narrows it down..." Except it did. London hadn't quite as many wineshops as gin shops, and few of those wineshops had French proprietors of sufficient means to presume to call on Miss Catherine Fairchild in mourning.

"Did this fellow wear an eye patch?" Colonel Orion Goddard sold wine, managed The Coventry Club, and had a sister married to the youngest Dorning brother. The colonel was half French, spoke the language like a native, and might have fooled a lot of menials into thinking he was French.

If Goddard had brought the dog around, that was another thread connecting Catherine to the Dornings, albeit an attenuated thread.

"Not Goddard." Thurlow took a long, loud drink of his ale.

"Auntie said his name. Monsieur Forester or Fromador. I don't speak Frog."

Thurlow had all he could do to manage his native tongue. "Fournier?" That made no immediate sense, but Xavier Fournier had begun making inroads into polite society. He'd been admitted to a lesser club. He'd been invited to a few informal social gatherings. A typically shallow, pleasant émigré who probably sought only to peddle his wines to the better households.

The man could wield a blade, though. He was said to be so fast with a foil the eye could not follow his attacks. A parlor trick, that, useful for setting him apart and making him seem more accomplished than the usual shopkeeper.

"Mighta been Fournier," Thurlow said. "With Deems out on his arse, there's nobody to oversee the cellars, is there? Harry don't know port from porter, and the young miss can hardly march into a shop and buy her own wine. With that lot, the merchants come to them. She's still not going out much, come to that, though she went somewhere today."

"Deems was pensioned. He wasn't sacked." Or so the lawyers had claimed.

"He were sacked." Another pull from the tankard. "Called to the library and told to pack his things. Young miss were doubtless polite about it—she's always polite—but Deems were in a right temper when Vincent and me hauled his trunk down to the mews. Good riddance, I say. Auntie agrees."

Armbruster did not. Deems, with his stuffy airs, had served a purpose. "Where is Miss Fairchild off to?"

"Richmond. Harry tried to give me hell because she wanted to take the dog to the countryside. Happens Caesar and me was on one of our constitutionals when she left."

"But her coach is still in the mews." Armbruster knew better than to lurk in alleys, but he did occasionally detour from the main walkways.

"The Frenchie took her. Auntie says the Frenchie brought a note from somebody, and young miss were changing her dress not a quarter hour later."

Good work, Auntie. "Find out where she went, Thurlow, and mind you don't let that dog turn you into a sot."

"Caesar is a perfect gent," Thurlow said, lifting his drink a few inches in the dog's direction. "A true gent, unlike some what just has a title and a bit of blunt."

"We all need blunt, Thurlow," Armbruster said, draining a third of his lady's pint. "Don't ruin a good thing that means some of my blunt becomes your blunt. Find out where Miss Fairchild went today and why she went there. I'll see you again Friday."

Armbruster left a few coins on the table, collected his hat, beamed another friendly smile at the barmaid, and sauntered out in plenty of time to keep his appointment with the tailor.

Fournier was a nobody, but he was an ambitious nobody, and he knew Goddard, and Goddard was connected to the Dornings. The situation wanted monitoring. If Catherine Fairchild ever found herself in difficulties—true difficulties—the fewer allies she had, the better for Lord Fortescue Armbruster.

Catherine settled onto the well-padded bench of Fournier's coach, not sure what to make of the day's outing.

Tea with Jeanette Dorning and Ann Goddard had been lovely and daunting. Both ladies were involved in the management of The Coventry Club. Mrs. Dorning took a mostly administrative role, over-seeing inventories, auditing ledgers, and serving as Mrs. Goddard's sounding board on menu ideas.

Colonel Goddard apparently supervised the club's day-to-day operations—when he wasn't immersed in his own wine business—while Mrs. Ann Goddard had turned the Coventry's kitchens into the envy of the Mayfair hostesses.

Over tea, the ladies had offered Catherine condolences, and then the talk had been of food, of the entertainments at the Congress of Vienna, of the vast crop garden enterprise Sycamore Dorning had envisioned for his Richmond property.

"Was it difficult?" Monsieur Fournier asked, climbing into the coach after her. "To be sociable?" He hesitated between the benches.

Catherine drew her skirts aside, and he joined her on the forward-facing seat.

"To socialize was... not as simple as it should have been. A diplomat's daughter learns the knack of attending conversations with half an ear, of keeping track of several discussions while appearing raptly focused on only the one. These ladies did not allow me to gather wool while I smiled and nodded politely."

"They are *formidables*. Ann Goddard is passionate about her cooking. Jeanette Goddard is passionate about everything, especially about projects she undertakes with her husband."

The coach moved off at a smooth walk. "You distrust her devotion to Mr. Dorning?"

Fournier removed his hat and put it on the opposite bench next to Catherine's bonnet and parasol. "I envy Dorning and wish him and his lady only the best. I ought not to have presumed on your person on the journey from Town, Miss Fairchild."

Oh, drat him. He would ruin what had been a sweet and unexpected comfort. "You ought not to bring up what needs no discussion."

His gaze went from serious to impassive. "I will apologize for my forwardness."

"I reject your apology. Had your overture offended me, I would have made that known at the time. And do not think I am the sort to be fortified by a good scrap, Fournier. I saw enough of intrigue and posturing with my father's work on the Continent. Be honest with me, or be silent."

To Catherine's horror, tears threatened. This had happened when Fournier had given her Caesar—lent her Caesar—but dogs were allowed to provoke sentiment. Needless apologies were not.

"You are fortified by a good scrap," he said. "So am I, especially in the fencing salon. I can be passionate there at the same time that I am self-disciplined."

"You speak of fencing as if it's lovemaking." As a sheltered near spinster, she ought not to have offered such an analogy, though it fit.

"Have you been reading Latin poetry, Miss Fairchild?"

"Now you are changing the subject. You and I cuddled for a time, Fournier. I enjoyed it. Nobody touches me, beyond an impersonal, gloved hand to assist me from a coach. Even my lady's maid can get me dressed and undressed without so much as brushing my arm. Now, you try to convince me you are covered in remorse over mere friendly affection, which I find more insulting than if you had hauled me into your lap."

He muttered something in French about the English and their insistence on details.

"Remorse is not a detail," Catherine said.

He shifted from gazing at the greening countryside to studying her. "What have you to be remorseful about?"

Double drat him to darkest perdition. "Much. I should have noticed sooner that Mama was failing, for one thing." Even that was not Catherine's greatest regret. Mama had not wanted any fussing, just as Catherine had no patience for being fussed.

"A diplomat's wife would of necessity excel at dissembling." He heaved up a sigh, which managed to sound French of him, and resumed his study of the countryside. "I was married."

Ah, they were making progress. "You are a widower. Do you wish you'd been the one who'd died?"

"I was never quite that selfish," he said, "but I have wished many selfish things. Marrying Gabriella was selfish, and I knew it at the time."

"Shouldn't both parties feel they are getting the best of a marriage bargain?" Mama had claimed that was the ideal foundation, but then, Mama had been married only the once, and to a diplomat.

"Marriage is complicated. Marriage in time of war is both

abjectly foolish and profoundly courageous. Gabriella had the courage. I was the fool."

"The greatest fool in all of France no doubt." While Catherine had taken top honors in that category in Rome.

Fournier resumed his fascination with sheep, hedgerows, and pastures. "In every union, one spouse loves a little more than the other, or so I believe. Perhaps in a long marriage, they take turns. One is a trifle more convinced of the marriage's rightness. One is more *épris...*"

"Smitten?"

"Enamored, perhaps. I was enamored of Gabriella. Of her hearty laugh, her warm smile, her robust energy. She was *intrépide*. The English word 'dauntless' comes to mind. The women of France became inhumanly determined on their objectives as Napoleon conscripted every man and boy fit to march. The ladies were left to manage, and manage they did. I adored Gabriella. She adored my family's vineyards."

Oh dear. "I'm sure your vineyards are to be much admired, but your wife was an idiot."

Fournier took Catherine's hand and pressed a kiss to her gloved knuckles. "Thank you for that, but you are only half right. Gabriella and I were simply idiots in different ways."

Catherine curled her fingers around his, lest he think to retreat into platitudes. "Go on."

"Gabby was as good a wife as she knew how to be, but when an opportunity came for me to remove to London, she insisted I go. Napoleon's disastrous march to Moscow was in train, his resources spread too thin. His blockade was increasingly porous, and France was starved for coin. I brought a shipment of excellent claret with me to London, and it sold quite well."

"You were a smuggler?"

"I relied on smugglers for a time. I no longer do. When Paris fell, we thought our difficulties were at an end, but the squabbling—Bona-partists, royalists, ultraroyalists, republicans—became just as deadly as the wars had been. To eschew politics was to be universally judged a coward. I should have returned to France permanently, but Gabriella would not hear of it. I came and went, and we managed until the Hundred Days."

Catherine allowed herself to lean against him, though only a little. "You had no one to talk sense to you when you contemplated making an ill-advised match and nobody to inspire you when you wanted to reestablish yourself in your native land. No wonder you are a demon when you get a sword in your hand."

His arm came around her lightly. "Do you know why I held you?"

"Because you are kind and know much of sorrow."

"I hope I am kind, but that is not the reason I presumed."

Catherine snuggled closer. "This is not presumption. Foolishness, yes, but not presumption. When I step down from this coach, I will thank you for a pleasant outing, you will bow over my hand, and we will pretend our little cuddling matches never occurred."

"If that is what you wish." He sounded amused.

"That is how it must be. Why do you hold me?" And how did he know to do so with a perfect blend of casual unconcern and secure embrace?

"I hold you because I have not embraced a lady I esteem in too long and because to do so is precious beyond words."

That admission also had something to do with his ferocious fencing, but Catherine could not articulate the connection. She was too consumed with the pleasure of resting again, physically and otherwise, in the arms of a man she esteemed. She also, by slow, careful degrees, turned her leaning into a mutual embrace, her arm around his waist, and that was more precious yet.

Before Catherine climbed from the coach some time later, she kissed her escort.

They were both lonely, they were both burdened by regrets and losses, and yet, she allowed a little desire to lace what was otherwise simply a gesture of thanks and affection. She was not fortified by senseless arguing, but she was fortified by bestowing a kiss where she pleased.

To her delight, Fournier kissed her back with exquisite restraint, then preceded her from the coach and handed her down.

He bowed, she curtseyed, and he courteously waited until she'd slipped through the garden gate. Catherine tarried on the other side of the high wall long enough to hear Fournier instruct his coachman to go on without him, because he needed to stretch his legs.

She lingered in the garden, knowing exactly why Fournier had eschewed the coach. He wanted the memory of the journey to linger, as Catherine did. Though he'd been speaking French, she had heard the smile in his voice as he'd dismissed his coach.

No harm in a smile, no harm in a simple kiss or a cuddle. Absolutely no harm at all.

Though it must never happen again.

To kiss Catherine Fairchild again... Nearly a week after parting from the lady, Fournier allowed the joy and frustration of that thought to fuel his attack, and with a flick of his wrist, he sent Sycamore Dorning's foil spinning through the air.

"How the hell do you *do* that?" Dorning panted. "I all but had you, and then... How in flaming hell...?"

He accepted a towel from former Major Alasdhair MacKay, a substantial Scot and one of Jeanette Dorning's cousins.

"Fournier focuses," MacKay said. "You have half a mind on what your lady said over breakfast and the other half on whether you can grow grapes in Richmond."

Dorning scrubbed at his face and grinned. "It's not what the lady said at breakfast..."

Fournier had once had a grin like that. Love-drunk, befuddled at any hour of the day.

MacKay ambled across the room, retrieved the foil, and shoved

Dorning aside. "Watch, English bumbler. Even Fournier can lose his weapon."

Dorning stepped away. "Not a fair match. You've had a chance to observe Fournier on the piste for hours, while he's never seen you take up a sword. I flatter myself that I've tired him, and you are fresh."

"The match will be fair," Fournier said, amused and touched at Dorning's fussing. "Though perhaps not even." As he took his place opposite MacKay, he calculated the optimal result of the contest.

Dorning had been preoccupied. MacKay was absolutely correct about that. Unless he had a knife in his hand, Dorning was usually preoccupied. That scattered focus limited his fencing.

MacKay's family sold whisky—good whisky—making him a useful connection.

MacKay was a member of The Aurora Club, heir to some sort of minor Scottish title, and much given to aiding streetwalkers.

And Fournier liked him. MacKay's humor was pithy without being mean, he was devoted to his wife and family, and he could pull Goddard or Dorning into line with a raised eyebrow. Beyond all of that, MacKay had the eyes of a man who'd seen into hell, as many of Wellington's surviving soldiers did.

Fournier cataloged that list in the time it took him to salute.

"Very well," Dorning said as MacKay saluted as well. "*En garde! Prêts? Allez!*"

Fournier played a bit at first, and MacKay did too. Bow and curtsey, a flutter of the fan, a veiled glance. MacKay was good, he was focused, and he was keeping his strength in reserve. A worthy opponent, then. A little of Fournier's restraint fell away, and the real fencing began.

He made MacKay work for it, left only the smallest openings, and parried quickly, but not as quickly as he might have. MacKay's expression never wavered. Absolute concentration, utter fixation on his task.

Until, yes... There. He'd made the decision to try to disarm his opponent. He danced back a few steps, advanced, retreated... He was good. Somebody had taught him carefully, and when he sprang his trap, Fournier obliged by allowing his foil to go flying.

"I'm rusty," MacKay said, laughing. "I would never have got away with that if you hadn't been spanking Dorning all over the salon for the past hour."

"You are kind," Fournier said, extending a hand. "Though let it be said that Dorning occasionally spanks back. You are impressive, MacKay. Perhaps Dorning should be fencing with you."

MacKay's genial expression subtly shuttered. He was dark-haired, blue-eyed, broad-shouldered, and not precisely refined in appearance. He dressed as a gentleman, and his manners at table were those of a gentleman, though his asides over cards could be earthy. Fournier had liked him at once, if for no other reason than he was as skeptical of England's self-declared perfection as Fournier was.

Liking did not, alas, confer trust.

"I'm for lunch at the Aurora," MacKay said, signaling an attendant to collect the weapons. "I am in thrall to my belly, Fournier. If I go for too long without eating, I lose all my charm."

"He falls on his face," Dorning said. "Keels over like a drunken sailor. I cannot join you for lunch, though you must bear up manfully under that disappointment. The tyranny of business calls. Ask Fournier about clarets, MacKay, and he will talk you into a swoon before the soup course is removed."

"I am enthusiastic about my art," Fournier said. "Ask Dorning about growing basil, and you will see the same result from him."

"I am a Dorning," Sycamore replied, as haughtily as another man might have announced membership in the Most Noble Order of the Garter. "We have botany in our blood. Ferns are actually my passion."

The lovely Jeanette was his passion, that and knives. A man could have worse compasses to guide his life. "I will be pleased to join

Monsieur MacKay for a meal, and we will toast your basil, Dorning. My regards to your lady wife."

Dorning collected his discarded shirt and waistcoat. "She'd like to have Miss Fairchild out to Richmond again soon. One hopes you are willing to serve as escort?"

Would Miss Fairchild be willing to be escorted? *"Bien sûr. I would be honored."*

A quarter hour later, Fournier was ambling along the street at MacKay's side. MacKay nodded to no less than a half-dozen young ladies of dubious repute, and to one, he passed some coins.

"One hears that you are devoted to London's unfortunate women, MacKay."

"One hears that you are devoted to London's unfortunate Frenchwomen."

"And Frenchmen," Fournier replied. "Mostly, I worry about the children. As the offspring of émigrés, they are neither French nor English. No matter their parents' politics, any who fled to London are regarded with universal distrust in France and universal resentment in England. A difficult legacy."

"The English excel at sowing discord on foreign soil. Ask any Scot precisely how that works. We spent too much effort fighting amongst ourselves while the English sat back and polished their bayonets."

Real bitterness lay beneath that remark, real suffering. "You did not invite me to lunch to discuss Jacobite uprisings."

"You allowed me to disarm you."

Fournier could demure. An Englishman might have, rather than risk insulting MacKay with a lie. "You had earned the right to provide Dorning a demonstration. Sycamore could be a phenomenal fencer. He has the speed, the reflexes, the power, the flexibility, but not the mind. He can focus for a single throw of the knife, or a series of throws, but fencing requires *strategy*. I wanted him to see that I am not invincible. He can best me, though that feat will require a level of concentration he likely has only when adoring his wife."

"You echo my own assessment of the situation. My Dorcas would like you. We should have you to dinner."

Dorcas was the preacher's daughter who'd brought MacKay up to scratch. They were raising a child, though the boy's antecedents were shrouded in discretion. *Orphaned kin* was as much as Goddard had said.

"I would be honored to accept such an invitation."

"You're wary of such an invitation. Good instincts. I told Dorcas as much."

"My good instincts tell me that your purpose in inviting me to lunch is not entirely social."

"What do you know of Miss Catherine Fairchild?"

Families, whether French, English, or Scottish, apparently were the same in any country. They fretted, they talked, and they meddled.

"Dorning asked me to escort her to his Richmond property last week. The lady appeared to enjoy the outing."

"She's good at appearing. She and Dorcas are connected through charitable committees, and Dorcas called on her yesterday. A condolence call, but also... My Dorcas is serious-minded and loyal. Miss Fairchild does not suffer fools. They get on."

Said with the economy of the articulate Scot and alluding to a universe of husbandly mystification.

"And what has this to do with me?"

"Miss Fairchild mentioned that you had been her escort. She also mentioned that she's sacked her butler, and Dorcas reported that the lady is using the firm of Belcher and Sons for her legal business."

"The butler needed sacking," Fournier said. "He seems to have learned of Miss Fairchild's irregular origins and disrespected her for it."

"You know of those origins?"

"I suspect half of Mayfair does, thanks to her lovely eyes, and the other half will as soon as the lady puts off mourning. She's wealthy, her firstborn son will be titled, and she is the sort of quietly magnificent woman who can make other ladies feel inadequate."

Which—again—raised questions. Had Catherine truly been intent on poisoning somebody with the Cahors? Why? Could she have been intent on self-harm?

"In the presence of a formidable woman," MacKay said, "some of the ladies turn up catty. My father used Belcher's firm for his London business for a time. He no longer does."

"They are lax?"

"They are thieves, to hear him tell it. The usual overcharging for services rendered, but they would also under-report inventory delivered and sums paid, and over-report expenses. Their larceny is one of the reasons I spend much of my time in London handling the family business personally. Dorcas does not like to think of Miss Fairchild's fortune being managed by such as them."

MacKay couldn't abide the notion either, and Fournier, who had not liked Belcher on general principles, had to resist the urge to make straight for Miss Fairchild's garden gate.

"What do you expect me to do about a pack of crooked English solicitors?" The oldest Dorning brother was Earl of Casriel, a distinguished if impecunious title. Casriel was respected, no fool, and to all appearances took his role as patriarch seriously.

He was the ideal party to intervene on Catherine's behalf, but he had not yet come up to Town from Dorset.

"I expect you," MacKay said, "to come to dinner tomorrow night. A quiet, informal meal with a few friends. Miss Fairchild has agreed to come as well. Dorning will not be there—he's off to Richmond tomorrow—but Goddard and his lady will join us."

Fournier tried to consider angles and outcomes. Catherine was grieving, and appearances to the contrary, no lady was at her best when sorrow was new. She was the equal of greedy attorneys, Fournier was almost sure of it. But then, why hadn't she sent Deems packing? Why slip away to buy wine in the middle of a downpour?

Why tell Fournier, pointedly, that nothing could come of her casual indulgence in a little affection with him...?

Though then—most intriguing conundrum of all—she had kissed him. A sweet, tender, unexpected gesture of trust shot through with a tantalizing hint of hope.

"I will cheerfully accept your invitation to supper. For our next meal, might we not dine at a little establishment I favor in Soho as opposed to abusing our palates at the Aurora?"

"Aye," MacKay said. "Give me soup, sandwiches, and a bit of shortbread, and I'm a happy man."

Also a good man. Fournier did not generally take non-French guests with him to émigré establishments, but MacKay was a decent fellow, and Fournier wanted the opportunity to study him further.

The Dorning family claimed they could not overtly monitor Catherine's situation, but they were concerned enough to find intermediaries who could. Fournier was concerned as well, but that aside—clandestine purchases of black wine aside and untrustworthy solicitors aside—he simply wanted to again spend time with the lady whose parting kiss could have awakened the sleepiest of princes.

CHAPTER SEVEN

Supper with family connections was the next step away from mourning. Catherine did not exactly dread the prospect—she was quite fond of Dorcas MacKay—but neither did she look forward to it.

What to wear, what jewelry to choose, how late to stay... Mama had developed unerring instincts for how to dress for a part. Catherine had learned from her, though Mama's lessons had not encompassed the transition from first to second mourning.

"You have a caller, miss," Harry said, nearly startling Catherine out of her chair. Harry held out the salver, and Catherine was assailed by ambivalence. Caesar, sitting at her feet, also looked to Harry with a question in his doggy eyes.

She wanted to see Xavier Fournier again—she wanted to kiss him again, speak with him, hear his voice, see him, and more, truth be told —and she did not. He was temptation and consolation and deliciously wicked longings tied up with a lacy violet bow.

That ambivalence was not to be her most pressing challenge, apparently. The ink on the card was plain black rather than imperial purple, and the name was not Fournier's.

"I can tell him you are not at home, miss."

"I'm in mourning, Harry. Where else would I be? He'll just call again tomorrow if I dodge him today." Lord Fortescue Armbruster was nothing if not persistent when pursuing a goal.

"Shall I bring up a tray?"

"You shall. We'll show him every courtesy, and then he can congratulate himself on having looked in on the bereaved."

If that was his lordship's aim. Catherine had initially dismissed Lord Fortescue Armbruster as just another spoiled younger son drifting about the Mediterranean coasts in the manner of the peripatetic Lord Byron. Fortescue, by contrast, saw himself as a master of the subtle game, the bored sophisticate drifting from diversion to diversion, dropping philosophical asides and flirtatious smiles by turns. Whatever he truly was, Catherine had ceased to be a diplomat's foolish daughter.

She chose a wing chair, did not check her appearance in any handy mirror, and schooled her features to the pleasant civility Mama had taught her to summon at will.

"Catherine." His lordship stopped just inside the door, a mannerism Catherine detested. To an observer, Lord Fort would appear to be tactfully waiting to be acknowledged. In fact, he was doubtless assessing her, the décor, the dog, the housekeeping, and the most advantageous manner in which to complete his entrance.

And, should Catherine be so hen-witted as to again fall for his theatrics, he was allowing her a moment to delight in his manly beauty and rush into his welcoming embrace.

Caesar glanced from Fort to Catherine, then yawned hugely.

Lord Fort approached her, both hands held out. "How are you bearing up?"

She gave him one hand, rose, and dipped a curtsey. *Let the bearing-up begin.* "My lord, good day. You are among the first to offer condolences."

He kept hold of her hand, another of his favored bits of farce. "I am so sorry for your loss, my dear. I'm sure you miss your mother very much. Shall we sit? You do look a trifle pale."

Once upon a stupid time, Fort's earnest blue eyes, his gentle grip, his manner of standing just two inches too close, would have imbued his platitudes with a sense of genuine sentiment and intimacy. An old and cherished friend, coming to offer support at a difficult time.

"I am not your dear, Fort. But let's not quibble over trifles." Catherine took her wing chair, lest he attempt to sit beside her. How well she recalled the quivering excitement of mere proximity to the man who'd captured her heart, the illicit thrill of his arm bumping hers, his hand brushing her waist.

She had been so innocent, and so eager, and he had played her so well—then.

She offered him a relaxed smile. "How is your dear mother? Her entertainments are always a highlight of the Season." Not that the marchioness had ever invited Mama, much less Catherine, to those entertainments.

His lordship came down on the end of the sofa nearest Catherine's chair. "Mama is concerned for you, and I am to report to her immediately. Here you are, alone in the world, bereaved, your ties to Society few because your dear Papa dragged you over half the known world. You must know I'd worry."

The wretched varlet managed to sound sincere. "You can see I'm well, and I'm well looked after. If I have few ties to the polite world, that will mean fewer demands on my time as I adjust to my loss."

God bless Harry for all eternity, for he chose then to bring in the tea tray and set it on the low table. "Anything else, miss?"

"No, thank you, Harry, but don't go far in case Caesar needs some air."

Harry bowed, and to his credit, he spared Lord Fort not so much as a glance. "Very good, miss."

"You've become a lover of canines?" Fort extended a gloved hand for Caesar to sniff.

The dog settled to the carpet and put his chin on his paws.

"Caesar and I are keeping each other company for the nonce. His owners are traveling, and I have always wanted a dog. Papa's changes of post precluded that joy, so I'm especially glad to have the loan of Caesar now."

Catherine busied herself with the tea tray, adding the smallest lump of sugar to a cup of steaming China black and passing it over.

"You recall how I like my tea." His lordship's tone held approval and affection.

Catherine recalled the days when she'd lived for his next approving, affectionate word. She also recalled that Fortescue Armbruster snored. He'd made love with all the restraint of a hog going at the slop bucket, and he'd laughed at her assumption that she and he would be married.

Laughed. She passed him his tea without allowing their fingers to touch. "Keeping track of a guest's tea preferences hardly requires thought. Shortbread?"

"Please."

She held out the tray, and he—predictably—chose a slice, dipped it into his tea, and bit off the end while holding her gaze. He'd probably practiced that maneuver in the mirror while at public school.

What in the name of Drury Lane's worst farces had she ever seen in him? The question brought a backward joy, because it acknowledged both her foolishness and the fact that, of all men, Fort Armbruster would never again command her attention.

Catherine poured herself half a cup, a trick her mother had taught her. Fort would get around to some other earnest declarations before he'd finished his tea, and then he'd sidle up to the real purpose for his call.

Mama had said in Rome that Lord Fort had gambling debts and ran with a bad crowd. He'd likely been sent abroad in an effort to treat both maladies, but to no avail. He had not called when Papa had died, and his gracious concern today surely presaged some scheme that would benefit him.

"You can be honest with me, Catherine," he said, putting down his tea cup. "How are you getting on? One hears rumors, but rumors are often the opposite of the truth."

"What have you heard?"

"Fantastic allegations. That you have become secretly engaged to a Russian prince. That you inherited a fabulous sum from an uncle in the fur trade. That you are rolled up and will soon be in service. Tell an old friend how you're managing and whether there's anything I can do to help."

Two lies—three including that bit about being an old friend—and one truth. Uncle had been in the fur trade. How like Fort Armbruster.

"I will be comfortable and have no plans to marry any Russians. What of yourself? Is this the year your mother will see you marched up the church aisle?"

He winced. If such a thing could be done manfully, he doubtless aspired to do it thus. "Must you be so dismissive? What we had was special, Catherine, but at the time... I was an idiot. I was in disgrace with my family. I did you a favor by allowing you to keep your freedom, and matters turned out for the best after all."

Caesar rose to sitting, such that his head came up under Catherine's hand. She stroked soft fur, pulled gently on a velvety ear, and ignored the temptation to commit murder.

Fortescue Armbruster had *allowed* her the freedom to be ruined, allowed her to risk sending her family into disgrace for all time, and—would the cost never cease rising?—allowed trysting with him to blight her days far into the future.

"You were an idiot," she said. "We can agree on that much."

"I'm still an idiot," he replied, his smile crooked. "You are wroth with me, and I understand that. You suffered terribly for daring some pleasure, but can't we put the past to rest, Catherine?"

She had not dared pleasure. She'd been lured, step by step, from the path of safety. She'd been seduced, as ignorant, lonely girls had been seduced by arrogant cads from time out of mind. Catherine would likely never have seen the situation clearly, except that she had confessed the whole sorry tale to Mama, who had become incandescent with rage.

At Lord Fort and at herself.

Mama, I miss you. The sentiment came so quickly and forcefully that Catherine wanted to order Armbruster from the house and demand that he never inflict himself on her again.

But no. Fort Armbruster had a long memory for slights, and to him, a former lover turning up difficult would be a slight.

"The past has a way of coming back to life," Catherine said. "Mama often said that half of diplomacy was recalling which secrets to forget and which to hint at and when."

"Was Lady Fairchild a spy? One doesn't mean to be insulting, but that's a shrewd remark."

"I would not have known what Mama got up to when she wasn't hosting Papa's entertainments, or waiting for him to return from some overseas assignment. The whole diplomatic corps struck me as a keen and noticing group."

Too keen, too noticing.

"Do you miss those elegant parties? The clever conversation?" His lordship's unspoken question was, *Do you miss me?*

Catherine did not. Hadn't for years. "I met many interesting people abroad, but no, I do not miss the sense of rootlessness. The forming of attachments just as one is expected to leave for a new posting. The same adjustment with languages, with customs, with fashions. My parents had the knack for it, while I just wanted a dog."

And she'd got Fort Armbruster's flirtation and fumbling instead. A sorry bargain.

"Should I bring you a puppy, Catherine?"

Xavier Fournier already had, a splendid puppy with great big teeth. "No need. If Caesar and I suit, I can find myself a replacement when his owners reclaim him. I do appreciate your call, Fort, but you must not let me keep you."

Condolence calls were to be kept short. Besides, Catherine needed to decide what to wear to the MacKays' dinner. Bettis would argue with her about her hair, then spend an eternity doing her hair however Bettis pleased anyway.

"You always were more prone to solitude than other girls," he said, finishing his shortbread. "I will call again, Catherine, even though you might not find the delight in my presence you once did. That's normal, given our past, but now is precisely when a friendly face, somebody who truly knows you, can be a boon. Mama is still trying to marry me off, and it would not hurt your cachet to be seen on my arm."

Merciful God. "You would escort me?"

"I've always been fond of you, beyond fond, but I did not feel I could offer for you honorably all those years ago. I was under the impression you understood the limitations upon me as a younger son on the outs with his family and his creditors." He affected a look of guarded woundedness, as if Catherine was to doubt the facts of her own history simply because they offended his vanity.

He had *laughed* at her fondest dream. Hugged her and patted her shoulder.

"And now, my lord?"

If he professed undying love now that Catherine was wealthy, she would be hard put not to go off into whoops. Even for Fort, that would be doing it a bit too brown.

"I thought you could use a friend. Not all of Society will be happy that your sorrow has been leavened with good fortune."

"Very few know of that good fortune."

"And those few have not kept their mouths shut, my dear. If you ever have need of my good offices, you have only to ask."

Just a few years ago, he'd been a stripling sent away in disgrace, but time had been kind to Fortescue. An uncle had left him a competence, he'd learned some discretion, and his older brother's marriage remained childless.

For a flickering instant, Catherine considered humoring Lord Fort. *I could do worse.* Perhaps taking a titled husband—this particular titled husband—would ensure her past remained a well-buried secret. Marriage to Armbruster would also ensure that Catherine's husband would never be able to deceive her with professions of tender sentiment.

Perhaps Fort had grown up.

And perhaps pigs would take to the skies over Hyde Park. This was Lord Fort, despoiler of innocents and bounder of the first water.

He rose and drew Catherine to her feet. "I know your opinion of me is not what it once was, Catherine, but I am your friend, and you matter to me. I was a foolish young man, and I behaved abominably, but I can do better now. If you are ever in difficulties, no matter how insubstantial, you must apply to me. I know how to be discreet, and I do have connections."

He bowed correctly and only then pulled his gloves from his pocket and slipped them on.

The air of genuine remorse and newfound good intentions was convincing, but then, Fort excelled at making the appearances convincing. Still, Catherine could put the moment to some use.

"Were you discreet all those years ago, my lord?"

Blond brows drew together. "I hope I was. I know the situation became delicate, but I did not bear tales. I did not, as the saying goes, kiss and tell."

"But you did drink to excess frequently, carouse at length with other ex-patriots, and perhaps lament our situation in a sympathetic ear or two?"

He'd run with a crowd of similarly disgraced young blades, not all of them British, not all of them gentlemen by birth. The risk to Catherine's reputation had nagged at her for years.

"I would never bandy a lady's name about in a disrespectful context, Catherine. I was young and sorely troubled by what developed between us, but I hope I kept my wits about me."

A fine declaration that amounted to an admission: Fort had no idea to whom he might have spilled the particulars of his affair with Catherine.

"Why?" he asked, peering down at her. "Has somebody said something untoward?"

"Somebody is always saying something untoward about me or within my hearing. That has nothing to do with our liaison."

"Your eyes," he said, raising a hand as if to touch Catherine's cheek, then letting it fall back to his side. "Bewitching eyes. I see them in my dreams."

"My eyes," Catherine said. "Which announce to all of Society that my mother was indiscreet. As I was indiscreet." A tame word for committing the worst possible folly in the varied annals of foolish young ladies.

"Drop a few words of Russian into your conversation, imply that you long to return to Saint Petersburg. The gossips will find something to notice about you besides your eyes—your fine figure, your witty conversation, your keen grasp of history—and they will do so in tones of respect and envy. Trust me on this. I know what I'm about."

He twinkled at her, bowed again, and saw himself out.

Caesar leaned against Catherine's legs and sighed.

"Tiresome," she said, stroking his head. "But for now, a task completed. I don't hate him. I hope I don't." But she had. For years, she had hated Fort Armbruster, and with good reason.

If she'd had the least inkling to whom he'd disclosed the details of their liaison, Catherine might have pressed him further. At the time, he'd murmured a few regrets, then shown the blithe unconcern of the strutting peacock.

Perhaps to him the whole situation hadn't even merited gossiping about, while Catherine's life had been shattered.

She was arguing with Bettis over how to style her hair—an argument she would win this time—when it occurred to her why Lord Fort's call had caused such a lingering sense of unease.

The twinkle in his eye. He was a good actor—not as good as he imagined himself to be—but good. That twinkle, though, that hint of delight, had been genuine, and Fort Armbruster should not have been delighted with any aspect of a simple condolence call on an old friend.

He'd be back, and he'd not rest until Catherine had allowed him to at least drive her in the park. She would refuse, and he would pester, and she would refuse him, again and again. She was not a sheltered girl, and this was not Rome, and she was done with charming men intent on their selfish games.

She would refuse until he did what he'd done with all too much alacrity in Rome: walk away from her and leave her to get on with her life as best she could.

Catherine Fairchild's attempted purchase of a case of Cahors would not leave Fournier's mind. While moving through the series of stretches that started his every day, walking London's streets, tending to his ledgers, and consulting with his customers, that humble claret bothered him like a sour aftertaste.

For a beefsteak dinner, she'd said. Was that the truth? A near truth? A young lady in mourning did not typically have gentlemen to dinner, and beefsteak was upper-class masculine fare.

Catherine was simply not a Cahors sort of lady. The wine was lovely in itself—forthright, robust, earthy—but not a fine lady's preferred libation.

Fournier regarded his reflection in the cheval mirror. "You are looking for an excuse to be stupid again. She does not want you for that. She said as much."

His reflection, an elegant fellow with a taste for understated lace and overstated embroidery, silently mocked him. For MacKay's supper, Fournier had chosen his favorite waistcoat, burgundy satin done all over in peacock hues with flowers and birds. His cravat pin was amethyst, a tribute to Miss Fairchild's eyes.

Had he not aspired to take the lady home at the end of the evening—an unlikely turn of affairs, given the proprieties—he would have walked to MacKay's house. Walking London's streets was not the same as wandering his vineyards by the hour, but it was exertion.

The gathering turned out to be small indeed. MacKay and his

wife had invited only Miss Fairchild, Fournier, and the Goddards. The meal was surprisingly convivial, with conversation leaping nimbly from French to English. Ann Goddard, compact, dark-haired, and passionate about her cooking—quizzed Fournier at length regarding wine pairings. Mrs. MacKay, a prominent preacher's daughter, wanted to know the state of religious affairs in France, about which Fournier could tell her little.

All the while, Catherine smiled graciously and offered only the occasional contribution to the discussion. When she did speak in French, Fournier realized that in his native language, Catherine had a slight Italian accent. He stored that detail away as he might have saved a letter from an old flame—or a new flame.

When Colonel Goddard professed a need to at least look in on The Coventry Club before the hour grew too late, Mrs. Goddard and Mrs. MacKay decided that for Fournier to take Catherine home would be *the only sensible thing*. The distance was short, and Fournier had brought his coach, after all.

Goddard and MacKay did not so much as glance at Fournier when he assented to this arguably dodgy arrangement, though Catherine spared him a small smile.

After five minutes of farewells that included having his hand shaken by the gentlemen and his cheek kissed by both wives, Fournier handed Catherine up, exchanged a few words with his coachman, and climbed in after her.

He took the place next to her and set his hat beside her bonnet on the opposite bench with a sense of relief. "We were managed," he said. "I confess I hoped we would be."

"As did I. They were very kind, and the evening was enjoyable."

Fournier wanted to remove his gloves, remove Catherine's gloves, and take her hand. "Something preoccupies you." He purposely did not use the English word *worry*, because Catherine would bristle at such presumption.

"I'm adjusting to a resumption of socializing. I was my mother's companion after Papa died. What few invitations we accepted,

Mama and I faced as a team. She had friends, from her embassy days, even from her time in Canada, but those friends had families, while Mama had only me."

Catherine leaned her head back against the cushions, and the coach lamps cast the planes and hollows of her face in shadows.

"Sorrow is keenly skilled at the art of the ambush," Fournier said. "Watching a family in the park, watching a damned cat with her kittens, your heart breaks without warning. Then you want to smash something fragile, because the whole day must be reconstructed to fortify you against a single bad moment."

"Another bad moment, but tonight was pleasant nonetheless. These people are not my family, but they are connected to my family, and that will be noted."

Fournier had noted that connection without *noticing* it. "Do you hate your father?"

"Papa? He was nothing but kind. Whyever..." Catherine fell silent, and her posture shifted, becoming less proper, more weary. "You mean the late Earl of Casriel. Mama had a miniature of him made for me. The current earl looks very like him. He stood up with me once—Grey did, when we were newly returned to London."

Had the present earl done that on purpose? To avoid rudeness before a crowd? To be decent to his half-sister? Why had he done it only the once? Had Catherine ever met her true father?

"You never danced with any of your other brothers?"

"Ash, at a house party. He was newly married, and we were both somewhat at sea, but there was trouble afoot, and I was a potential ally. I quite like his wife. Lady Della is fiercely devoted to him, and he to her, though more quietly."

Such longing imbued that observation. Such wistfulness.

"You never made your bow at court?" Odd for a diplomat's daughter. Very odd.

Fournier again had the urge to take her hand, and he again ignored it.

CHAPTER EIGHT

"We were in Italy when I was seventeen," Catherine said, and the careful detachment in her voice told Fournier her seventeenth year had been difficult.

"You did not want to be there."

Her smile was brittle. "I resented not having a London Season as only the young and self-absorbed can aspire to bitterness. No daughter had ever withstood such inconsideration from her parents, no injustice could compare to the wrong I suffered. For years, I'd been dragged about wherever my father's work took him, and I had consoled myself with the thought that someday I would have the elegant dances, the latest London fashions, the afternoons driving in Hyde Park. I wrote whole novels in my head about what a sensation I would create upon my come out."

How he would love to read those novels. "Were your parents trying to protect you?"

"Because I am a bastard? Perhaps, but even I know that Lady Emily Cowper's paternity is considered more dubious than my own. She's also said to have borne children by one if not two men other than her husband. If her ladyship can be the most popular patroness at Almack's, why couldn't I at least lurk among Mayfair's ferns and companions?"

The question had the ring of an old conundrum. "The young have a nose for hypocrisy, and proper English Society thrives on hypocrisy. Do you aspire to dance at Almack's?"

"Of course not. Most of the Mayfair Season is a genteel version of the Covent Garden street corners after the theater lets out."

Fournier laughed. "*Touché*, mademoiselle. You would have terrified polite society at a younger age. Perhaps you will terrify the hostesses now."

She shook her head. "I have no ambition to behave like a slighted seventeen-year-old. That way lies nothing but regret."

Fournier could be only so strong for so long. He took off his gloves and held out a hand to Catherine. To his great delight, she pulled off her gloves as well and not only clasped hands with him, but turned to rest against his side.

"I've missed you, Fournier. I do not want to miss you. Missing you is a problem. No more coach rides for us."

He tucked his arm around her. "I've missed you too. That is a sign that I am alive and that I still have a heart. If we are not to ride in coaches, would you like to hack out with me some fine and misty morning?"

"I ought not."

"Because of whatever it is that preoccupies you." Whatever *worried* her. Whatever kept her from admitting that she wanted to waltz at midnight beneath glittering chandeliers and attire herself in the latest fashions.

"Be quiet, Fournier. You told the coachman to take *un itinéraire indirect*. Presuming of you."

"Hopeful of me. I did not realize I could still have hopes, beyond hopes for a good harvest, or for my friends to prosper."

"I want to kiss you again."

Bon Dieu. "What stops you?"

The coach made a slow turn, while Fournier's fingertips

wandered over Catherine's features. Strong jaw, smooth brow, velvety lips. Desire began as a whispered longing, and even that was encouraging.

Enjoyable.

"I don't seek to marry," Catherine said. "I saw what my parents had, a partnership of sorts. They were loyal in a way that transcended mere fidelity. I suspect my father conducted liaisons that furthered his diplomat aspirations, and my mother... I was conceived out of her loyalty to my father in a sense. They esteemed one another, and they loved me, but I haven't the fortitude for such an arrangement."

Nothing in that recitation struck Fournier as untrue, but neither was it relevant. "And your brother Ash and his wife. They are also married. Sycamore is married. Could you not tolerate a man who adores you as they apparently adore their wives?"

"Adoration is for paragons and saints. I am neither."

"God be thanked for small mercies." Fournier took the initiative and kissed her, because he realized they had come to that. Catherine had stated her wishes, had acted on those wishes, and now she was stating terms as well.

No entanglement. No expectations. No assuming she would hand over her future and her fortune for the sake of a few pleasurable moments. Good terms, terms to inspire a man to negotiate better terms yet.

Catherine shifted to take a proper hold of him. As Fournier freed a hand to dim the coach lamp, he had the thought that Catherine Fairchild would have made an admirable Frenchwoman.

Then he could not think anything at all, because her kissing was beyond admirable. She had the knack of exploring a man as if he were her fondest wish and the most exciting adventure ever laid at her feet. Her fingers winnowed through his hair, then gripped him by the nape. She slipped a hand beneath his waistcoat, pressing her palm flat so he felt his heart beat against her caresses.

All the while, she kissed him, he allowed himself to revel in the pleasure, then the touch of her tongue to his lips dashed cold reason on the flames of eagerness.

Fournier lifted away from certain bliss and cupped the back of Catherine's head against his palm. "If we continue as we've begun, this coach will burst into flames."

She snickered, a wonderful sound. "Not very discreet of us, to make a bonfire of your town coach."

"Discretion matters to you very much."

She smoothed her hand over his cravat. "Discretion is mandatory, Fournier. I am, much to my surprise, contemplating the unthinkable with you. I cannot afford to court scandal, and your own standing in polite circles will not benefit from gossip either."

"But you are tempted, and my kisses are irresistible?"

"Your kisses are exquisite, but it's your... your genuineness that tempts me. You do not posture and pretend. You admit your regrets. You live life as it is, not as you wish it or demand that it should be."

He would not, in other words, make trouble when she discarded him. "Who taught you to choose your intimate partners for their ability to weather abandonment without complaint?"

With his arms around her, Fournier could feel the shock of his question reverberate through Catherine. She was no old hand at the game of dalliance, then. Far from it.

"I haven't exactly conducted myself like the whore of Babylon, Fournier."

He put a finger to her lips. "Never speak so ill of yourself, please. You are not that seventeen-year-old girl plotting rebellion against the parents who denied her a come out. I am not a randy squire who has come up to Town for some sport. I care for you, else you would not be in this coach."

Catherine remained silent as the coach made another turn. They were circling, meaning they'd reached their destination despite Fournier's direction to the coachman.

"A liaison with you—with anybody—is not what I had planned," Catherine said, straightening. "To be so preoccupied is inconvenient, but you... If somebody asked me to sketch a man who could hold my interest, I would have said he must be honorable above all, also sensible, able to laugh at himself, worldly, have a purpose beyond his own entertainment, be astute, and honest, and kind. Then you come along, and I find myself adding to the list. Handsome in a dashing, Continental sort of way would be nice. Facile with languages is always delightful. Well traveled, worldly... an excellent kisser..."

She'd forgotten patient. Did she but know it, Fournier had learned many and strategic forms of patience.

"To long for some affection and closeness in the midst of grief isn't unusual, Catherine."

She peered over at him, then positioned her bonnet atop her head and tied the ribbons. "I know. I accord myself some latitude because of it."

Catherine used grief to excuse her behavior with him, in other words. A pity, that. She passed him his hat and pulled on her gloves. Fournier rapped once on the roof and donned his gloves as well.

"How do we do this?" she asked.

"The coach pulls up. I get out first. I hand you down—"

She smacked his arm. "Be serious."

"No, Catherine," he said gently. "I shall not be serious. You have been too serious for too long. I will be earnest and passionate, but also warmhearted and affectionate. I will be as pleased to ride out with you as I would be to lick honey from your bare breasts. If all you want is a bedmate, then I will envy some other man that joy. You and I shall remain friends as we explore other forms of closeness, or we part friends."

He had surprised her, and himself. With Gabriella, he'd yielded all such discussions entirely. There had been no terms on his part, only his attempts to keep her happy.

And look how that had ended.

The coach rocked to a halt, and Fournier got out, hoping he hadn't overplayed his hand. Hoping he hadn't underplayed it either. Catherine alighted from the coach, and Fournier bowed politely.

She curtseyed with equal decorum. "Thank you for seeing me home."

"*Mon plaisir.*"

Catherine looked away. She studied his cravat pin. Fournier had no intention of making the moment easy for her. A man who had been warned to expect eventual dismissal was entitled to some dignity.

"If the weather is fair on Friday morning," she said, "shall we hack out? My mare is nothing fancy, but she does need the exercise."

Unseemly joy coursed through him. Ebullient, sparkling, wordless joy. "I'm sure your mare is elegance on four hooves, and yes, we shall hack out. I will call for you at seven. Your groom will accompany us."

"I will look forward to it."

Fournier leaned closer, treating himself to a whiff of roses and hope. "Into the house with you. The next time you put honey in your tea, think of me."

Her smile was demure, her eyes lit with mischief. "I will look forward to our ride."

She made a stately progress up the steps, and Fournier waited as any gentleman would until she was safely in the house. Then he dismissed his coach and prepared to enjoy a good, long evening ramble while he sorted and labeled developments.

He had reached only the nearest street corner before a diminutive shape emerged from the shadows beneath an extinguished porch light.

"Mee-shure. Good evening."

"*Bonsoir*, young Victor," Fournier replied, touching a finger to his hat brim. "You almost have it. *Monsieur.* You must think the r but not strive to pronounce it, and the first vowel is closer to the *i* in 'miss you.' Try again. *Monsieur.*"

"Miss-sue."

"Better. Now what have you to report?"

Victor hitched up the trousers sagging around his skinny hips.

"Some toff called on Miss Fairchild this afternoon. Fancy gent, crested cabriolet, didn't stay long."

"Coach wheels?"

"Red, gold trim, fancy gray in the traces. Coachy wore black livery with red and gold trim."

"Fancy indeed." And not the Dorning family livery either. "Did you notice any details of the crest?"

"The usual nonsense," Victor said, with the exquisite dismissiveness hungry boys aimed at the trappings of luxury. "Birds, arrows, rosebuds, and the like. Something else you should know."

"Yes?"

"That undergroom, Nevin Thurlow? He's a sot. He's fair worn a path to The Boar's Bride and calls it walking the dog."

Fournier passed the boy some coins. "You have an aptitude for this, my friend."

"I'm good at it. The colonel says the same thing."

"Has Colonel Goddard asked you to keep an eye on the Fairchild household?"

"No, sir. He says I'm on assignment to you for the duration."

"If Dorning or Goddard ask for a report, be truthful with them. That also means if they ask for a report on my own comings and goings, Victor."

The boy took to studying the worn toes of his boots. "What about Mrs. Dorning?"

MacKay would call Victor a canny lad. "The same, and that applies to Mrs. Goddard, Mrs. MacKay, MacKay himself, or the Welsh cousin, if he's back in Town."

"He's not. Not yet."

"Then be off with you, and my thanks for your vigilance."

"Bomb-swoir, miss-sue!" Victor melted into the shadows with a jaunty wave, and Fournier resumed walking.

~

"You like your French competitor," Ann Goddard said, tipping her chin up to allow her husband to untie her bonnet ribbons.

Colonel Sir Orion Goddard took his time with the ribbons because he was going mostly by feel in the shadowed foyer of their home and because he treasured any moment of domesticity with his wife.

"I respect Fournier. I always have."

Ann undid the frogs of his cloak. "You *like* him, Orion, and your standards in this regard are quite high."

He turned so she could sweep the garment from his shoulders, then performed the same courtesy for her. Theirs was not a grand household, and Goddard saw no point in asking a porter or under-footman to remain awake when a key to the front door would suffice instead.

"Fournier is honest," Goddard said, lighting a carrying candle from the sconce above the umbrella stand. "When he saw that my champagnes were superior to anything he could procure or make himself, he ceded the field to me at the Coventry. I felt I owed him some pointers on the newer methods for making champagne, and he's been more than gracious critiquing my clarets."

Ann slipped her arm through this. "And you'd become so unused to anything approaching civility from most of London that a French-man's decency caught your eye?"

Goddard let himself be escorted up the steps, knowing quite well that Ann—having allowed him to look in at the club—wasn't about to permit him to look in on the ledgers or the inventories, or any other late-night temptations waiting for him in the office.

As if her company on a rare early night wasn't temptation enough? As if she, too, hadn't wanted to see how the Coventry's kitchen had fared without her directly supervising the making of every sauce and side dish?

"Fournier grasps, as my cousins do to some extent, what it is to be an outsider," Goddard replied. "And yet, he carries on. I eventually put to rest the rumors surrounding my military career."

"Thank God."

"But he will never put to rest being French in London, and when he goes to France, he's likely regarded with equal suspicion, even as he gives employment to dozens of families, and his winemaking brings in revenue and cachet for the French government. He won't be scorned, exactly, but neither will he be thanked for the choices his family likely made for him."

Ann yawned behind her hand as they gained the first floor. "Socializing takes effort."

"For us. For others, remaining at home of an evening is the greater chore. The Coventry thrives on keeping such souls entertained."

Ann leaned into him. "I thought Fournier came to London more or less as an adult."

"He was here as a child as well, then sent back to France as Bonaparte stabilized matters, then apparently came back to London at the urging of his wife."

Ann straightened. "I should have known he was married. He's patient in the way a husband learns to be patient, a good husband. He's also... Maybe there's a word for it in French. Unto himself? Self-possessed? Self-contained? Those words don't convey quite the solitariness I sense in him."

The word Ann sought might be *lonely*. "*Seul mais complet.*"

"Yes," Ann said. "Alone but complete. In that, he and Miss Fairchild seem alike. Did Fournier's wife survive the war?"

"She did not. Nobody seems to have the particulars, though the stated cause was influenza. The situation in France was horrific before Paris fell, with the French army pillaging what little was left in the countryside to pillage. Since Waterloo, the French have again fallen into raging factions. Even the king says the royalists are more royalist than he is."

"I'm glad we don't live there." Ann preceded Goddard into their sitting room. "I love the thought of sampling the cuisine, reading the cookbooks, and sitting at Carême's figurative knee, but the rabid

ideals, turning neighbor against neighbor... England flirts with
upheaval on that order, but so far, we've learned some restraint from
our neighbor's violent example. Besides, you have had enough of
mistrust and rumors."

Goddard closed the door and didn't bother lighting candles in the
sitting room. He and Ann would undress, as they always did at the
end of an evening from home, assisting each other, talking through
the day's events, and easing away from the day's worries. If Ann
wanted a nightcap, she'd enjoy it with her slippered feet up on a
hassock before the fire.

"Fournier doesn't say much about France," Goddard replied,
turning Ann by the shoulders and starting on her hooks. "But the look
in his eyes... He says even less about his late wife or his family. I know
he visits his château regularly and takes a personal hand in the
blending of the clarets, but I suspect the memories are mostly sad."
Goddard indulged in a kiss to Ann's nape and slipped his arms
around her waist from behind.

Everything came right when he held his wife. Even when everything already was right, something inside him settled into place when
Ann was in his arms.

"Fournier has a look in his eyes when he beholds Miss Fairchild,
Orion."

"Noticed that, did you? Jeanette said the same thing. Says he's
smitten." To Goddard, Fournier appeared more to be a man longing
for the unattainable.

"Jeanette has been corresponding with her in-laws."

"My sister is a conscientious correspondent." Orion started on
Ann's stays. "What is the news from the Dorning wives?"

"Lady Casriel was some peer's widow before marrying the
present earl. She moved in Society. Lady Susannah was raised in
polite circles as well. Lady Jacaranda simply knows all and sees all,
probably because her husband is a financial advisor to half the peerage, or he was. The ladies recall hearing some talk. Ye gods, to be
unlaced feels divine."

"I should unlace you more often, then."

Ann sent him a look over her shoulder. "A devoted husband is worth more than vanilla beans."

"Such flattery will surely cause my clothing to fall off."

She turned and hugged him. "I don't tell you often enough how happy I am, Orion. I love being your wife, and I love you."

He held her and mentally blundered about for some pretty declaration, but as usual, none came to hand in any language.

"I love you too. Madly."

They embraced for a long, sweet moment, one more step in the nightly progress toward a shared bed and the daily miracle of a shared life.

"About Miss Fairchild," Ann said, stepping back. "She was with her parents in Rome. She would have been sixteen or seventeen."

"A dangerous age."

"A dangerously stupid age, you mean. I thought I was ready to cook for the king when I was seventeen, and I hadn't even finished my articles."

"I was ready to conquer the world at eighteen," Orion said. "The world soon sorted me out. What of Miss Fairchild?"

"Lord Fairchild took his wife to Italy supposedly because her lungs were delicate from braving winters in Canada and Russia. He wasn't there in any official capacity. Considering that Napoleon's reach included Rome, his lordship ought not to have been there at all."

"Though without much of a navy, the Corsican had to deploy resources carefully. So there was Lord Fairchild in Rome, with his supposedly ailing wife and a daughter who very likely did not care to be kicking her heels anywhere but in Mayfair."

"His bastard daughter, with the distinctive Dorning eyes. The only way to avoid a court presentation would have been to take her away from England for a time. She and her mother did not return to London for nearly two years, though the war was ongoing, and they apparently left Rome nearly a year before Lord Fairchild did. Then it was Saint Petersburg again, the Congress of Vienna, or mourning his lordship. Miss Fairchild has not moved nearly as much in Society as the daughter of a titled family should."

Goddard peeled out of his evening coat. "Perhaps Lady Fairchild was indiscreet again in Rome?"

"She had an understanding husband, Orion. She'd have no need to disappear to Switzerland to hide her misstep."

Ann settled on the vanity stool and began removing jewelry. "Something happened. An illness, a broken heart, nervous exhaustion. Lord Fairchild's various postings made the whole matter less noticeable at the time, but Miss Fairchild is an heiress now, from a titled family, and with titled connections. If somebody knows the specifics of her past, it could go hard for her."

"The past in question might be her mother's. Perhaps Lady Fairchild's health, her gambling habits, her fondness for patent remedies necessitated a repairing lease on a Greek island."

Ann regarded him in the mirror's reflection. "You are gorgeous when you are half undressed."

"Not when I'm entirely undressed?"

"You are irresistible then, so please be about it."

He had his waistcoat and shirt off in less than a minute. "I assume the Dorning women have a strategy in place for dealing with a lot of old gossip?"

Ann slipped off her earbobs, necklace, and bracelet. "They do not. Casriel and his countess will soon be in London, and Jeanette will confer with her ladyship personally. Without knowing particulars, it's hard to form a plan. I'm more concerned that Miss Fairchild thinks her past will keep Fournier from offering for her."

"If Miss Fairchild is, in fact, married to some Albanian adventurer, then it damn well should give Fournier pause."

Ann's perusal in the mirror turned thoughtful. "You are protective of Monsieur."

"He was protective of me, Ann, not in any obnoxious way, but he defended my interests when few others would. He's been helpful to MacKay as well, and Powell likes him."

"Sir Dylan is discerning."

"Powell is pernickety." Also very happily married, thank the ministering angels. Sir Dylan had finally gone home to Wales and taken his bride with him. "What's to be done about Miss Fairchild?"

"I don't know, but somebody ought to acquaint Fournier with what we know of Miss Fairchild's past."

"All we know is that she went to Italy, and at some point before returning to London, she left Italy for a time. If there's more to the situation, then Miss Fairchild ought to be the one conveying particulars to Fournier. He doubtless has a few regrets of his own to share as well."

Ann turned on the vanity stool to regard her husband directly. "I love you, Orion, but you are being too gentlemanly. The logical explanation for the gap in Miss Fairchild's travels is that she was indiscreet and bore a child. If that's the case, it complicates everything."

He moved behind the privacy screen. "How I hate proper society. Are you sure we can't move to France?"

"The Coventry would close in a week if we truly abandoned our posts, and then Sycamore would pout."

"A dire result indeed." Goddard considered shaving and discarded the notion. Ann liked him a little bristly at bedtime. "What's to be done?" For that was the point of this discussion.

Ann and Jeanette, along with Dorcas MacKay and the Dorning ladies, would naturally be concerned for a young woman cast on her own devices before the wolves of polite society. That the young lady in question had family connections made the matter pressing, and thus the menfolk—like so much horse artillery—must be maneuvered into position.

"You will drop a hint or two in Fournier's handsome ear that Miss Fairchild might face more than the usual gossip when she puts off mourning. You will send notice to Lord Tavistock that Miss Fairchild might be a guest on one of your French properties. You and I will make a condolence call on her next week and take her some of your excellent champagne."

Goddard brushed his teeth, washed, and traded his knee breeches for a banyan.

"You do realize," he said, standing at Ann's back, "that my hints won't put Fournier off? If he thinks Miss Fairchild faces judgment for a youthful indiscretion, his loyalty will become unwavering." Though if the look in Fournier's eye was any indication, he was already a man sorely smitten.

"I do believe the ladies and I are counting on his gentlemanly instincts, Orion. Might you lend a hand with my hair?"

"Of course." Goddard began the delicate process of extracting pins from Ann's coiffure, undoing bits of silk ribbon, and unbraiding plaits. The result was a riot of curling, waving tresses cascading down her back. He took up the brush and restored order in the form of a single thick braid, a task that soothed him probably more than it did Ann.

And yet, as he wrapped himself around her beneath the covers a contented hour later, a thought niggled at his peace.

Fournier would defend Miss Fairchild's interests like the gentleman he was, but he was also an émigré with a dubious past of his own. If Miss Fairchild told him to quit the field, Fournier would bow politely and disappear from her life.

And that would be a shame for all concerned.

CHAPTER NINE

Catherine rose on Friday morning after a night of fitful rest. She half hoped for rain, and she desperately wished for fair weather. She hadn't worn her habit in so long that she'd tried it on the day before to ensure it still fit.

It did, loosely.

She had forbidden herself to fuss over her hair, over the angle of her veiled toque, over the color of her stock. With a dark blue riding habit, she usually wore a black stock, but she'd reached the limit of her tolerance for black.

Fournier was waiting for her in the mews, looking quietly splendid in his riding attire. "Miss Fairchild." He possessed himself of her hand. "A pleasure to see you, as always. May I introduce you to Bertold? Bertold, make your bow."

An equally splendid bay gelding tottered into an equine bow. When Fournier touched the beast's shoulder, he straightened and nuzzled his owner's pockets. Fournier slipped him a bite of carrot.

Catherine had the oddest urge to curtsey. "Bertold is impressive."

"He's impressively loyal to his belly, somewhat like our friend

Major MacKay. Give him an apple, and he will be more devoted to you than your mastiff. How fares Caesar?"

This was small talk, idle chatter likely produced for the benefit of the grooms, and yet, it was small talk with Fournier, and he wasn't asking about the dog.

"Caesar is an adaptable sort. He appears contented, and the whole household likes him. I enjoy his company tremendously."

Nevin led out Catherine's mare, who'd come through the winter in good weight. A bit too good weight.

"Morning, miss. Herself will need to walk a bit first."

"Of course." Catherine took Franny's reins and checked the girths, then led the mare to the ladies' mounting block. Franny stood like a statue while Catherine settled into the saddle and arranged her skirts.

"You leave a man with no gallantries to perform," Fournier said, swinging onto Bertold's back. "I will have to be inventive. As we will be plodding along for some time, your groom can catch up to us at his leisure. Shall we be off?"

Fournier brought Bertold alongside Franny, and the horses walked side by side down the alley. The day was lovely, to be in the saddle lovelier still. The trees weren't finished leafing out, and the light still had some of the sharp brilliance of early spring.

A season for beginnings, or at least for fresh air. "I nearly sent you my regrets." Not what Catherine had planned to say.

"Your decision to go for a pleasurable outing in the park will be remarked, as will your choice of escort."

"Yes."

"And?" Fournier sat atop his grand horse, entirely at ease.

"The time has come to stop hiding. I have no plans to take Mayfair by storm, but neither can I make the life I want if my sole aim is to avoid gossip." At some point during the night, Catherine had realized that Armbruster was likely every bit as invested in keeping her secrets as she was—they were his secrets, too, after all, and Fort was nothing if not careful of his standing.

Catherine wasn't *safe*, precisely—she truly would not socialize any more than she had to—but neither was she as worried as she had been.

"I agree," Fournier said. "If all children were held perpetually accountable for their parents' indiscretions, we none of us would dare leave our homes."

"You are a forgiving sort, Fournier." Would he be as forgiving if he knew the greater indiscretion had been not Mama's, but Catherine's?

"I am an imperfect sort. Have you dreamed of me?" He asked the question as they approached the mouth of the alley.

He was also the flirtatious sort, though his flirtations felt different from the calf-eyed, surreptitious pawing Armbruster had offered her.

"Should we wait for my groom?"

Fournier watched the passing traffic. "May I be blunt?"

"Of course."

"Your mare has not been kept in condition. Your groom failed to saddle her in time to walk her for you, though you doubtless made the exact hour of our appointment known to your staff. She has not been conscientiously groomed in the regular course, or she'd have less winter coat left. Your groom also failed to have his own mount ready such that we need not delay for his convenience."

Catherine had focused on the outing itself—and her escort—but she'd also noted those facts in passing.

"I can't sack Nevin. He's Mrs. Trask's nephew."

"You cannot tolerate his slacking, Catherine. My business depends on those I employ respecting me and respecting themselves enough to put in a fair day's work for a fair day's wage. That Nevin acquits himself poorly now, after you've dispensed with Deems, suggests the fellow is *un homme stupide et arrogant*."

No clatter of hooves came from the direction of the mews, suggesting Nevin had been quite behindhand preparing for the outing.

"Is scolding me your version of not being serious, Fournier? Of warmhearted affection? I confess I haven't much experience with *affaires amoureuses*, but I'm sure lectures are not how an outing of this nature is to begin."

He urged his horse forward. "Have you had *any* experience with *affaires amoureuses*, Catherine?"

His tone was merely curious, but Catherine would not lie to him. Not about this. "Some."

"Then you must have been with selfish dunderheads. I am concerned for you, as a friend is concerned, as your family would be concerned did they know what you contend with. Whether or not we ever become lovers, I am your friend."

Franny, a somewhat shaggy, pudgy creature in her present state, toddled along next to Bertold, a charger in his prime.

"You are so French, Fournier."

"Thank you. I am also a gentleman, which is far more relevant to the discussion. If you refuse to allow me to court you, at least allow me to befriend you as we become lovers."

"Court me?"

"Nobody would find my presumption unusual. I am known to be socially ambitious. The French are no respecters of rank—this is universally believed—and only a fool would turn up his nose at your fortune. When you dismiss me, all of Mayfair will applaud that you have come to your senses."

"No."

He looked peevish, and on him, that was attractive. "Why not? I make a credible suitor."

"Because friends don't use one another like that. I am honestly puzzled as to how any dalliance between us can progress, because my household is full of servants who will gossip, no matter how much I pay them. I am watched, you are watched, and..."

"And you have convinced yourself that unless we find ourselves stuffed into another coach late at night, a few kisses will be the limit of our pleasures?"

"I am resourceful, too, Fournier, but I'm no longer a schoolgirl whom all would rather not have underfoot. I cannot claim to be sketching the nearest vista by the hour while my obliging maid looks in on her auntie. I cannot slip out of my bedroom to meet you in the orchard, confident that nobody will question how the hems of my nightgown somehow got soaked between midnight and dawn."

"You aspired to be devious."

He did not shy away from the word, meaning Catherine didn't have to shy away from it either.

"I was awful. I was beyond ridiculous, and I paid dearly for my recklessness. That I am contemplating the same sort of folly with you both fascinates and appalls me."

The streets had grown wider, the vehicular traffic more elegant, the pedestrians fewer and more fashionable. Still no sign of Nevin.

"You are telling me," Fournier said, "that your adventures were long ago. We have that in common. My wife has been gone for some time, and I was faithful to her."

From another man, Catherine might not have believed that declaration, but from Fournier, it was simply a statement of old business.

"You endured long separations from her."

"I was a man without a country, without family on hand, without a place in London society. Loyalty to my wife was an anchor and kept life simple. To be honest, Gabriella found my fidelity a touching oddity."

One should not speak ill of the dead, but one should also not allow a friend to labor under a misconception.

"Then she was a selfish dunderhead."

Fournier smiled. "I begin to agree with you, though I must quibble over one point."

"Only one?"

"Only the one for now, but it matters. You refer to youthful folly, Catherine, probably undertaken with somebody of similar inexperience and more a matter of rebellion than joy. I married in part as a matter of duty—my aunts wanted me wed, though I knew Gabriella coveted my vineyards rather than my person. You and I are done with such tedium. What we embark on will be for joy and friendship and pleasure, *non?*"

He'd put his elegant finger on why Catherine was even tempted to frolic with him. In Rome, she'd been resentful of every stricture. Why behave like a nun when no London Season awaited? What did a reputation matter if one's very birth meant scandal was a foregone conclusion?

She had been too young, and too sheltered, to realize scandal and fallenness came in degrees, some far easier to bear than others. She'd squandered her good name for Armbruster's promises and a few fumbling interludes fraught—on her part—with more terror than desire.

Little of joy colored those memories, and the sorrow they'd bequeathed to her was a daily burden.

"Joy and friendship and pleasure sound too ambitious," Catherine said, "but lovely."

"Then choose one, and we will start there."

The comment was meant to be lighthearted, to begin a bantering repartee that would take them through the gates of the park and onto some misty bridle path.

"I choose friendship, Fournier. I would dearly like to have your friendship and you have offered that freely, so let's begin there."

He sat up a little taller. "You flatter me. Friendship first, then." He tossed a coin to a crossing sweeper and, by some subtle cue, signaled Bertold to pick up the trot.

Catherine's choice had apparently surprised him—she'd certainly surprised herself—and the whole pretty, sunny morning grew one degree brighter still.

∿

Fournier had not wept when he'd learned that Gabriella had been lost. That bereavement had had an inevitable quality. Sooner or later, in post-revolutionary France, the reckless paid for their boldness, and Gabriella had been very reckless.

He'd not wept when news of the tremendous casualties suffered on all sides at Waterloo had become known. He'd not wept... He could not recall the last time he'd wept. At his mother's funeral, perhaps.

Amid the greening trees and gentle mists of a Hyde Park morning, he battled an ache in his throat born of both sorrow and hope. Catherine Fairchild valued his *friendship*. More than she sought a clandestine hour of pleasure, she sought his companionship, caring, and trust.

Something akin to relief threatened to overwhelm Fournier's dignity. A man who had friends was never truly in exile, was he? Friendship was an anchor that transcended time, nationality, and distance. Friendship could be more durable and comforting than marriage.

A home for the soul, a refuge for the heart.

Goddard, MacKay, and even Dorning might someday number among Fournier's friends, by virtue of long acquaintance and an occasional muttered admission over a hand of cards. Their friendship would be understated, not the public display Catherine made riding at Fournier's side.

"Does my choice disappoint you?" Catherine asked as they trotted through the park's gates. "Would you rather we instead trysted on the staff's half day and pretended not to know each other otherwise?"

"Trysting on half day is for those who lack courage and imagination, though I will happily accede to that plan if such is your wish. A lady's offer of friendship is no small treasure."

"My poor Franny is truly out of condition," Catherine said, slowing her horse to the walk. "I suppose I am too."

Bertold adopted the walk as well, after the requisite protest. Parks, in his equine opinion, were for galloping, not wooing.

"Out of condition in what sense?" Fournier asked.

"Mourning for Papa, then Mama's advancing illness, meant I did not have to brave the wilds of Mayfair. I worried for my mother, of course, but I also enjoyed having an excuse to bide at home. I went to my charitable committee meetings, I accompanied Mama on her increasingly rare social calls, but mostly, I..."

"The great boon you'd once sought—the social whirl of polite society—had become a purgatory to avoid. Returning to France became like that for me. Why do you look at me so? Friends confide in one another."

"Tell me more about your purgatory, Fournier."

The horses *clip-clopped* along, the mare's breathing a trifle labored, while Fournier sought to find words for emotions he'd barely acknowledged.

"Gabriella came to treat me as her London factor. She was never overtly unwelcoming, but neither was she overjoyed when I risked my neck to visit home. I had no legitimate offspring, so the vineyards would go to her should death befall me. She did not wish me dead, but with each trip to France, I became less the absentee owner of the château and more the tolerated guest whose wishes were ignored in favor of Madame Fournier's orders."

"I'm sorry," Catherine said, nudging her mare up onto the verge so a pair of gentlemen could trot past them. "Your experience smacks of the toleration I was shown by polite society. Nobody was overtly cruel, and yet, my fondest dream, to take my proper place in London's drawing rooms and ballrooms, soured one whisper, one glance, one silence at a time. In my case, though, I can say the dream I cherished was foolish. For you to expect a warm welcome from your wife was not foolish at all."

"For me to be angry at a woman who'd never held me in much personal esteem would be more foolish still."

"And yet, you were angry. Are you still?"

Fournier considered making some quip about friendship being more work than trysting, but quips and bon mots could also show a want of courage and imagination.

"I am angry at Gabriella for dying, because her death denied us any sort of rapprochement, any resolution. I begged her to take refuge away from the château, but she refused that request until traveling became perilous. Her coach was held up, and she had to walk miles through wretched weather before she found an inn. A lung fever set in, and that was the end of my ambitious wife."

"You are angry at yourself."

"This pleases you, because you are still angry at yourself as well."

Catherine saluted with her whip. "A fine riposte, monsieur. I try to have compassion for the younger woman I was. Some days, I meet with more success than others."

"Splendidly honest of you and well put. Shall we trot again? The mare will never regain her conditioning if we don't offer her the occasional challenge."

"Subtle, Fournier. As it happens, a challenge is in the offing."

Mr. Ash Dorning approached on a handsome bay. Fournier had been introduced to most of the Dornings, and he was somewhat acquainted with Ash as a result of that fellow's interest in The Coventry Club and his formidable skill with a sword.

"Miss Fairchild." Dorning halted his horse and touched a gloved finger to his hat brim. "Fournier. A lovely morning for a hack, is it not?"

He was merely offering pleasantries, and yet, Fournier knew that the encounter was anything but a chance meeting. Dorning had stopped his horse when he might have trotted right on past with a nod, and he had started a conversation with Catherine where any number of gossipy equestrians would observe his courtesy.

And yet, Catherine had no facile reply for him.

"In spring," Fournier said, "early mornings carry a double load of hope, for the day and for the season both. We crave the light and warmth as at no other time of year."

"And when we grieve," Dorning said, "light and warmth are especially dear. My condolences on your loss, Miss Fairchild. How are you managing?"

Dorning had the extraordinary eyes that Catherine probably regarded as a curse. On him, in the morning sun, the color shaded nearly indigo, and his gaze held a world of honest compassion.

"'Managing' is an apt description," Catherine said. "Good and bad days. Life goes on between sorrow's ambushes. Please thank Lady Della for her note of condolence."

"Della lost her mother at an early age," Dorning said, "and she well knows the burden Society can place on a lady due to circumstances beyond her control. She will pay you a call next week at the latest, and I will likely accompany her, if that suits?"

Catherine had stopped fiddling with her reins and inspecting the canopy long enough to aim a direct gaze at Dorning.

"I am always happy to receive friends, Mr. Dorning. They are a singular comfort in difficult times."

"Just so. I will bid you good day. Enjoy the fresh air. I find it a much-needed tonic when the blue devils beset me. Fournier, perhaps you'd oblige me with a sparring match or two at the fencing salon?"

"I would be delighted. My regards to your lady wife."

Dorning nodded and trotted off. Catherine stared after him as if he'd materialized from the fairy realm, a being out of context among mere mortals.

Fournier signaled Bertold to resume walking, and Franny fell in beside him.

"One could hardly believe that deft, soft-spoken gentleman is Sycamore Dorning's brother," Fournier said, "but he is, and what's more, he and his sibling are dearly devoted."

"Lady Della is a bastard," Catherine said. "I'd forgotten that. Mama told me. The Quimbey spare went frolicking with the late Earl of Bellefonte's second wife. Mama knew all the old secrets. Lady Della is petite and dark, while her siblings are all tall and blond."

"And Ash Dorning reminded you, here in Hyde Park, that you are not the Dorning family's only changeling. I gather Lady Della manages well enough."

"Her ladyship is an earl's changeling, claiming a discreet connection to a ducal family, while I am..." She fell silent.

"An earl's by-blow," Fournier concluded. "A baron's changeling. But you were about to say that you were nobody."

Catherine blinked, then pretended to shade her eyes against the slanting beams of sunshine. "I would not have said that, but I nearly thought it."

"Except that you did not. I realize the mare is out of condition, but even she is capable of a short canter on such a lovely day. Shall we?"

He did not wait for Catherine's assent, but cued Bertold to pick up the pace. A few strides on, Franny gamely broke into the canter, laboring mightily to keep up with the larger gelding. When the horses came down to the walk, Franny's sides were heaving like bellows.

Catherine, flushed and smiling, patted her horse. "Well done, darling lady. We'll have you back on your mettle in no time."

Yes, we will. "Perhaps you will ride out with me again next week?"

"I would enjoy that, and I will have a pointed word with Nevin about his slacking. Franny needs more exercise, and Nevin needs to spend less time at The Boar's Bride. I owe you my thanks, Fournier."

"For?"

"I would have made one excuse after another to avoid the park. I would have let Franny go entirely to pot, and I would have told myself I was being prudent, taking things step by step."

"For a time, perhaps, but your good sense would have asserted itself eventually. The polite society you so longed to join is not worth your misery."

She cocked her head as if trying to identify the call of a distant bird. "I do believe Lady Della Dorning would agree with you, but then, she is surrounded by family happy to support her opinions."

You have me. Fournier did not entirely understand why that was so, why Catherine Fairchild of all women should rouse him to once again enter the lists of doting swains, but enter them he had.

"The issue at hand is whether *you* agree with me," Fournier said. "Have you cast off mourning for social acceptance from a lot of gossips and buffoons?'

"Have you?"

She'd pinked him, again. "Friendship with you is most invigorating, Miss Fairchild. One delights to anticipate becoming lovers as well as friends. In my case, I do not seek the acceptance of London Society. I seek Mayfair's custom. An émigré in trade must know his place."

Catherine grinned at him, an open, gloating, merry smile that made those extraordinary eyes of hers sparkle. "A *comte* in trade, one who owns vast vineyards and whose winery blends the finest clarets ever to grace discerning palates."

"I should never have told you about the title. Titles work differently in France. They can result from a family holding public office over a period of generations, or from..."

He trailed off, following the direction of Catherine's gaze. Her smile had disappeared, and in its place was the cool, gracious mask.

A gentleman on a prancing gray came down the path.

Catherine nodded. "Lord Fortescue, good morning."

"Miss Fairchild, and... Fournier, is it?"

Hard to ignore the creditor to whom one owed a sizable sum. "My lord, good day. A fine morning to take the air, is it not?"

Armbruster's gaze went from Catherine to Fournier and back. "It is that. Good day, Miss Fairchild, a pleasure to have seen you."

Fournier merited no parting courtesy from his lordship, and when Armbruster had trotted off, Catherine was no longer smiling.

"Come, Fournier. Franny has had her outing, and I have condolence replies to write."

Fournier did not question the lady's change of mood. He escorted her home and bowed politely over her hand in the mews. Friends did not pry, after all.

Though they did keep a careful watch on one another.

The outing to the park with Fournier changed something fundamental for Catherine. She wasn't ready to turn her back on propriety entirely, but neither was she terrified of quoting the wrong philosopher, wearing the wrong bonnet, or holding her parasol at the wrong angle—all sins she'd committed during her very first month back in London.

Fortescue Armbruster's veiled curiosity hadn't put her into a panic, in part because Fournier had told her that Armbruster didn't pay the trades. Once a scoundrel, always a scoundrel, apparently, and even Fournier hadn't seen Armbruster's untrustworthiness at first glance.

Who else numbered among those whose trust Fort Armbruster had abused?

A tap on the parlor door had Catherine putting down her pen. The condolence cards had slowed, such that now the mail was mostly from Mama's more far-flung acquaintances.

"Come in," Catherine called.

"A caller, miss," Harry said, holding out the silver card tray. "A lady."

Lady Della Dorning. "Gracious. Has the fire been lit in the guest parlor, Harry?"

"'Fraid not, miss. Mrs. Trask isn't one to waste coal."

"Then here will have to do. A tray with all the trimmings and the silver teapot."

"Very good, miss."

Harry was trying to step into Deems's shoes, but Harry was young, and at the moment, he was blushing.

"Was there something else, Harry?"

He drew himself up and stared over the mantel at the portrait of the third Baroness Fairchild. "We haven't a butler, miss, but somebody should see to the cellars."

The cellar was stocked with many fine vintages collected on

Papa's travels. "Have you somebody in mind, Harry?"

"I thought perhaps I could drop around to Monsieur Fournier's shop and ask for a few pointers. I know a claret from champagne, but there's more to it than that. When to decant, what wine to serve with which dishes. Mrs. Trask and Cook were talking about it."

Catherine's first reaction was surprise. Harry was getting very much above himself, for all that he was right. Polite society would laugh Harry to scorn. But then... why not support a footman's ambitions when he showed some initiative?

Why not? "I will have a word with Monsieur, and I'm sure he will be happy to assist. I will also have Cook review the menus with you so you can hear her suggestions regarding the wine pairings, but, Harry, you are not to lord it over the other staff. You are merely curious, and if you ask the occasional question when running an errand at the wineshop, that is nobody's business but yours."

Catherine did not add that she'd discussed wine selections with Mama by the hour and enjoyed Italian, Greek, and even American vintages undreamed of by most British butlers. She could share what she knew with Harry casually and see how he went on.

"Thank you, miss. Thank you. I'd best fetch her ladyship."

He all but bolted from the room, the antithesis of Deems's stuffy dignity—and what a pleasant change that was.

Lady Della numbered among those small people who exuded a large presence. How she did that, precisely, Catherine did not know. Her ladyship did not dress with an extravagance of ruffles and lace. She did not speak loudly or conduct herself with any flamboyant airs.

And yet, she was—to use Fournier's word—formidable.

"Miss Fairchild, good day."

They exchanged curtseys. "My lady, a pleasure. I've sent for the tray. Please do have a seat. Your husband warned me you might visit, though I wasn't expecting you quite this soon." Fortunately, Catherine was properly attired to receive a caller, in part thanks to Fournier's scolding.

Lady Della smiled as she sank into Mama's wing chair. "If you are up to an outing in the park with Xavier Fournier, then you can endure a visit from my humble self. Ash was off to Angelo's salon this morning, or I would have dragooned him into escorting me. I gather a chance to spar with Monsieur Fournier is not to be missed."

Lady Della's manner was brisk and friendly. She wasn't collecting gossip, but rather, inviting a confidence: Was Catherine *sparring* with Monsieur?

"Monsieur is a charming escort. I cannot speak to his skill with a sword." *Yet.*

"You will need several charming escorts. Ash is available for that purpose, and Valerian and Oak will be in Town shortly. Casriel has many demands upon his time, but I can call upon Nicholas if you're casting about for gallants."

"Nicholas?"

"My oldest legitimate brother. Lord Bellefonte. He's actually very sweet, and Leah—Lady Bellefonte—isn't as sociable as Nicholas. Nobody is as sociable as Nick. He's the world's largest butterfly. He'll be calling you darling and dearest before he's finished his first promenade with you, and then he'll start bragging about his children."

Lady Della appeared to chatter, but she was, in fact, opening negotiations. Catherine had served as her father's amanuensis at enough diplomatic meetings to grasp what was afoot.

Her ladyship had been born a Haddonfield, the youngest child—to appearances—of the late Earl of Bellefonte. Her ramblings had already made the point that Nicholas, the present earl and Della's oldest *legitimate* brother, had an older half-brother who was *not* legitimate. The present earl also had a by-blow, if Mama's intelligence was accurate, a young lady whom the earl and countess included in their household along with their growing brood.

All that, subtly conveyed before her ladyship had even taken off her gloves.

"I am not particularly sociable," Catherine said. "Life attached to an embassy required that I learn how to comport myself, but to be honest, I prefer a quiet life."

Harry brought the tray in and withdrew, though he paused with his hand on the door latch and sent Catherine a questioning look. She nodded, and he closed the door.

Good riddance, Deems.

"You must not let that old Miss Dubious business haunt you," Lady Della said. "That was years ago, and the gossips aren't calling you that now, I'll wager."

The nickname still had the power to wound. "How much would you wager?"

"My best bonnet. One lump and a dash of milk, please. The Dorning ladies are gathering at Richmond next Wednesday. Oak and Valerian will be in Town, though we will never get Hawthorne to leave his acres this time of year, and Daisy has positively taken over rural Hampshire. Kettering and Jacaranda are already on hand, Willow has agreed to bring Susannah to London next week, and Casriel ought to be here any day."

"I will be mobbed if I join this gathering?"

"Of course, but in the nicest possible way." Lady Della's smile was commiserating. "The womenfolk are dedicated correspondents, the menfolk not as much. If we get together, then our fellows can also congregate without having to make a fuss about it. Sycamore enjoys making a fuss, though, and I suspect he bought the Richmond monstrosity in part so we'd have a family respite near Town."

"Sycamore wants to grow ornamental ferns in addition to spices and vegetables," Catherine said. "Ferns are apparently soon to be all the rage."

Fournier had told her that. Something about Lady Della's regard as she sipped her tea suggested she'd divined the source of Catherine's knowledge.

"I recall the first time I heard you referred to as Miss Dubious," her ladyship said. "You were dancing with that dreadful Fortescue Armbruster. He wasn't staring at your bodice, wasn't trying to charm you. That struck me as most odd behavior for him."

"That was my pity dance," Catherine said. "We'd come across his lordship a couple years earlier in Italy, and he could not ignore me." The waltz had been more painful than if Armbruster had offered her the cut sublime. The last vestige of Catherine's innocence had died in that Mayfair ballroom, not when Armbruster had danced with her, but later, when she'd seen his friends condoling him on the ordeal of having to dance with the Diplomat's Dubious Daughter.

"Armbruster is the one deserving of pity," Lady Della said. "Not a groat to spare, and the hostesses invite him only to make up the numbers. Ash says his lordship greeted you cordially in the park when you rode out with Fournier."

Catherine poured herself a cup of tea and decided that with Lady Della, she would begin as she meant to go on.

"Diplomatic service is much like having a large family, my lady. One is always observed. We didn't all admit to being spies, but we all noticed details and guarded our privacy in equal measure. If the Dornings are to mob me, I am up to that honor."

"I told Ash you would be. He likes Fournier, by the way. Says Monsieur knows more of melancholia than appearances would suggest. Ash is a melancholic, though we're learning how to keep the beast on a leash. I am prone to panics, episodes of extreme, irrational dread. You will hear it from the others, so you might as well hear it from me."

"I'm... sorry." Catherine was also not about to reward Lady Della's bold disclosures with reciprocal gestures of trust. Not yet, probably not ever. "Mama suffered the occasional bout of melancholia. She was better when she and Papa were together."

Her ladyship finished her tea and set the cup on the tray. "Interesting. I am much better when Ash is on hand. You'll join us at Richmond on Wednesday, then? We'll make a day of it, and I will introduce you around. Have Fournier escort you. He's good company, and he and Jeanette get to arguing in French, and we are all left quite in the dust, save for Colonel Goddard. It's marvelous."

The day would be overwhelming, but it would be only a day, and these people were Catherine's *family*. She had longed for their notice,

for the loan of their consequence, and now that she was to have it...
She would beg for Fournier's escort if she had to.

"Was this gathering your idea, my lady?"

Lady Della pulled on her gloves. "No."

"But inviting me to join you was your idea."

"Ash's idea, actually, though I wish I'd thought of it. He said that
you, too, know more of melancholia than appearances suggest. My
husband is never wrong in these matters. If he says somebody has a
gambling problem or a guilty conscience, they do. He suspects Lord
Fortescue has both, but extra spares tend in those directions."

"Melancholia nearly killed me at one point." Oh God, where had
that come from?

"But here you are, all healthy, wealthy, and wise instead. Well
done of you. You and Ash can compare notes about how to keep the
beast on its leash or, better still, out of the garden altogether. You
must bring Caesar with you to Richmond."

Her ladyship rose, while Catherine needed a minute to gather
her wits before she got to her feet. "How is it you know the name of
my guest dog?"

Della hugged her. A thoroughly presuming, wonderfully casual
hug. "Jonathan Tresham is my half-brother, the Duke of Quimbey is
his uncle, and Caesar belongs to Uncle. I know the dog at sight, but
Fournier was the one who had the sense to bring him to you. Willow
will approve, and Willow does not give his good opinion of any two-
legged person lightly."

Her ladyship left without bothering to curtsey her farewell, and
Catherine returned to the tea tray, this time taking Mama's wing
chair.

She sipped her cooling tea, probably feeling somewhat like
Franny at the end of a vigorous canter. Winded, a little befuddled to
once again be out and about, but pleased.

Very pleased, and happy, but also a little like crying.

CHAPTER TEN

"You were smart to come peaceably to the inspection," Worth Kettering said, falling in step beside Fournier uninvited. "If you ignore the Dorning family summons, they just start paying calls on you. There are a deuced lot of them to clutter up one's calendar, particularly when they feel no compunction to decamp after a polite fifteen minutes. Best to simply brave them en masse."

"I am but a humble escort. Miss Fairchild is the one braving the masses." And how was she faring among the ladies who'd swept her off to *catch up over the teapot?*

Kettering was big, dark-haired, and usually as restless of body as he was of mind. He was an informal investment advisor to the Crown —a dicey proposition when the Regent was afflicted with a compulsion to spend money. At Fournier's request, Kettering had discreetly arranged business loans for a few émigrés. His terms were more than fair and his advice invariably sound.

Kettering was also married to the oldest Dorning daughter, and he was brother to a northern earl. Not a man to be trifled with.

Fournier had sold Kettering a quantity of wine over the years, including some interesting rosés. Here in Sycamore Dorning's walled garden, Kettering exuded none of his usual brisk restlessness. He ambled instead of charged. He stopped to sniff a pot of hyacinths instead of spouting off about promising ventures or shaky banks.

Marriage clearly agreed with him.

"Miss Fairchild," he said, "has been a thorn in the collective Dorning conscience for years. I was married with a child on the way before Jacaranda told me that she had at least one other sister that she knew of. The Dorning eyes don't lie."

"More's the pity, when one is an illegitimate young woman facing the London tabbies."

"Now those tabbies must face Miss Fairchild, and they will do so knowing she stands among allies. The family is of one mind in that regard."

The walled garden was peaceful, awash in red and white tulips punctuated by a few presuming purple irises. Water trickled softly over the edges of a three-tiered fountain, and benches at intervals along the crushed-shell walkway invited a guest to tarry.

The day was lovely, almost but not quite warm, as Kettering was being almost but not quite friendly. Fournier would be almost honest, in the spirit of the occasion.

"If the point of this cozy chat is to ascertain my intentions, Kettering, you may be assured they are both honorable and doomed. Miss Fairchild likes me well enough, but she does not seek to be courted."

Kettering made a face. "I hate it when that happens. Then a fellow is left all at sea, smitten and not exactly dismissed. I can assure you the finest brandy, a fortune in coin, and pretty acres are no consolation at all under those circumstances."

"One hears that you and Lady Jacaranda are devoted." Kettering had his own minor title, and thus the lady was no longer strictly Lady Jacaranda. In a characteristic display of contrariness, Kettering rarely used his honorific.

"We are devoted. Another Dorning trait. They marry for love."

"And why do Ketterings marry?"

Kettering gestured to a bench. "I am to be interrogating *you*, if you please, not the other way 'round. Ketterings marry for love. Why do Fourniers marry?"

Fournier took the bench, the wood warm against his backside. Spring had arrived. Winter might get off a few parting shots, but they would be only that.

"I am the sole Fournier extant from my line," he said. "I married once out of what I mistook for love, but I was merely infatuated and suffering the excess of animal spirits that makes fools of most young men. I did not see my intended clearly, while she was very certain of the bargain she struck with me. She cared for me, in her way. I could not endure another such union."

That marriage had been careful, polite, increasingly distant, and so terribly lonely, at least for Fournier. He had ceased pondering Gabriella's half of the union.

"Then you are wooing Miss Fairchild with an eye toward a love match? She's rich, Fournier. Marrying her will earn you resentment from the very people who sustain your business."

Fournier understood why Kettering was prying. The family needed to know his intentions—quaint of them, given how long they'd ignored Catherine—but Kettering also needed to solve the riddle of Catherine Fairchild and Xavier Fournier. Kettering was drawn to puzzles, as Xavier was drawn to exploring different blends of claret.

"Miss Fairchild will not have me, Kettering. We are friends. An émigré learns to thrive at the margins of London Society, and Miss Fairchild has studied in the same school. We have that in common. She can choose to expand her social circle now, though I doubt she will."

Kettering stretched out long legs and crossed them at the ankle, leaning his head back and closing his eyes.

"Why not? Why not swan about Almack's, forcing all the hostesses and fortune hunters to lick her dancing slippers? Every wallflower, bachelor uncle, and dowager would applaud her for it."

"As would you, but Catherine is not so petty."

Kettering opened his eyes and speared Fournier with a look. "Pettiness has nothing to do with it. You fence. Quite well, I'm told."

"I enjoy an occasional match." Those matches had kept Fournier sane when he'd first returned to London.

"You could put Angelo out of business, and yet, you don't. That would be petty. For Miss Fairchild to exert her influence would be in the nature of administering discipline where needed. Society was unkind to her. If she does not assign them a punishment, they will think they can be unkind again."

"Does that not puzzle you, Kettering? Catherine was merely a minor diplomat's only child, neither a great beauty, according to the fools who judge such matters, nor an heiress as far as anybody knew. She should never have merited so much notice. Why was Catherine, of all the young ladies in all their imperfections, made to suffer so inordinately?"

"Her eyes made her an easy target."

"Easy targets abound. There's Lord Palmerston, panting after Emily Cowper, though he's panted after Lady Jersey and Princess von Lieven with similar ardor. He is nicknamed Cupid, and always, this is mentioned with a smile. Castlereagh and Canning dueled over politics, and their stupidity merits more knowing smiles. Why focus on a relatively obscure young lady who was no threat to anybody?"

"You have brooded on this."

Catherine's choice of the Cahors was never far from Fournier's mind. Why would a fine lady order such a wine if not to drug some disobliging fellow? Why come to the shop without any escort or coach? Why live under the tyranny of a martinet of a butler?

"I am concerned for a young woman whose path has been difficult," he said. "She has had no useful allies, save her mother, and that good lady has gone to her reward."

Kettering rose. "She has us now, and you. In my experience, if one cannot win a lady's hand, he can still strive to win her respect—and her trust."

Fournier got to his feet as well. "No small treasures."

When Kettering ought by rights to have loped off to report to his wife, he instead remained in the garden, ostensibly studying the fountain.

"Have you earned Miss Fairchild's trust?" he asked.

"She can trust me to be at all times a gentleman, Kettering. Cease your meddling and go adore your wife."

"We missed breakfast," he said, gaze shifting to a corner of the building that overlooked the garden. "Adoration can play hell with one's schedule."

"Also one's dignity. Be off with you. Like a good escort, I will loiter about in the garden until I am summoned for the noon meal."

"We must meet over foils sometime," Kettering said. "Sycamore claims you move more quickly than the eye can follow. Ash says he's not far wrong."

"You flatter me, and yet, I am warned. I will do nothing to jeopardize Miss Fairchild's good name, and you lot will not now interfere with the wishes of a young lady who has grown independent of necessity. *Partez*, Kettering, *s'il vous plaît*. I have pondering to do."

Kettering bowed. "Until I see you at table. Enjoy your brooding."

He strode off with his characteristic vigor, while Fournier returned to the bench. The question of who had borne Catherine malice all those years ago plagued him. She had been treated with inordinate meanness, considering her modest standing at the time. Nonetheless, it was Kettering's last question—about earning Catherine's trust—that remained foremost in Fournier's mind.

"Where is she off to this time?" Fortescue Armbruster hadn't meant to let his irritation show, but really, what could Catherine be thinking? "All her haughty footman would tell me is that she's from home. She's supposed to be in mourning, prostrate with grief."

"Auntie says first mourning for a parent lasts only a month,"

Nevin replied, "and Miss has gone to Richmond to call on family, which is allowed during mourning in any case."

Fort set his hat on the scarred table, signaled the barmaid to bring him a small pint, and slid onto the hard chair opposite Nevin. "The almighty Dornings are not Miss Fairchild's family, not legally. Did they at least send a coach for her, or was she forced to take her own conveyance?"

Nevin saluted with his tankard and grinned. "The Frenchie wine nabob took her, same as last time. Has a lovely coach, if I do say so my own self, being a con-is-sewer of carriages and all."

"You are a lazy undergroom."

The smile faded. "I work for my bread, true enough. Unlike some. Why all the questions about the young miss's comings and goings? She's a decent sort, and she doesn't need any trouble. You said you wanted to court her, but I don't see you doing much in the way of courting."

The barmaid, a slender blonde this time, set a foaming tankard down before Fortescue, though ale was hardly sufficient fortification, given his frustration. For Catherine to jaunt all over the home counties was bad enough, but with that damned Frenchman for an escort...

"Émigrés are all either spies, revolutionaries, or charlatans," Fort said. "They make fortunes teaching French to the daughters of cits and putting on airs as lady's maids. The lot of them would spend the whole day eating bonbons and gossiping if we allowed them to."

Nevin and the barmaid exchanged a glance.

"Well, they would," Fortescue said. "Why is she loitering at our table?"

The maid held a half-full pitcher of ale and studied Fort's favorite top hat. He'd paid dearly for it, despite having three others, but it fit ever so well and had such a delicious shine to it.

"*L'argent, monsieur,*" the barmaid said. "*La bière n'est pas gratuite.* Nothing in life is free, and you shall pay the money for your ale."

She said the English words slowly, as if Fort's hearing might be impaired.

He put a coin on the table. She picked it up and flounced off.

"She'd poison my drink if she had her way." Fort took a sip nonetheless, the day being warmish and the ale having been paid for.

"No, she would not, my lord. You come in often enough that she'd rather have your custom than your death on her conscience. Nan is a practical sort. Are we done here?"

"We are done when I say we're done, Thurlow. Has Miss Fairchild kept up with her correspondence?"

A small boy set a pan and shovel inside the door and sauntered up to the bar while Nevin appeared to study the age-blackened rafters overhead.

"Miss gets mail from all over," Nevin said, "and she sends her replies all over."

"What does 'all over' mean?"

Nevin watched the boy scramble onto a stool and put a carefully chosen coin on the bar. "Canada, Portugal, the shires, France, Italy. Saw one the other day with writing on it that wasn't in proper letters."

"What does that mean? Were the letters Greek?"

"They weren't like the letters in Aunt's Bible, I can tell you that."

"Cyrillic, I suppose, from Lord Fairchild's time in Saint Petersburg. What of the Italian letters?"

The boy at the bar tucked into a meat pie, and Nevin took a leisurely sip of his drink.

"I don't now a ruddy thing about the Italian letters, your lordship, or the Canadian letters, or any of the letters. Some have black bands, some don't. Young miss answers her mail on Thursdays and Mondays, and I take the lot of it here to be posted. His lordship always franked the mail when he was at home, but the young miss pays for hers. Not everybody does."

Most mail was paid for by the receiver, a custom that ensured the mail was, in fact, delivered.

"Focus on the letters from the Continent. Does Miss Fairchild's French correspondence come from Paris?"

"How would I know? I can barely make out simple English."

"Get that haughty barmaid to look it over for you."

Nevin finished his ale and set the tankard down with a *thump*. "Seeing as I don't speak a word of Frog, and Nan gets along just fine in the king's English, I'd have to pay her for that service, wouldn't I?"

A gentleman was at all times in control of his temper, but Armbruster was sorely tempted to dash his ale in Nevin's face.

"For your information, Thurlow, Miss Fairchild has in the past exercised poor judgment, and her youthful folly could at any moment redound to her discredit. She was on the Continent when she committed her worst blunders, and she is vulnerable now to gossip. I seek to prevent such misery from befalling her, and your intransigence is not helping."

"In-tran-si-gence." Nevin rose and pulled on his cap. "Is that like stubbornness? Maybe it's more like I have work to do—honest work—and snooping about the young miss's affairs for the sake of your self-proclaimed saintly intentions has grown tiresome."

Armbruster well knew how to deal with insubordinate underlings—humor them as long as needful and not one second longer than that.

"Fine," Armbruster said. "Go wield your muck fork when you could be whiling away the morning over a pleasant pint. Far be it from me to interfere with a man's honorable work. Mark me on this, though, Thurlow. Miss Fairchild is due to receive, or has received, an epistle that will put an end to her careless frolicking with encroaching Frenchmen. She will soon appreciate the support of an old friend, and her Dorning connections will have nothing to say to it."

"How fortunate for the young miss that you are so gallantly willing to ride to her rescue. Excuse me, my lord. I am powerless to resist the allure of my muck fork."

Nevin blew a kiss to the barmaid, nodded to the boy wolfing down his meat pie, and departed, cap in hand.

The urchin at the bar was eyeing Thurlow's empty tankard, probably hoping to cadge the dregs, the little vermin. Armbruster finished his own ale in no hurry whatsoever, lest the brat get ideas, and considered the day's developments.

Catherine was enjoying her freedom, and that was understandable. She did, after all, have a wide streak of reckless rebellion in her soul. The Frenchman wasn't bad-looking, and he'd slink off to cozen some other wealthy Englishwoman when Catherine tired of him.

"I do not have time to indulge her bad taste," Armbruster muttered. The barmaid, damn her disrespect, had been right. Nothing in life was free, and the time had come for Catherine to pay for her sins.

Armbruster finished his ale and tapped his hat onto his head. From behind the bar, the serving maid watched him with a disdainful gaze.

"You are issuing me a challenge of some sort," Armbruster said, ambling over to the bar. "That translates plainly enough. Cease your attempts at subtlety, and tell me what you know."

"Your hat," she replied, holding out her hand. "I want your hat."

Ye gods, she had cheek. "You'll not get my hat."

The scruffy boy watched this exchange from two yards away, his meat pie half eaten.

"I will have your hat, and then you will know from precisely where in France your Miss Fairchild gets a monthly letter. Has since I started working here a year ago."

"Every month, without fail?"

"Every month. She receives the black-banded letters from all over. But the monthly letter has no marks of mourning."

Well, damn. This was intriguing. "A man's hand or a woman's?"

"Fine penmanship, educated, but I cannot say whether from a man or a woman based on the handwriting."

A shrewd and probably honest answer, implying more information was available.

Armbruster flashed his best *trust me, I'm a lordling* smile. "Where is the letter from, Nan?"

She snapped her fingers at him. "The hat, monsieur."

He loved that hat, and the hatter wasn't about to extend him more credit. Married to Catherine, though, he could afford a different hat every day of the week. Besides, this Nan person was a cold-hearted creature, and he had no wish to waste half his morning parleying with her.

Armbruster passed over the hat.

"Cahors," she said. "A small town two long days' journey east of Bordeaux in good weather. Every month, this letter comes, and every month, Miss Fairchild replies. To learn more than that, you will have to pay in coin."

"You know who sends the letters."

"I know who sends the letters and from exactly which household. You do not know, and one fancy hat will not gain you the information."

Armbruster's next quarterly allowance was due to him in a fortnight. He weighed benefits and burdens and the tedium of relying on a half-soused stable hand for his intelligence.

"Tell me, Nan, why do you recall the direction of one letter among hundreds that must pass through this inn?"

"My mother was from Cahors. She was killed spying for the English at the Siege of Toulon. They promised to evacuate her, but alas, the English—for the first time ever and surely the last as well—did not keep their word."

Toulon had not ended well for Britain or for the French royalists. "I'm sorry for your loss."

Nan stared at him, and Armbruster felt keenly that his head was bare when he was preparing to be out of doors in public.

"You will pay," she said, "for the information I pass you regarding the next letter from Cahors. Come back next week."

She named an audacious sum, but not beyond Armbruster's means.

"I will be back in two weeks, and you will tell me everything you know about these letters."

"Bring the money. Good day, monsieur."

He was being dismissed by a French barmaid. The boy went back to eating his meat pie, and Armbruster nearly snatched the hat back, so naked did he now feel without it.

"Why the hat?" he asked. "Why not my watch, or some coin, or... Why that hat?"

"The watch is engraved, and I do not need a watch when the church bells tell me the hour all day. You have more coin every three months than any humble family needs for a year, but you caress the hat. You adore the hat. You are stupid."

He nearly slapped her, but for her, taunting and flirting were probably of a piece. Not a game Armbruster had ever enjoyed. He liked his women adoring and submissive.

"You cannot wear that hat. You cannot eat that hat. Perhaps you, mademoiselle, are *stupide*."

"Nevin will wear the hat while he shovels horseshit, my lord. Soon, the hat will smell as rank as your soul, fine aristo that you are."

She smiled at him sweetly, while the boy snickered into his pint. That snickering had Armbruster bowing and taking his leave rather than returning fire. The exchange stayed with him, though, as he loitered at Tatts and worked up a sweat over foils at Angelo's.

By the time he'd gone home to change for his evening entertainments, he decided that he'd got the best of the exchange with the fair Nan. All she had was a hat, while he was poised to get hold of what could be one of the Fairchild family secrets.

Perhaps his late lordship had a French by-blow. For an English diplomat to dally with the enemy would not have been the done thing at all. Or perhaps Lady Fairchild owed an outrageous sum of money to some Continental debtor, and the monthly correspondence was a tally of sums paid and still owed.

Armbruster was still pondering possibilities when he dropped by his club to start the night's revelries. The fellows were having a good laugh at the expense of some duke's spare, forced to flee to Brussels ahead of his creditors.

Armbruster was declining an invitation to play a few hands at The Coventry Club when he recalled what exactly had made the encounter with the devious Nan so distasteful.

The filthy, snickering imp. The boy had been entertained at the expense of his betters, or so he'd believed. Armbruster hadn't heard that particularly robust version of derision since the day he'd dubbed Catherine Fairchild the Diplomat's Dubious Daughter.

Though, on that occasion, the laughter had of course been directed at a deserving object.

~

"Were you expecting me?" Catherine asked.

She stood in the doorway between the parlor and bedroom of the guest suite Fournier occupied. Her manner exuded gracious poise, while her eyes gave away uncertainty. She was attired for bed, covered more modestly than she would have been in any evening gown, and yet, the aubergine velvet did marvelous things for her eyes, and for Fournier's imagination.

He rose from the bed and set aside the pamphlet on ferns he'd been staring at. "I was waiting another hour for the household to settle before I discreetly tapped on your door."

"The Dornings put us directly across from one another. Do you suppose that was on purpose?"

Fournier drew Catherine by the hand into his bedroom and closed the door. Her fingers were cold. Nerves or a country house on a chilly spring night?

"Sit with me by the fire, Catherine. Or perhaps you'd enjoy a game of chess?"

She disdained to take a seat, dropped his hand, and paced before the hearth. "If I were more sophisticated, I would say yes to the chess, and we would banter over the board, with all sorts of subtle innuendo and teasing."

"Not teasing. Teasing is cruel. Flirtation, which is enjoyable. I thought to venture to the stable to see if my coach has truly developed a loose axle, all undetected by my excellent and conscientious coachman. Then I thought, no. Providence has provided you and me an opportunity for time together, if not for intimacies, and your family means well."

"Do they? I haven't enough experience with family of this sort to know."

"For a woman bent on trysting, Catherine, you seem annoyed. What troubles you?"

She wrapped her arms around her middle and stared hard at the rumpled quilts on the majestic four-poster that dominated the room. "What if you are disappointed in me?"

Gracious, she was brave, but he'd known that. "What if you are disappointed in me? I am out of practice and was never much for frolicking."

"You weren't? Whyever not? You are handsome, well fixed, charming, and a man."

"Is that a list of sins?"

She took the reading chair by the fire. "I'm nervous. Forgive me."

"I would rather love you. I am nervous too, *mon coeur*." He scooped her out of the chair and sat with her in his lap. "I am also very pleased to see you. You should wear aubergine frequently."

She was awkward in his arms, neither resisting nor surrendering. "I can't. That hue emphasizes my eyes."

"I adore your eyes. You ask why I am not drawn to intimate encounters. I am, in the animal sense, but being an émigré, the situation grows complicated. If I show attentions to a French lady, she will develop expectations. Her prospects in London are few, and among my own kind, I am *un eligiblé*."

Catherine laid her head on his shoulder. "Poor lad."

"I could take up with an English widow, and because I am French, she would feel a little extra wickedness about our illicit dealings. I do not wish to be anybody's tawdry convenience."

"Well said." Catherine scooted around, rearranging her dressing gown and misplacing a few of Fournier's wits. "What about a mistress?"

"Miss Fairchild, you shock me."

"Monsieur Fournier, you are prevaricating."

While she, in the role of inquisitor, was relaxing. "I was married until a few years ago. I tried to set up a second household in the fine old pious English tradition, but the whole business... The scheduling, the having some clothing here and other clothing there, the complication of having to travel between dwellings, the expectations... I am not suited to calculated self-indulgence. The lady and I parted on good terms, and she has returned to France."

"You made that possible."

"Gladly. She was homesick, and in France, nobody would pry into how she managed among the heathen English. She is married now and a very devoted wife."

Catherine kissed Fournier's cheek. "She could have been your devoted wife."

"I had a devoted wife. Devoted to my vineyards, to my consequence, to my name."

"I hate her," Catherine said, hugging Fournier close. "She destroyed your innocence."

"A man does not think of having *l'innocence*." Fournier was fairly certain the meanings were comparable in both languages. "Who destroyed yours?"

Catherine mashed her nose against his throat. "A laughably typical younger son from a 'good' family. He was on holiday, traveling the Mediterranean, and I was in a rebellious phase."

"I am not laughing, Catherine. At least you did not marry this cad and find yourself bound to him for all time. You never had to support a fiction of accord with him, never had to waste your time and devotion making a home for him and currying the favor of his friends. Trusting this scoundrel could have cost you even more than it did."

Catherine gave Fournier an odd look, as if she recognized him, but could not recall his name. "The things you say... Take me to bed, please."

He rose with her in his arms. "Are you again being rebellious, Catherine?" He would have to finesse the moment if she was. Rebellions ended, and Fournier did not want to be a casualty of the return of her good sense.

"You talk to me," she said. "You demand nothing. You are patient and kind and blazingly honest. You brought me Caesar. You worry over my choice of wines. You haven't even inquired into the extent of my appallingly large fortune. As rebellions go, you are a miserable failure."

"Delighted to hear it, but if this *liaison* is not a rebellion for you, then what is it?" He laid her on the bed and sat at her hip.

"I am with you for joy and pleasure, my friend. The candles, Fournier. Please."

He hoped to be more to Catherine Fairchild, and he wasn't about to waste this opportunity to make progress in the direction of greater intimacy with her. He tended to the candles and the fire while Catherine wrestled free of her dressing gown and drew up the covers.

Fournier left the bedside candle burning while he disrobed, and Catherine frankly gawked at him. He met her gaze, blew out the candle, and got a quiet chuckle for his reward.

"My lady asked me to extinguish the candles."

"I was enjoying the view."

"Enjoy the whole man," he said, climbing beneath the covers and lacing an arm beneath her neck. "Be bold, Catherine. Be greedy and curious and have your pleasure of me."

Kettering's words, about earning Catherine's trust, echoed in the silence. Fournier had puzzled over those words, examining them from all directions. Catherine's trust had been abused in the past, but she had found her courage again.

What was needed was patience. She managed best when allowed to follow her own instincts, without hurry or expectation. She managed best, in other words, when Fournier trusted *her*.

"Where do I start, Xavier?"

His name. In bed, she used *his name.* "Wherever you please. If I find your attentions objectionable, I will inform you. If you were, for example, to cuddle up along my side and run your hands over every inch of my naked flesh, I would be amenable to your caresses."

"Good to know. Likewise, of course."

His great displays of articulation came to an end as Catherine traced his features with deft fingers, explored his chest and belly, sniffed his shoulder, and straddled him. She pinned his wrists to the pillow beside his head and commenced kissing him with such a blend of curiosity and boldness that he was soon in a state of raging arousal.

How long had he contented himself with passing self-gratification and hard work? He wanted for nothing by the standards of either French or English societies, and yet, he had been starving.

For tenderness, for closeness, for honest desire.

The fog of pleasure revealed another truth to him. A woman who kissed with Catherine's fire and passion, a woman who took her lover's hand and placed it over her breast, who fondled him with diabolical gentleness... Such a woman might very well delight in the earthy, robust joy of a good Cahors wine.

The Mayfair damsel Catherine showed to the world was not a lie, exactly, but she disguised the true lady, with whom Fournier was delighted to share a bed.

As Fournier learned what touches Catherine liked and what touches she adored, regret tried to edge out his joy. This might be their only encounter. Why hadn't he met Catherine years ago, before she'd staged her ill-fated rebellion, and he'd embarked on his ill-fated marriage? Why must the woman he loved struggle against the betrayal she'd suffered from a dishonorable rogue years ago?

Catherine crouched over him and snuggled close. "Xavier, I need..."

"I am yours." He'd spoken French. *Je suis à vous.* Then the import of her hesitation became clear. "We can make love like this, Catherine. You need not be on your back."

"How...?"

"Your rebellion was undertaken with *un idiot.* You simply take me inside you. You control matters in this position, while I lie in a pool of unbearable pleasure."

In the shadowed firelight, her expression became determined, though her intimate touch remained careful.

"Like that," he whispered. "Precisely like... *Mon Dieu, Catherine.*"

She drew out the moment of joining, sinking and retreating, pausing, feinting. Fencing analogies came to mind and just as quickly dissolved in that pool of unbearable pleasure. That *ocean* of unbearable pleasure.

"I like this," Catherine said. "I like this much better than being half smothered and mashed and... Oh, I like this so very much."

Fournier could not recall how to say *one rejoices to hear it* in English. He was too busy contending with the rising tide of desire threatening to swamp his self-restraint. That Catherine was still wearing her nightgown was only the smallest boon. When he thought he could endure no more, Catherine's rhythm shifted, and her undulations became purposeful.

The honor of France, or at least of one drafty château in Bordeaux, rested upon Fournier's self-control, and by the barest margin of desperate willpower, he held himself in check as Catherine keened softly against his shoulder.

She clutched at him as if he were her last prayer of salvation, and a small eternity passed while pleasure reverberated through her. When she at last subsided onto his chest, Fournier gently withdrew and spent in the warm press of their bellies.

Messy, but honorable.

Also a far greater satisfaction than he'd known in years. He stroked Catherine's hair and resisted the urge to assess his performance further. That habit, like the habit of regret, had been born of his marriage. Bad habits could be broken.

"This is how it's supposed to be, isn't it?" Catherine asked, sitting up and passing Fournier the handkerchief from the bedside table. She watched as Fournier swabbed his seed from her skin and then his.

"The whole point is that great explosion of sensation on both sides," she went on. "I assumed that for the man something momentous occurred, or else what was all that sweating and panting in aid of, but for the woman... You caressed my breasts, didn't merely grope and squeeze..." Her expression became thunderous. "He went about it all wrong, didn't he?"

Fournier could tell her that comparing lovers aloud was not the done thing. He could tell her that *explosions* were not the point of intimacy for many people. He could make excuses for a selfish, dishonorable young man who should nonetheless have known better.

But above all else, Catherine Fairchild deserved the truth.

Fournier tossed aside the handkerchief and gathered her in his arms. "I do not know this *he* you refer to, but I promise you, Catherine: Any man fortunate enough to earn your intimate notice has every possible inspiration to exert his amorous talents for your pleasure. You should also know that while spending my seed means I am *hors de combat* for a time, a lady has no such limitations."

Catherine passed her tongue over his nipple. "*Hors de combat*. I have much to learn. For how long?"

Dieu au paradis. "Not long at all, if you keep that up."

She laughed, the most knowing, feminine, delighted laugh, and Fournier's heart ached with joy. Catherine Fairchild might take her time inspecting his wares and yielding her trust, she might dither over the actual commitment to marry—wise lady—but Fournier had finally found a woman who would never, ever play him false.

CHAPTER ELEVEN

Catherine endured a relentlessly cheerful breakfast among her Dorning siblings. Fortunately, Xavier had prepared her for that ordeal. He would be polite, he'd explained. She would be gracious, and the Dornings could all go to perdition.

A simple and effective plan, if one could ignore knowing smiles and a meal that included ample portions of billing and cooing among the married couples.

"I am astonished," Catherine said quietly as Fournier waited with her for his coach to be brought around. Sycamore and Jeanette Dorning were seeing them off, though the Earl of Casriel had escorted Catherine down to the porte cochere and had warned her to expect a condolence call from him and his countess within the fortnight.

"Astonished that my coach could be so quickly repaired?" Fournier replied.

"That my siblings could be so... so... blasé about their own scheming. I had some acquaintance with Sycamore and Ash prior to this occasion. I thought they would naturally be less reserved, less formidable than their elders."

The coach rattled around the circular drive, coming to a halt at the foot of the steps.

"Sycamore and Ash are both men to be reckoned with," Fournier said. "Mr. Ash Dorning is quiet, but his fencing reveals considerable determination and shrewdness. Sycamore is as quiet as a hurricane, and that, too, is a form of shrewdness."

"Because a family can accommodate only one hurricane at a time?"

Fournier offered her his arm as they descended the steps. "Something of the sort. They like you, Catherine, and they will not abandon you after this little show of support. The quiet Ash, the charming Kettering, the cordial Lord Casriel, they are allies who command respect in Mayfair. Nobody trifles with a Dorning lest the whole horde take offense."

Sycamore completed his role as host by kissing Catherine's cheek in parting, while Jeanette hugged her and beamed at Fournier. He and Jeanette exchanged some words in French, too quickly for Catherine to follow precisely. Something about an uneventful journey home, and some adventures being quite pleasant.

The coach was soon on its way, and Catherine was tucked up against her escort.

"Do you know what astonishes me most of all?" she asked.

"The explosions," Fournier replied, setting his hat on the opposite bench, untying Catherine's bonnet ribbons, and divesting her of her millinery. "You are a woman clearly fascinated with a new discovery, and may heaven be thanked, I am the lucky fellow with whom you have begun your explorations. These benches fold out to make a bed, in case you were about to ask."

"Perhaps if our destination were York, I'd have enough time to put your traveling coach to good use," she said, "but we will be in London in little more than an hour."

Fournier took her hand. "If the pleasure we share is not the greatest revelation of the past twenty-four hours, then what astonishes you most, *chérie?*"

He was the same self-possessed, articulate, conscientious escort, and yet, the look in his eyes had changed, becoming more tender and more... sad? Catherine would try to sort the difference later, when she had solitude in which to think.

"The pleasure is so far beyond astonishing," she said, "that words fail me in five languages."

"As many as that?" He kissed her gloved fingers. "Such flattery."

"You are astonished as well," Catherine said. "We can talk about that later. What has taken me completely aback is that I don't feel in the least ashamed. I have no regrets and, in fact, cannot wait for another opportunity to spend a night in your arms."

"You go beyond flattery now. Soon, I will be blushing. This is not manly, according to you English."

"Soon, you will be strutting. You and I were a couple at the breakfast table, and it was lovely and nobody's business, and nobody made it their business."

"The Dornings' meddling had gone as they'd intended. I am still torn between gratitude and annoyance."

Catherine rested her head on his shoulder. "Your annoyance sounds suspiciously smug, Fournier."

"I have every reason to be smug. Nap if you like. Some passionate fellow deprived you of a full night's rest."

She'd slept in his bed, the first time in her life that she'd spent the night with a lover. The passionate fellow now sitting so placidly beside her had been magnificent, and the pleasure answered so many questions Catherine had not put even to Mama.

And the affection, the cuddling, and warmth... That was dangerously alluring too. So was watching Fournier rise, pull on a pair of loose pajama trousers, and move through a series of slow, graceful stretches unlike anything Catherine had seen previously.

That he would observe his morning routine while she looked on was a gesture of confidence in her, a silent request for her to accept the whole man, not only the gallant lover.

"You are thinking," Fournier said. "Marveling at my amorous skills? Or perhaps at your own?"

"Yes. Marveling at both. Here I thought I was a half-disgraced wallflower, not an ardent acolyte of Eros. I wish I'd met you sooner."

"We have now, and the mistakes and regrets that weigh on our hearts make us appreciate *now* more than we would if life had been a bed of clover, *non?*"

Well, perhaps, but no amount of Gallic philosophizing would move Catherine to forgive Fort Armbruster for laughing at her. *Marry a schoolgirl who barely knows how to kiss just because I've endured her fumblings on a few occasions?*

At some point, Catherine would have to tell Fournier the rest of it, the whole, sorry, heartbreaking tale. Fournier was worthy of that confidence, but Catherine would have to reveal it on her own terms, in her own time.

When she wasn't aching in places private and pleasurable. When she could make sense of what had changed with a single joyous night in Fournier's arms. It occurred to her a quiet, cozy mile later that Fournier was perhaps also rearranging his expectations and trying to make sense of their situation.

"Are you pondering and marveling?" she asked.

"Both," he said as the horses increased their pace. "You have called me blazingly honest, albeit a miserable excuse for a rebellion."

"Just so. I esteem your forthright manner greatly, Fournier. Don't think to turn up diffident or coy on me now."

He shifted, wedging himself more into the corner of the bench and wrapping an arm around Catherine's shoulders.

"I value your esteem, though that word is too reserved for the sentiment I bear you. I am *captivé*, or perhaps your English word 'enthralled' applies. One can hardly think in the state I find myself."

In the past mile, his silence had become brooding, his expression distant. Not cold, but lost in thought.

"If your wife is still alive, then simply tell me, Fournier. I have no need to marry and no real wish to marry. A wife is not the impediment to our friendship that you might think her to be."

Not a sentiment the proper Miss Catherine Fairchild should be able to think, but that same Miss Fairchild had seen life in diplomatic circles on three continents. She'd observed Mayfair's best families from among the ferns and potted palms bordering many a fine ballroom, and—most significantly—she was no longer a furious, lonely seventeen-year-old bumbling through her first affair.

"My wife has gone to her reward," Fournier said, "but you should also know that there was a child."

If highwaymen had stopped the coach, Catherine could not have been more taken aback. "You lost a child?"

"No." He spoke near her temple. Catherine realized he'd chosen to make this disclosure when they were cuddled such that she could not see his face. "Yes, rather. The girl was legally my daughter. Though, given my extended travels to London, she could not possibly be my daughter. Still..."

"You loved her."

"Of course I loved her. How can one not love a child? She wasn't mine in the sense that I was present at her conception, but she was mine to love, to care for, to raise, and to protect."

That last word was spoken in a near whisper.

"Go on."

"I thought, I had hoped, that the child might bring Gabriella and me together. My wife apologized to me—a first in our marriage—and said she could not regret Mignon, but neither was Gabriella pleased to have slighted my pride. What matters pride when an innocent child needs two parents? I had hoped a daughter might mean a fresh start, that Gabriella might at least join me in London for a time."

"She refused."

"We compromised. By then, Napoleon had escaped from Elba, and traveling anywhere had become more perilous than ever. Gabriella agreed to take Mignon to her cousins' farther inland for safety. I agreed to return to London with another shipment of brandy and claret, knowing I could fetch exorbitant prices for it. All of France was in an uproar, and our own Grand Armée was pillaging the countryside as viciously as any invading enemy could ever hope to."

"I recall the devastation." The British forces, so eager to plunder their fallen enemy, had found nothing left to steal or destroy. Napoleon's soldiers had kindly seen to the destruction of the French countryside for them. Nine months after the fall of Paris, the exiled Napoleon had returned. The army had rallied to his side as he'd marched from the Mediterranean coast north to Paris.

"*Exactement*," Fournier said. "Devastation and more devastation. Gabriella should have taken a humble cart and attired herself as a farm wife, but she took the carriage, and of course the coach was held up. The bandits stole everything—the horses, the pistols, even Gabriella's cloak and boots. They shot the coachman and groom, but spared the females. The weather turned foul, and Gabriella walked for miles before she came upon a coaching inn. By then, she was already on the way to a lung fever, but she lasted long enough to bury the child. Mignon fell ill even more quickly than did her mother. They are buried together, though the innkeeper could not recall the exact location of the grave."

Fournier's elegant coach rolled on as before, swaying gently on its springs. Outside, another morning advanced in sunny spring glory, and yet, all the joy Catherine had arisen with, all the wonder, had subsided in the face of Fournier's tale.

"Do you blame yourself?"

"Not anymore. I will even confess to some relief that I am free of Gabriella. She tolerated marriage to me because I offered her a way to realize her ambitions. She was neither loyal nor faithful nor honest, in the end, but all of that is bearable. What breaks my heart is the child's fate. Her mother loved her, though not as a little girl deserved to be loved. I had the legal right to take Mignon with me to London, to safety, but I did not. I blame myself for that. Her death is a sorrow I will never put entirely behind me."

What comfort could Catherine possibly offer in the face of such a loss? What comfort had anybody offered her?

"You loved that child, Fournier. You welcomed her into your heart and treated her as if she were your own. I can tell, as one who was not related to my legal father, how much that meant to Mignon. Her mother is responsible for making reckless decisions, but as skilled as you are with your sword, you could not have fended off murderously desperate men."

"I could have died trying. I could have argued for my wife to be allowed to keep her damned boots."

"And starving bandits would have taken her boots anyway, stripped you naked, and shot you too. Would that have been a better outcome? Three deaths instead of two?"

"I might have been naked and dead, but my honor would have survived the encounter."

Men. *Honorable* men. "While your honor is no small trifle, Fournier, half the émigrés in London would be in worse straits without your generosity. More to the point, I could not have fallen in love with you had you wasted your life arguing with villains over your idiot wife's boots."

The next silence was more fraught, until Catherine felt Fournier's posture ease.

"The formidable Miss Fairchild does not approve of such a death for me," Fournier said. "I will not argue with a lady."

"But you will have your regrets. We all do, Fournier." Catherine certainly had hers, and Fournier's disclosure gave her much to think about, though she did not at all regret declaring her regard for him.

No wonder he wasn't interested in casual dalliances. No wonder he was so generous with other émigrés. The loss of his wife and child also explained his ferocious devotion to sword practice and his mixed feelings about a permanent return to France.

Catherine laced her fingers with her lover's and wrapped an arm around his waist. She could not sleep, but she could close her eyes and ponder what had just happened in Fournier's comfortable coach.

He had trusted her with the truth, with his most devastating sorrow, and with his greatest disappointment. The lovemaking had been a revelation, greeting the day as a couple had been astonishingly comfortable, but the true surprise was the degree to which Xavier Fournier had decided to trust her.

How was she ever to reciprocate such a display of courage?

"Fournier is rich," Worth Kettering said as he swung into the saddle and prepared to accompany Grey Dorning, Earl of Casriel, back to Town. "We need not worry over his means."

"Catherine might well be richer," Casriel replied. "The settlements would require setting up trusts, protecting her wealth from his creditors, and so forth."

"Child's play." Boring child's play for Worth Kettering, though he did like to keep his legal drafting skills honed. "Catherine's fortune is significant, but Fournier has the greater wealth. He took terrible risks during the war, and his risks paid off. He inherited from all sides, being an only surviving son, and he has diversified. Even a bad harvest won't substantially reduce his coin, and now Goddard has taught him the new method for making clear champagne."

"Why would Goddard do a thing like that?"

"You should ask him." Kettering knew Colonel Orion Goddard only in passing, but the colonel managed both Sycamore Dorning and The Coventry Club with apparent ease.

"One does not pry, Kettering. One asks one's wife about her recent correspondence and muses aloud regarding passing questions. I gather Fournier took up for Goddard when half the military was ready to hang him for treason he did not commit."

Kettering was well connected. He had the ear of the influential dowagers in Mayfair and most of the younger sons. No less person than the Regent himself sought Kettering's financial advice, and that same august personage occasionally passed along excellent insights about the market for art.

But Fournier was something of a puzzle, and Kettering was helpless not to solve a puzzle. "A wealthy émigré who will take up for a disgraced British colonel is his own man. I generally like that quality in a fellow, though Fournier's situation does pique the curiosity."

"Goddard is half French," Casriel said, "and entirely smitten with Sycamore's cook."

"Jacaranda says Catherine is smitten with Fournier."

"My countess concurs. She further relates that Miss Fairchild's whereabouts at the time when she ought to have been making a come out are something of a mystery."

The day was beautiful, if one could ignore the pall of smoke hanging over the metropolis across the river.

"Mysteries want solving," Kettering said. "We need to get to the bottom of it before some jealous tabby does."

"I am not concerned with jealous tabbies," Casriel replied. "The Dornings have the standing, connections, and sheer numbers to face down all but the worst scandals."

Kettering, who prided himself on his quick thinking, took a moment to unravel the earl's reasoning.

"You are concerned that Catherine will be blackmailed. Everybody already knows she's a Dorning, so what other secrets could be used to prey on her?"

"Precisely. Everybody will soon know the Dornings are through ignoring our sibling, but what of that extended period when Miss Fairchild and her mother were apparently in neither Rome nor London? Where were they, and who knows why they went there?"

Kettering managed assets, but Casriel managed a family. Different spheres, and yet not that different sometimes.

"It might be nothing. Diplomatic couples often endure separations."

Casriel, the picture of lordly elegance in his Bond Street riding attire, said nothing.

"It might be a disaster-in-waiting," Kettering muttered. "Jacaranda will make her inquiries. What else can we do?"

"Oak will raise the topic with his portraiture clients. Sycamore is keeping an ear out at the Coventry. Ash has the fencing and boxing salons covered. I'm more in evidence at my clubs and of course among the parliamentary committees. Willow has put the Haddonfields on alert, and when Their Graces of Quimbey return to Town, Lady Casriel and I will pay the requisite call."

A formidable army. "What does that leave for me to do?"

"Who do you know in the Foreign Office?"

"An undersecretary or two, a few attachés from among the younger sons. Why?"

"Lord Fairchild was in Rome in no particular official capacity that I can ascertain," Casriel said. "That in itself is odd, given that Bonaparte was in control of much of Italy at the time. See what you can find out, and, Kettering?"

"Of course I will be discreet. Don't insult me when we're getting too old for fisticuffs, Casriel."

"A Dorning is never too old for fisticuffs, pistols, or swords. I know I can trust your discretion, but given that Fournier and Catherine were brushing hands over the teapot at breakfast as shamelessly as you and my sister ever have—"

"Meaning as shamelessly as you and Lady Casriel still do."

"—I fear time is of the essence," Casriel concluded in one of his signature lordly understatements.

"So why are we plodding along at a drunkard's trot?"

Casriel tugged down his hat brim. "To the bridge, then. On three."

Unlike most Dornings of his acquaintance, Kettering waited the entire count before cuing Goliath into a glorious, heart-pounding gallop. The earl still beat them to the bridge by a nose—age and guile and all that—but only by a nose.

～

Fournier had told no one in London about Mignon. Jacques probably knew, as did a few other émigrés with connections to Bordeaux, but they had done Fournier the courtesy of leaving him to mourn privately.

Why tell Catherine Fairchild of the child? He mused on that question as the coach rolled ever closer to London, and the urban pall robbed the sky of its pristine sparkle. Catherine was a warm weight against his side, but she was not sleeping.

Already, he knew how she breathed in slumber and how she breathed when lost in thought.

"You should put up a marker," Catherine said. "For your Mignon."

"I would not know where to put it."

"Put it anywhere. On a pretty spot in your vineyard, in the yard of the château's chapel, if that's still standing. The important thing is to make a gesture that acknowledges the loss."

"You speak from experience." And she spoke quite emphatically.

"When I left Rome, I was a heartbroken mess. I'd been angry before, in the sullen, powerless way many frustrated young people are, but I left Rome furious. My mother worried for me, and I worried for me, but I did not know how to part from my bitterness. Young women are ruined every day. Young men flee their creditors even more frequently. But I was stuck fast, convinced my sorrow and outrage were the worst betrayal ever visited on any undeserving fool."

"You were innocent."

"I knew better."

"I knew better too, Catherine. I knew better than to leave Mignon in France." Saying the words aloud brought pain, but not the burning sorrow of fresh grief. What had been self-castigation was now a lament, a prayer for the dead.

Catherine sat up. "No, you did not know better. Nobody can predict the future, much less in time of war, Fournier. Gabriella apparently managed the vineyards competently. Why wouldn't you trust her to manage motherhood as conscientiously? You must get past this."

"By putting up a marker?"

Catherine was quiet for a time, and Fournier schooled himself to patience.

"When I left Rome in near hysterics, Mama was desperate for a way to ease my torment. She suggested we cut up the dress in which I'd first met my... I don't know what to call him. I thought he was a suitor, but he was just another lying scoundrel."

"When you met the perfidious, lying scoundrel, then."

The carriage slowed for a toll gate, while Catherine stared at her bonnet. "Perfidious, lying, randy scoundrel. He wasn't even a decent kisser. I know that now. In any case, he'd complimented me on that dress, and I wore it the first time he had it off me."

God help the scoundrel if Catherine ever decided to seek revenge. She had the means now, the standing, the family connections, to ruin anybody.

"So how did you put up your marker, *mon coeur*?"

"I cut that dress to ribbons, snipped until my thumb burned and my palm had a blister. I cut and cut and cut, and then we threw the whole mess into a pile of brush the gardener was burning in the stable yard. All that beautiful fabric and exquisite workmanship—Mama and I had done the embroidery ourselves—turned to ashes. A sacrilege, to simply burn it, but the sight eased something in my heart, Fournier, as did the sound of the scissors slicing the fabric and the pain of that blister on my thumb. I could look forward after that and look beyond myself."

She subsided against him. "It's not as if the dress fit me by then, but Mama's suggestion was a way to put the past behind me. When I am exceedingly vexed, I think of that acrid black smoke curling into the blue summer sky, and it settles me. The affair ended in humiliation, but my life went on."

Fournier pulled the shades down and wrapped his arm around Catherine.

"I did not think you a woman suited to drinking the Cahors, you know. All refined and poised, full of dignity and self-possession. Cahors is too bold and vivid for such a woman. Too earthy and proud."

Catherine slid her hand inside his jacket to rest against his chest. "But?"

"But I see more clearly now. I never did deliver the case you ordered."

"Bring it around on the staff's next half day."

She'd made him smile, which should have been impossible, given the seriousness of the discussion. "As Mademoiselle wishes."

He would also start shopping for a ring and think about having a marker put up, not only for Mignon, but also for Gabriella.

"There's a reason I like the Cahors, Fournier."

"Cahors is a wonderful wine, though underappreciated."

The sound of the coach wheels acquired the hard rumble of a vehicle navigating one of the Thames's bridges.

"Not only that," Catherine said. "We can put up markers and burn dresses to settle the past, but I sample the Cahors when I can find it to celebrate and mourn the present."

Catherine's earlier comment, about the dress no longer fitting her by the time she'd destroyed it, popped into Fournier's head, as did his first impression of her. A woman made cautious by bereavement, as a widow might be.

"You fled from Rome to Cahors?"

"To a little manor house several miles outside the town. Papa had connections across diplomatic lines, favors to call in, and nobody would think to look for a disgraced English girl in France of all places."

"Clever." Also brave. "You speak French with an Italian accent, which made the choice even easier."

"And Mama's French was nearly that of a native speaker, though she threw in occasional asides in Russian for the sake of our safety. I could not be happy in Cahors, but I could heal somewhat."

A dress might not fit because a young woman had lost her appetite. A dress might also cease to fit because...

Fournier mentally crossed himself—old habits died hard—and spoke gently. "Does the child yet live, Catherine?"

She tucked her face against his chest and nodded.

And that nod explained much. All of it difficult and so very dear. "I'm glad," Fournier said, hugging her close. "I am so very, exceedingly glad that your child thrives. Tell me more. I must know everything about this wonderful child of yours."

First, he must of course hold the woman he loved while she cried tears long overdue. Catherine stopped short of hysterics, though he would not have begrudged her such an indulgence. She did weep and cling to him and soaked his handkerchief to a gratifying degree.

As she gradually composed herself, and the carriage navigated yet more toll gates, she did tell him everything, or nearly everything.

The girl—Marie, after the late Lady Fairchild's mother—was ever so smart. She was dark and tallish like her mother, but her eyes were thankfully a celestial blue rather than the telltale violet. She was fluent in French and English and starting to work on German and Italian, because she enjoyed languages. She loved animals, and her governess, and she was beginning to send short notes to her mama along with the governess's monthly letters.

"She wants me to visit her, Fournier. She does not beg, but she invites, and that breaks my heart. I had six months with her, before Papa sent word that we must meet him in Lisbon. I've seen her once since then. I begged Mama to tell polite society that I was dead so I could remain in France, but Mama needed me too. The hardest thing I've ever done..."

"Was leave that child in France."

Catherine peered up at him, her face blotchy, her eyes sheened with tears. "No, because I knew I would someday, despite war, scandal, or the wrath of God, return to be a mother to my child. The hardest thing was *pretending*, standing up with the young men who considered me a pity dance and then standing up with Marie's father. I smiled at him when I wanted to put a knife in his heart."

"He deserved that, at least."

"He doesn't know," Catherine said, a thread of triumph in her voice. "He has no idea that I bore his child, and I will never do him the courtesy of enlightening him. Don't think to argue with me about this. Not now."

"You are that child's mother. I am nobody to question your judgment."

A subtle tension drained from her. "I had not planned to confide in you to this degree so soon after your own disclosures. I want you to know that you are not the only parent with regrets, Fournier."

She thought of him as a parent, from which he derived precious comfort. "You think I would judge you for not bringing this child to England?"

"If you *were* to judge me, I'd rather know that now and not six months of half days from now."

"Don't be ridiculous," he snapped. "You did what you thought was best for your daughter at the time."

"So did you."

Three fierce little words, but they clobbered Fournier with their simplicity.

"I did." Of course he had. Maybe Gabriella had too. He would at some later time examine the notion that forgiving himself meant forgiving Gabriella as well.

Complicated business, forgiveness, but not impossible.

"Marie's father is awful, Fournier. I don't trust him any more now than I should have trusted him in Rome." A note of fear laced Catherine's words, suggesting Marie's father might be powerful in addition to conscienceless. A younger son, she'd called him, implying that a title or an old fortune was involved.

"You have been careful, and you dallied with him long ago. If you choose to move to France and never set foot on English soil again, that is your business."

"I want to," Catherine said. "When the peace came—the real peace—I could not leave Mama, but my heart was in France. All I want, all I wish for, is to be a mother to my daughter and raise her with all the love in me. I cannot do that here in England, which makes the whole business complicated. The Dornings will not understand."

"You underestimate your family. Casriel is raising an illegitimate daughter conceived prior to his marriage. She is very much one of the family."

Catherine regarded him again, her features showing less evidence of her earlier tears. "Lady Della mentioned that. Mama claimed that Hawthorne was rumored to be as much cousin as brother, and then there is Lady Della herself."

The coach was no longer rolling along, having reached the congested streets of London, but Fournier was not in any hurry for the journey to end. He could move to France—with Catherine—and they could live at the château with Marie and grow grapes and have babies, and...

Be happy. The prospect stunned him, and made him cautious. The intimacy of the bedchamber was delightful and precious, but to share a future, to share dreams...

Perhaps Catherine was contemplating the same awe-inspiring possibilities, because she had grown silent as the coach gained the quieter streets of Mayfair. Fournier handed her down in the mews and bowed politely over her hand.

He did not want to leave her, did not want for the miracles—plural—of the past twenty-four hours to end, but he also needed solitude in which to contemplate those miracles.

"I will come around tomorrow with your Cahors," he said. "The best of that vintage I possess."

Catherine smiled at him, not the gracious, poised expression of a polite woman, but a lover's beaming benevolence.

"We will drink a toast, to friendship."

He bowed, she curtseyed, and Fournier signaled the coachman to move on without him.

"You will walk?" Catherine asked.

"I need to move the better to clear my head of all the tender sentiments befogging my thoughts."

"Clear your head if you must, monsieur, but leave the tenderness in your heart undisturbed."

He bowed and managed to walk away without bursting into song or twirling his walking stick like a callow swain, but it was a near thing.

A very near, wonderful thing indeed.

The last two weeks of the quarter were always interminable for a younger son making do on an inadequate allowance. Fortescue Armbruster had learned, though, that one could cope with those two weeks. A call upon the solicitors, and one of the junior Belchers would pass along a few banknotes as an advance on the next installment of Papa's largesse.

Sons burdened with an overly long-lived father understood life's unfairness, whether that father was of the peerage or a lowly attorney. The banknotes came, not from next quarter's total, but from the firm's petty cash accounts. A bit of goodwill toward one who might still end up with a title on some distant day.

In the last two weeks of the quarter, Armbruster acquired no new clothes, snuffboxes, fashionable accessories, or gambling debts. He moderated his socializing and frequented only the lesser establishments serving food and drink. He might even, if the shortage were dire, do his drinking at his lodgings and forswear the company of the fairer sex.

Because nobody who was anybody knew him at The Boar's Bride, and because the ale was passable and the meat pies decent, Armbruster did not exactly dread his return to that venue. The same scruffy boy was at the bar, and Nan was polishing glasses with a dingy towel.

"*Encore*, Victor," she said, whipping the towel at him. "*Dimanche, lundi, mardi, mercredi.*"

The boy repeated Nan's recitation, his accent surprisingly good.

"*Jeudi, vendredi, samedi.*"

Another parroting of Nan's words, followed by a cheeky smile. "I'm getting better, aren't I?"

"Your days of the week are intelligible. Now tell me that the food is good."

Young Victor frowned. "The word for food is big."

"Like your word for nutrition," Nan said, resuming her polishing.

Armbruster watched this exchange, both impatient with it and charmed. The boy likely hadn't seen the inside of a schoolroom in all his grubby years, and yet, he was eager to learn—or to cozen another pie from Nan.

"That's it!" Victor said. "*Nourriture. La nourriture est bonne.*"

Nan tousled Victor's hair. "*Bravo, mon jeune ami,* but no more free ale for you today. Back to work before somebody steals your patch."

Victor shook his tankard above his mouth, several drops landing on his cheeks and a few in his open maw. He wiped his face with his sleeve. "You'll watch me things while I step around back?"

"*Bien sûr.* Away with you."

Victor sent Armbruster an assessing glance that could have come from a much older male, then scooted under the bar, and passed through a beaded curtain into the kitchen.

"My lord is thirsty?" Nan asked, draping her towel over her shoulder.

"My lord needs information."

She gathered up the detritus of Victor's meal. "Then my lord had best have some coin."

Armbruster took the stool the boy had vacated. "What if I have something more valuable than a handful of coins?" What Nan had demanded amounted to a very substantial handful when a fellow was pockets to let.

She looked him up and down as if he were a fractious colt on the block at Tatts. Good bloodlines, questionable temperament. A gamble at any price.

"What could you possibly have that would appeal to me more strongly than money?"

"A lucrative post." He took off his hat—the plain black he wore on Sundays—and set it on the bar. "That means a position that pays quite well."

Nan spared his hat a glance, then said something in French.

"Languages have never been my forte," Armbruster replied, "but one need not be fluent in French to grasp that a lot of money over an extended period is better than a single payment."

"Your favorite wealthy auntie has developed a bad cough?" Nan asked, pulling a lady's pint from the barrels behind the bar. "Your godfather has found some *sinécure* to bestow on your undeserving self?"

Her utter indifference ought not to wound him, but it did sting a bit. "Why do you say I'm undeserving?"

"You earn nothing. You make nothing but noise and trouble. You aid nobody. Your definition of friendship is some fellows to get drunk with or win money from, but you aren't smart enough to win very much. You are good-looking through no doings of your own, and you could have learned several languages, but you are too lazy. Why should the stalwart John Bull spare you so much as a farthing to encourage your many bad habits?"

The French made everything about politics, and look where that had got them. "Some of my naughty habits are quite enjoyable."

"For you, but what of the valet who must clean the vomit from your boots? Not very enjoyable for him, is it?" She took a sip from the tankard. "Either buy a drink or leave."

Her boldness was both offensive and refreshing—stirring even. "I'll soon be able to pay for much more than a drink."

"Your older brother is to be set upon by highwaymen? Not very original, but then, one wonders if you could pay the highwaymen enough to do the job correctly. They do like their ale, those highwaymen."

"You've had truck with highwaymen?"

She gave him that same look again, though this time he would have said the fractious two-year-old colt was also a bit off behind.

"I have had truck with worse than that, but I do not care to have truck with you. Good day."

"You offer free French lessons to a boy who smells worse than a muck pit, but you don't want to hear my offer?" An offer Armbruster had concocted while trying to total his unpaid bills over last night's gin. Not so much an offer as a means of getting something for nothing.

"I am a busy woman, and listening to your vanities and presumptions is a waste of my time." How haughty she sounded, and yet, she did not set the drink down and decamp for the kitchen.

"I can make your life much easier," Armbruster said. "I'll set you up in your own place, and you will have nobody to wait upon but me. Your duties will be pleasant, and you will have most of the daylight hours free. How does that sound?"

She laid the back of her hand against his forehead. "Are you unwell, my lord? I have assumed that your afflictions are simply the usual wealth, arrogance, and idleness, but perhaps you have a true malaise of the mind."

"I am of quite sound mind."

She took another sip of the drink and set the tankard down, her manner as dainty as a duchess's. "I am not for sale. You and I have one bargain, on my terms. I will give you the direction of a certain letter, and you will give me coin. That is our bargain, and if your lordly brain cannot grasp those terms, then our business is at an end."

"I want all your passion naked in bed with me," Armbruster said, because he knew a bluff when he heard one. "I want you panting beneath me, begging me—"

The boy emerged from the kitchen, and his surprisingly clean little paws were balled into fists.

How quaint.

Armbruster set a coin on the bar and helped himself to a deep swallow from Nan's tankard. "I am soon to marry quite well. My intended has yet to learn of her good fortune, but it has come to my attention that she was absent from polite society's notice without leave for more than a year. When I ponder that curious development, I am led to only one conclusion." His conclusion being that blackmailing the lady for a few coins would not serve when he could get his hands on her whole fortune instead.

"*Tu me dégoutes*," Nan said, her voice low and mean. "You prey on women, some fine gentleman you are."

"You disgust her," the boy translated. "Not the good-manners *you*. You, like you rank pile of filthy, steaming—"

"Victor, *ça suffit*."

"Insult me all you like," Armbruster said, rising and tapping his hat onto his head. "But my prospects are about to improve enormously. In another few days, you will give me that direction and wish you'd offered me much more."

A fine line upon which to exit the stage, except that Nevin Thurlow stood in the inn's doorway, Armbruster's favorite hat on his head. The hat had come down in the world, acquiring a stain on the underside of the curled brim and sporting a wilted red tulip tucked into the band.

"Is the toff bothering you, Nan?" Nevin asked.

"He's leaving," Nan said. "Victor, you may finish his lordship's ale rather than let it go to waste."

Victor snatched the tankard from the bar as Thurlow sidled into the common. The boy held the door open and swept a bow. The look in his eyes was unnervingly cold, considering the lad had just been given a free drink—another free drink.

Armbruster left at a dignified pace, which was a mistake. Once he had gained the walkway, the boy dashed the ale at him and managed to spatter his best pair of Hoby boots.

"Next time, I'll ruin your prissy damned waistcoat, *milord.*"

"Vile puppy." Though the little beast had an eye for style. The waistcoat was exquisitely embroidered. Armbruster sauntered off, exuding his best not-a-care-in-the-world attitude, but in his head, he was buying The Boar's Bride and burning it to the ground. He'd have Victor arrested for theft and, for good measure, accuse Nevin Thurlow of assault.

When a man married money, he married power, and Armbruster was very much looking forward to having both money and the power once he'd made Catherine Fairchild his wife.

CHAPTER TWELVE

"My fencing has become sublime," Fournier said, taking a spoonful of his ice. "This is all your fault, mademoiselle. I have always been quick, but now my accuracy is faultless as well. I know what the other fellow is thinking before he thinks it. My arm is tireless and my energy without limit. The younger fellows are quite dispirited."

"You sound more astonished than boastful," Catherine replied. She was certainly astonished. The past two weeks had been an exercise in admitting that Mama had been right. A man had finally come along who'd captured Catherine's heart. Fournier brought her pleasure, laughter, comfortable silences, and *such* passion.

Oh, to have met him earlier. To have met him *first*. Mama had also said the fellow might be quite unexpected, out of the common way, and she'd been right about that too. Had Catherine met Fournier years ago, she might have dismissed him as another charming Frenchman.

"I am also *étonné*," he said, "you are correct. Never before have I made love in a wine cellar, and me one of the foremost wine merchants in Europe."

He'd been touring the vast stores beneath The Coventry Club as a favor to Colonel Goddard, and Catherine had tagged along out of curiosity. She was familiar with Continental vintages, but her curiosity about Xavier Fournier would never be satisfied.

He could make love against a wall.

Also in a moving coach, and the things he could do with his mouth were beyond shocking and well past delightful.

He spoke Russian quite well and sold wine to the imperial court. He had his shirts and small clothes made in France and patronized Bond Street only for his outer finery. When he shaved, he hummed French folk tunes.

And his favorite flavor of ice was vanilla.

"The last bite is for you," he said, passing Catherine the spoon and bowl. She traded, giving him her chocolate ice. They did nothing so fatuous as feed each other in public, but for Catherine to sit beneath the greening maples across the square from Gunter's was boldness enough.

"We are being watched," she said, savoring the treat as a pair of young ladies trundled by with their chaperone. "Judged."

"Assessed," Fournier replied with his signature calm. "I have won the notice of a lovely woman, and the male half of London is jealous of me."

"You have won more than my notice, Fournier."

He collected their dishes and set them aside on the bench.

"What have I won, Catherine?" he asked, rising. "One must not be precipitous or presumptuous, but with me, I hope you are honest."

He offered his hand, and Catherine got to her feet, slipping her arm through his. This outing for an ice was a pleasant social commonplace for most of London's decent society.

For Catherine, it had been a revelation. "The only man to bring me here previously was my father, and always, my mother accompanied us. I dreamed of ices at Gunter's when I was exiled in Rome, of the carriage parade, of dry cake and witty conversation at Almack's. What I wanted was not the ices or the fashionable diversions. I wanted acceptance."

"And now?"

"Being Marie's mother cured me of that stupidity. These people live to judge and find fault. They politely snipe at the Regent, Wellington, the French, the Americans, one another... They didn't want me when I was Lady Fairchild's by-blow, and they don't want me now that I'm an heiress with a title stashed in my trousseau. Their approval would gain me nothing of merit."

"And yet, you worry for your daughter. Her birthright is here, your wealth is here."

Catherine was enraptured with Fournier's lovemaking, but the quality that drew her the most was his talent for listening. She could tell him anything and know that his response would be thoughtful and kindly. He knew instinctively that her concern was for her daughter, so small and innocent.

And so scandalous.

Fournier was a gentleman, in other words, not a petulant lordling. He looked upon human foibles with compassion, rather than with an eye toward his own advantage.

"In France," Catherine said, "legitimacy is much less of an issue, and in France, as far as anybody outside the household was concerned, I was a tragically young Italian widow, not a headstrong English idiot."

"You are saying that Marie has a greater hope of happiness in France."

"She *is* happy. I have letters every month from her governess, and I know Marie is happy. My daughter begs me for a pony in her notes, but that is the extent of her discontent."

"She must earn her pony, *mon amour*. By reading a number of books, by keeping a journal every day for some months in her best handwriting, by tending a patch in the garden for the whole summer. By learning to ride when no pony has been promised to her."

Fournier matched his steps to Catherine's as they made their way toward her home. He tipped his hat to passing dowagers, and he bent nearer when Catherine spoke. His smallest gesture announced to the world that nothing pleased him more than being Catherine's escort.

He understood London Society in a way Catherine didn't, something else for her to ponder.

"I wrote back to Marie that she may begin taking lessons, and I sent her a list of pieces to learn on the pianoforte. She has a natural talent for music, but the garden is also a good idea. Children thrive on fresh air, and she is a Dorning by blood. They seem to thrive on botany."

"Do you thrive on botany?"

"I have always been drawn to the garden, for its peace, for its beauty. I have no particular botanical education, but I enjoy your discourses about grape varieties, soil, and altitude."

"I have discourses now, like a man of great learning. How you flatter me. What will you do with the rest of your day?"

"Dream of you while trying to tend to a mountain of neglected correspondence. What of you?"

"One hopes your dreams will be pleasant. I will be dreaming as well, of wine cellars and the rustle of your skirts when you raise them above your knees for our mutual pleasure." He said this as casually as if remarking the weather.

"I adore your ability to be naughty in your mind and polite in your manners."

"I am not naughty. I am a properly respectable wine merchant, though I am also besotted."

They turned the corner onto Catherine's street. "That worries you."

"Not as much as it should. We could live in France for much of the year. I don't miss my homeland, with all of its upheavals and sorrow, but I miss my home." He tipped his hat to another pair of dowagers, both of whom smiled back at him.

Customers, perhaps.

The import of Fournier's words took half the length of the street to settle in Catherine's mind. *"We could live in France?"*

"With Marie, if you wish. A parent and her child should not be avoidably separated."

"Are you proposing marriage, Fournier?"

He paused at the foot of her front steps. "I am, though I bungle the matter badly. Call it thinking out loud, or making a fool of myself out loud. I see us together, Catherine, but the details are lost in a fog of passion and hope."

A younger woman would have been offended at this bumbling offer of marriage, but Catherine was no longer a girl, and she was a mother, and Fournier was not bumbling.

He was *trusting* her. "*C'est compliqué, non?*" she said, continuing in French. "You have a business which ideally requires you to be in two countries at once. I have a child in France whom I cannot acknowledge and a fortune in England I did not expect. We both have reason to be cautious, and yet, I, too, see us together, Fournier. I don't know where or how, and Marie's situation will always have first claim on my loyalty, but I do see us together."

"That is good, then. Our objectives are in accord."

Not precisely. Catherine's first objective was Marie's safety and happiness, but thereafter... Who was to say that mother, child, and suitor could not all have happiness, in time?

"I am desolated to leave you," Fournier said, taking her hand in his, "but our discussion offers me reason to rejoice. What time shall I come for you tomorrow?"

"Dorcas's invitation stated that supper would be at eight, so come by at seven." That would leave them thirty minutes to inventory Catherine's wines, or to send the coach wandering London's streets.

Or to simply converse over a glass of wine. Catherine had altered her menus to admit of more than an occasional glass of Cahors.

"Very well, until tomorrow at seven." Fournier bowed over her hand.

"You could come in for a cup of tea."

"If I come in for a cup of tea, I will find an excuse to make love with you between your library bookshelves or on the sofa in your personal sitting room. My business requires that I deny myself those pleasures, and you have correspondence requiring your attention. We must have some dignity, Catherine."

She brushed her hand over his lapel. "Must we?"

He groaned and muttered something in French. "Until tomorrow evening. Dream of me."

She blew him a kiss, he laughed, and they parted with a smile.

We could live in France. That was a solution of sorts, though not ideal. Through trusts and clever lawyering, the Fairchild fortune would one day become Marie's. That meant involving London solicitors, while at the same time keeping the facts of Marie's parentage secret.

The French were fanatical about public records, though for an illegitimate child, not even the mother's name appeared on the birth documents. Though what mattered documents when human memory lasted at least long enough to make matters difficult for a girl of irregular origins?

Catherine was still pondering possibilities as she sat down to the stack of correspondence she'd been neglecting for the past fortnight. Dealing with notes of condolence while falling in love had seemed hypocritical, but the replies could not be put off forever.

She made good headway, inspired by thoughts of tomorrow night's supper with the MacKays, until only a few notes remained to be dealt with. The next epistle sported no black band and had no return address.

That meant the sender had paid the postage, a common courtesy with a letter of condolence. Catherine slit the seal and prepared to read more kindly platitudes.

I know your secrets.

She dropped the note onto the blotter as if the very paper could poison her. Her first instinct was to burn the message, but she was a diplomat's daughter, and Papa had received many anonymous threats. She instead made herself study the note.

The script was elegant, not a drunken scrawl. Black ink. The paper was merely folded foolscap, the seal off-center in the wax blob, as if somebody wanted to obscure the specifics of the design—a flower of some sort—and the wax was not the standard red, but rather more of a burgundy.

The scent of the wax was cinnamon, suggesting wealth—or a clerk who worked in a spice house. Spies came from all walks of life, and someone had apparently been spying on Catherine in Rome, or France.

She was still staring at the note when Harry brought in the tea tray.

"That stack can be mailed," Catherine said, gesturing to the replies she'd penned. "Harry, do you pick up the mail, or does Nevin?"

"Nevin, usually, when he's walking the dog."

"Please have Nevin meet me in the garden."

Harry's increasingly smooth demeanor faltered. "In the garden, miss?"

"He won't be comfortable abovestairs if he's been at his labors." More to the point, Catherine wanted privacy for the discussion she was to have with her lazy stable lad. She was no longer assured of that privacy even in her own home.

"I will tell Nevin to await you in the garden, but, miss, you have a caller."

The tray had been arranged for two, now that Catherine bothered to notice. Harry passed over a card. Plain black ink. Elegant script.

"Show him in, and leave the door open. I will see this guest to the door myself, but you will please remain within calling distance while I endure Lord Fortescue's visit."

Catherine was looking damnably well, but then, why shouldn't she be in the very pink? According to Armbruster's spy, in the past fortnight she'd been out to Richmond to visit the Dornings twice, to the British Museum twice, and to Gunter's twice. She'd called upon Jeanette Goddard Dorning and on Lady Della Dorning, all in the company of the rubbishing French wine nabob.

And those were just the outings Nevin had learned of. If she was larking off to Vauxhall, Nevin might well not know of it or care to add that development to his report. Divided loyalties in a subordinate were tedious.

"My dear," Armbruster said, taking both of Catherine's hands. "Has the gossiping horde descended yet?"

Catherine withdrew her hands. "The condolence calls are a great comfort, and yes, they've begun. Lord and Lady Casriel led the charge, closely followed by Lord and Lady Trysting and their various relatives. Shall you have a seat, my lord?"

Armbruster's note should have arrived days ago, and yet, he searched Catherine's countenance in vain for any hint of disquiet. The younger Catherine had been an open book—eager, shy, lonely, curious, and much put upon to find herself far from Mayfair as she'd left the schoolroom.

Begging to be seduced, in other words.

This Catherine was everything that young lady should have been —poised, gracious, pleasant, and utterly self-possessed. A vague twinge from the mental vicinity of Armbruster's conscience suggested he might have had something to do with Catherine's transformation.

Or perhaps the apparent support of her titled family was to blame. They would drop her fast enough once they learned how far she'd strayed from propriety.

"I have been worried about you," Armbruster said, taking the corner of the sofa nearest Catherine's wing chair. "It's the wrong time of year to be grieving the loss of a parent."

Catherine lifted the lid of the teapot. "There's a right time of year for bereavement?"

"Of course not, but spring is an especially hard time to be out of the whirl."

Catherine poured two cups of tea and passed him his without adding any sugar or milk. "The lovely weather, the emerging foliage, and the flowers have been a consolation, my lord. Life goes on, and Mama loved spring. To battle fresh sorrow as winter descends would try my spirit sorely."

Armbruster sipped his tea while Catherine did likewise. She wasn't exactly pretty, but she was more attractive for having gained a few years. She'd taken to wearing her hair in a simple chignon that accented the planes and hollows of her face. Her eyes, for all their lamentable color, looked out on the world with a woman's gravity rather than a girl's passing moods.

"Does anything in particular plague your spirit of late?" Armbruster asked.

"The loss of my mother, of course. The business of taking charge of a fortune I never expected to manage."

"The solicitors are on hand to deal with the boring financial matters. You know you can apply to me for advice as well, and if I might offer a passing observation, contributions to any fashionable charity will go some way toward quieting the talk."

Catherine set her cup on its saucer. "Don't be coy, Fortescue. What talk?" She seemed amused, though Armbruster knew very well how much she valued Society's good opinion.

He studied the vase of daffodils on the windowsill and schooled his features to reflect reluctant honesty. "You've been seen, Catherine."

"I do not aspire to invisibility, so this is hardly news."

"I know how badly you deal with being ignored, Catherine, but I am not your enemy. I am, in fact, your friend."

She glanced at the clock. "So as a friend, you are about to warn me of some dire rumor that will see me hounded from London?"

"I suspect it's not a rumor." He spoke gently, because Catherine's world was about to shift, and she did not deal well with upheaval unless it was of her own creation.

"Out with it."

While her expression remained serene, her words bore a hint of agitation, and that was encouraging.

"It has been remarked that you left Rome with your mother well ahead of your father. For more than a year, his lordship tarried in Rome and then traveled the Mediterranean and Adriatic, while you ladies...? Nobody seems to know what you got up to, and in a time of war, what could possibly prompt two unescorted women to wander at large? You and I had lost touch by then, so I could not offer any specific defense in your name."

Catherine offered him the plate of shortbread. "Lost touch, Fortescue? You dismissed me as if I were some dolly-mop who'd asked for too much coin after an evening's romp."

Of course he had. Any man would given the expectations she'd developed. "My dear, you wanted my entire future when I hadn't even the coin to pay my creditors. What sort of husband would I have made?"

"Vexatious, I'll grant you, and I am not your dear."

He waved away the shortbread. "I was your first. Can you honestly tell me that no affection for me, for the stupid, brash, passionate fellow I was, yet remains in your heart?"

Catherine dunked a piece of shortbread in her tea and munched in silence. This was her version of telling him to sod off, to take his rumors and leap into the Thames with them.

She was still headstrong, and curing her of that affliction would be a husband's privilege.

"Catherine, I'm trying to help. Sooner or later, somebody will remark how loosely supervised you were in Rome, and whatever it is that befell you thereafter—melancholia, a repairing lease at some sanitarium, overindulgence with the poppy—they will find out. The Continent is no longer blockaded, and many a fine family is pinching pennies in Brussels. You cannot hide your past forever."

Plainer than that, he hoped he need not be. If Catherine had a by-blow somewhere in Tuscany, then the child was likely his, though a fellow never knew for certain. Catherine had been *very* headstrong.

"I am not ashamed of my past, my lord. I have regrets, as I expect you do, but nothing for which I will allow polite society to scorn me."

"They called you Miss Dubious, Catherine. What do you think the scandalmongers will dub you if they learn that you eloped with some dashing Italian count and bore him a child?"

"How odd that polite society begins this speculation only after my mother, who never left my side, is no longer extant to dispel the attack on my good name."

She delivered that observation with a barely discernible twitch of her brow, the equivalent of a flinch that only a former lover would notice. Catherine Fairchild was hiding something that troubled her.

Such a pity when a wealthy young woman without family or friends had a shameful secret to guard. Reminding Catherine of her vulnerability was enough delicate work for one day's effort, particularly when the next quarterly installment should be waiting at the solicitors' office.

Armbruster rose. "I am on hand to dispel any attacks on your good name, Catherine. Never forget that. I was not at my best years ago, but I am a wiser and more worthy fellow now. You can trust me, and I will not fail you."

He used the pretense of his parting bow to stand closer to the lady than propriety allowed, and she did not step back. She'd probably missed him and, like all neglected women, intended to make him pay for a separation that had gone on longer than she'd intended.

He hadn't ignored her when she'd finally showed up in London, though he had made sure she didn't become bothersomely popular. He'd felt bad about that, but a fellow had a quarterly allowance to think of.

"You can call on me at any time, Catherine," he said. "And I ought not to say this, but as a friend, I will risk your disapproval. Xavier Fournier is respected within the limits of his trade, and the ladies tell me he makes a fine diversion, but if you need a gallant, you can do much better than that."

Armbruster patted her hand and would have taken his leave on that avuncular note had Catherine not spoken.

"Are you volunteering to be my gallant, my lord?"

"I am, and more than that. We are friends, Catherine, but when you need me to be more than a friend, I am prepared to serve in a more substantial capacity."

"I am not looking for a passing diversion, my lord."

He beamed his charming-bachelor smile at her. "Neither am I. The time has come to do my bit for the succession. Mama lectures me without mercy on that very topic, and you and I are well acquainted with one another."

Catherine's smile was cool. "How very generous of you. I'll see you out." She linked her arm with his and escorted him to the front door. No footman or butler was on duty, so Catherine herself handed him his hat and walking stick.

"I appreciate the call, my lord. Please give my regards to your mother."

"Of course." He'd do no such thing. Mama would have to be talked into accepting Catherine Fairchild as a daughter-in-law, and that discussion required familiarity with figures Armbruster had yet to winkle out of the lawyers.

So much to do, but the objective was in sight. Next steps required a stop at the solicitors' office and then a pleasant evening at Lady Haddigan's card party. After a few drinks, Armbruster would indulge in some discreet speculation—more discreet speculation—about where Catherine Fairchild had got off to during her protracted absence from Society.

But not too discreet. He pulled on his gloves and prepared to enjoy the rest of his day.

"One question before you take your leave, my lord?"

"Ask me anything, my dear. That's what friends are for."

"When did you take to wearing a cinnamon scent? It's most distinctive."

He smiled down at her, such as an adoring swain smiles at a particularly noticing damsel. "My valet suggested it. He's French, and what such fellows lack in humility, they make up for in style. I am cinnamon to my toes these days—shaving soap, pomade, cologne. If you're free on Sunday, might you enjoy the carriage parade with me?"

"I am already promised to Lord and Lady Trysting for the carriage parade. His lordship has agreed to handle my financial affairs, and his wife seems to know everybody worth knowing. I find them good company."

Worth Kettering was taking over her finances? That would never do. He'd tie the whole fortune up in trusts and *heretofores* and *notwithstandings* and then stand sentinel over the lot of it like some jealous fairy godmother.

"Another time, then, but soon, please?"

"Perhaps," Catherine replied.

And perhaps Fortesque would redouble his efforts to spread those rumors about Miss Dubious. He bowed again over Catherine's hand and wished her a pleasant rest of her day.

"Such gracious people," Fournier said as the coachman gave the horses leave to walk on, "though French spoken with a Scottish accent will always sound alarmingly fierce to my ears."

"Dorcas likes her husband's fierceness," Catherine replied, "and I gather Alasdhair MacKay adores everything about his wife."

"A wise man, to choose a wife he can adore. MacKay is also formidable with a sword."

As had become their habit when sharing a coach, Catherine's bonnet sat next to Fournier's top hat on the opposite bench. She sat beside him and was even holding his hand, but in some regard, she was as distant as if she'd taken a diplomatic posting in Cathay.

Perhaps Catherine was having second thoughts about a shared future.

Perhaps her menses troubled her.

Perhaps the servants were squabbling now that the household had no butler.

Fournier had spent most of his marriage trying to fathom the moods of a woman who had enjoyed a fine command of several languages. Much of the time, he'd been ignoring the obvious. His wife had loved another—probably a string of other fellows—and the time she'd spent with her husband had been a needful penance.

Twenty minutes of gloomy thoughts later, Fournier faced a choice as the coach turned into the alley that led to Catherine's mews. He could bow over her hand and offer to meet her in the park on the next fine morning—the equivalent of rolling over and feigning sleep, at which he and his late wife had both excelled—or he could remind himself that his late wife and Catherine were very different women.

He handed her down and bade the coachman to proceed home without him. "I will walk. The night is mild enough and the hour still early."

The coachman saluted, and Fournier held the garden gate for Catherine.

"Let's sit a moment," he said, "and enjoy the peace of the evening."

She led him to a bench in heavy shadows, there being only a quarter moon and the usual complement of London's smoky night air. They again sat side by side, as proper as a bishop and his maiden auntie.

"I am poor company tonight," she said. "The socializing is not as effortless as it once was. For Mama and Papa, it was an enjoyable art. For me..."

"Drudgery?"

"Work, at least. I know Mrs. MacKay mostly from her charitable endeavors. I wanted to ask if she'd ever heard me referred to as Miss Dubious or the Diplomat's Dubious Daughter."

Fournier shed his gloves and eased off Catherine's so that he might feel the warmth of her hand. "You have had many occasions to put that question to her, and she strikes me as a woman who would answer honestly."

"Maybe I don't want her to be honest."

Fournier rested an arm along the back of the bench. "The more upset you are, the more reserved you appear, and you have been very composed since I poured you a glass of exquisite rosé nearly four hours ago. Is something amiss, Catherine?"

He'd put similarly ambiguous questions and nonquestions to Gabriella time and again. *Is everything well? How have you been? I've missed you. The château appears to be thriving. Would you like to someday see London? What news is there of our neighbors?*

And she had provided him cheerful, meaningless answers.

Catherine rested her head on his shoulder. "I would like to be very unreserved with you, Fournier. I'd like to take you up to my bedroom and keep you prisoner there until dawn."

"Can one be a willing prisoner, or does that ruin all the fun?"

She said nothing in response to his attempt at gest.

"You are serious?" he asked quietly. "You wish me to spend the night?"

"I wish you to come inside and directly upstairs with me. The staff are all long since abed, it's my house, and I desire you madly."

She kissed his cheek and cuddled closer. She was being honest about the desire, but was she being dishonest about other matters?

"Catherine, I trust you. If you are searching for a way to tell me that we shall not suit, that you have decided to move to France without me to live quietly with your daughter, then please be honest. You need not offer me a farewell romp as if I were a callow youth whose ardor has grown tiresome. I will be sad if we are parting, I will be devasted, but I will not stand in your way."

"We would suit," Catherine said, rising. "I know that in the marrow of my soul, Fournier. Please take me to bed."

Would was conditional phrasing in English. *Please take me to bed* was imperative.

The old litanies rose up in his mind. *Do not make too much of a passing mood. Do not create friction when a woman is so obviously trying to be agreeable. Do not make the situation worse with interrogations and fuming silences.*

He gathered up their gloves and escorted Catherine to the French doors that led to her personal parlor. She'd left the latch unlocked, apparently, or Harry—who had pestered Jacques endlessly about wine pairings—had been lax about securing the house at the end of the day.

No lamp illuminated the path to Catherine's bedroom. No fire burned in her grate.

"A pity we have so little light," Fournier said. "I would love to inspect your bedroom down to the last detail."

"You will have to content yourself with having your person inspected down to the last detail, monsieur."

Catherine offered him her back and swept the hair off her nape. By feel, he eased the hooks of her gown free, then loosened her corset laces. How often had he performed these courtesies for his wife? How often had other men done the same for Gabriella?

He kicked that sad, bitter thought away. "Shall I take down your hair?"

"I will see to my hair. You have clothing to remove."

No matter how Fournier tried to convince himself otherwise, Catherine's words held no hint of seduction. He disrobed until he wore only his breeches. His attire was draped neatly over the reading chair, his boots positioned beside the bed.

And behind his falls, his cock was all but taking a nap.

Catherine wore a robe over her chemise, and her feet were bare. By the dim moonlight, her pale garments made her stand out like a ghost, her braid a dark rope over one shoulder. She tucked herself against Fournier, her arms slipping around his waist.

"To bed with us, then?" she asked.

"This is what you wish?"

"You've said your fencing has become sublime. I would like to experience sublime lovemaking with you, Fournier. Experience it again."

He suspected his fencing was about to become horribly inept, but when Catherine kissed him, he kissed her back. By degrees and caresses, his misgivings were gradually submerged under a tide of desire.

No woman could fake this degree of passion, this near desperation. Catherine soon had him on his back in the bed while she lavished upon him every consideration likely to increase his arousal. Her hands, her mouth, her breasts, and then finally, her heat, sheathing him in a luxurious slide into heaven.

She started off slowly, teasing him with a relaxed rhythm of thrust and feint. When he retaliated with openmouthed kisses and deft caresses to her breasts, her tempo became demanding.

"I want you to spend, Fournier. Share this with me."

"*Non.*"

Her undulations turned desperate. "Please."

"*Non et non.*" He caught her to him and drove into her with a determination that had been unthinkable a half hour past.

Catherine yielded to passion, the pleasure shuddering through her and threatening to unravel Fournier's resolve. She battered herself against him, her breathing a harsh counterpoint to the creaking of the bed ropes.

This much was real and true, and this much, Fournier could give her. When she subsided onto his chest, he pulled the covers up around her shoulders.

"You are not satisfied," she said. "I want you to be satisfied."

She doubtless did. Catherine was a generous and enthusiastic lover. She also, though, had wanted him to be distracted. He'd drifted off in a fog of marital exhaustion often enough to see the pattern.

"I want you to have your rest," he said, easing from her body and shifting them to spoon himself around her back. "Sleep, *ma chérie amante*, and if the weather is fine, we will gallop in the park tomorrow morning."

Catherine said nothing, her breathing as even as if she had already succumbed to dreams, though Fournier knew her and knew she hadn't.

He was accustomed to frustrated desire—Gabriella had emphatically not wanted a child with him—and as Catherine fell into true slumber, he ignored his body's clamorings to focus on the unrest in his heart.

A demon had entered the paradise he'd been building with Catherine, a demon of doubt at least and possibly of the human variety. Catherine had mentioned that old slur—Miss Dubious—and as Fournier silently dressed and let himself out of the house an hour later, he turned his mind to why that insult should trouble her now.

"*Monsieur, bonsoir.*"

The voice accosted him before he'd reached the end of the alley. "Victor, you are out late."

A portion of shadow detached itself from the darkness. "Saw your carriage pull around, thought you'd want a report."

"I want you to be safe at home in bed, my young friend, but what have you to tell me?"

"Somebody is watching Miss Fairchild's house. I can't tell for certain, because the clothes are all wrong, but I think it's that butler fella she sacked."

Deems. "Tallish, unhappy, a face like a tired hound?"

"Could be him. He tries to pretend he's a clerk out on an errand, but he never comes 'round The Boar's Bride. If Nevin is walking the dog, the fellow disappears. No real clerk dawdles about on the walkway when he could be having a pint."

"A fair point. Anything else?"

"Nevin is spying on Miss for some toff. He meets the toff at the Bride, and Nan don't care for the toff *at all*. She says he's *puant* this and *vil* that. *Vil* means vile, but I don't know about that other."

"Stinking, reeking, malodorous. The feminine form is *puante*. *Une truie puante* would be a stinking sow. Nanette does not care for aristos in the general case. Has this toff given her particular offense?"

"Interfered with her, you mean? I'd like to see him try. Knows her way around a knife, does our Nan. He paid her to spy on Miss Fairchild's letters for him."

French curses rolled through Fournier's mind. "And does Nan plan to accommodate him?"

"Spy for him? She told him what he wanted to know when he dropped in this evening. The letter he was waiting for is ready for Nevin to pick up tomorrow morning. He paid Nan in sovereigns, monsieur. A bag of 'em."

"Good for Nanette." An enterprising creature, because she'd had to be. Fournier sold a lesser Merlot to The Boar's Bride, and Nan had made an impression. "If I pay you a sovereign, Victor, what will you do with it?"

"Never had a sovereign before. Buy some flowers for Nan, I s'pose, and give her the rest to keep safe for me."

Chivalry was not dead, after all. "A sound plan," Fournier said, passing over a shiny gold coin. "If you ever want me to invest a sum for you, you have only to indicate, Victor."

The money glinted dully in the moonlight, then disappeared into Victor's pocket. "*Merci beaucoup.* Why pay me so much? Nevin probably don't make but five times this much in a year."

"You work harder than Nevin ever has."

Victor melted back against the shadows from whence he'd sprung. "Nevin says a bastard will never rise, no matter how hard he works, so why bother? I say that's an excuse to sit on his arse and makes sheep's eyes at Nan."

"Do you blame him?"

A smile gleamed. "No, monsieur. Mind how you go on the way home. The streets can be dangerous."

"My regards to Colonel Goddard and Mr. Dorning, Victor."

The only reply was a silent swaying of the branches above the alley.

CHAPTER THIRTEEN

Catherine needed a whole week of rainy days to find her balance after yesterday's developments—and last night's developments—but the weather refused to oblige her. She woke to a gloriously sunny spring morning, complete with tulips blooming along the garden wall and birdsong accompanying the morning chores in the stable.

"Fournier, you are prompt."

He looped Bertold's reins through a hitching ring on the ladies' mounting block. "On this beautiful morning, I had good reason to rise early. You are looking well rested." He bowed over Catherine's hand with mere politeness, probably for the benefit of the groom. Nevin not only had the horses ready, but also had his own cob saddled.

"I am well rested, thank you," Catherine replied, a glaring falsehood to the man who'd asked her to be honest with him. "Shall we be off?" Her voice held a damnable note of forced good cheer, one Fournier would detect easily.

He nonetheless boosted her onto Franny without comment and swung onto Bertold's back. They kept to a walk most of the way to the park, and when Catherine should have manufactured some friendly conversational gambit—a discussion of the rosé he'd brought over for her to try yesterday evening—her mind produced only worries.

And anger.

"Thurlow," Fournier said when they turned onto Park Lane, "I believe Miss Fairchild left her whip behind. Perhaps you'd retrieve it for her?"

"Good heavens," Catherine said. "I'd not even noticed. Please do fetch the whip, Nevin. Franny is regaining her former condition, but a fashionable lady ought not to be seen on the bridle paths without the proper accoutrements."

Nevin tugged his cap and steered his mount back the way they'd come.

"I did not forget my whip on purpose," Catherine said.

"Of course not." Fournier directed Bertold through the open gates. "The sight of me in all my equestrian finery turned your head. Bertold and I do cut a dash. One must acknowledge the obvious."

Catherine had not missed Fortescue Armbruster. She'd cursed the day she'd met him, cursed the evening she'd let him kiss her. Invoked foul imprecations in several languages upon the night she'd allowed him under her skirts.

If she parted from Xavier Fournier—and part from him she must —she would miss him for the rest of her life.

Last night had proven that, if there'd been any doubt. "You cut a dash wearing nothing at all, Fournier."

"The sunshine is more golden, the birdsong sweeter because you think it so. I have news to convey to you that is not in the least sunny or sweet."

Catherine steeled herself to remain composed. She was good at remaining composed. Could make small talk while her heart was breaking, could smile politely when she wanted to be sick. Fournier had not used a single endearment with her on this outing. The news must be quite dire—or perhaps, in a backhanded way, fortuitous.

"Say on, Fournier. Nevin will come trotting along eventually, or we will run into some Dorning or other out to prove they've finally recalled the meaning of family loyalty."

He turned Bertold down a leafy bridle path. "Would you miss me if business required that I return to France for a time?"

"Yes." The horses *clip-clopped* along, and a rabbit loped across the path. "I missed you last night. I fell asleep in your arms and woke wondering if I'd dreamed you in my bed."

"Last night was lovelier than any dream, Catherine."

Last night was how it should be with a woman and her lover, all except for the part about Catherine being desperately upset and Fournier stealing away when she'd drifted off. Fournier deserved to know about the note, deserved to know that Catherine's enemy—or enemies, plural—were preparing to tarnish her good name in earnest.

Or blackmail her, which amounted to the same thing.

"Share your news, Fournier, because I have some news for you too."

"You will tell me that our idyll has come to an end," he said. "Tell me that the time has arrived to put our pleasures in the past."

How could he know that? "Why would I make such an announcement?"

"Because some fine London gentleman is spying on you. Nevin is in his employ, and Deems might be as well. Your house is watched by Deems, at least, and this fine gentleman has been noting the addresses from which you receive regular mail."

Without Catherine willing it so, Franny stopped in the middle of the path. "I *beg* your pardon?"

"Bad news, but we are honest with one another, *non?* Colonel Goddard provides room and board to a host of children who would otherwise be at large on London's streets. Among their number is the crossing sweeper working the intersection nearest your home. I teach him the occasional word of French."

"I know Victor. He has permission to sleep in the mews, and he's done the occasional errand for Harry. We used to feed him regularly, but he seems to have come into room and board elsewhere."

"The colonel has taken an interest in him, as have I. Victor has seen Nevin meeting at The Boar's Bride with a fine gentleman, the same gentleman who bribed the appropriate parties to share with him the address on your regular epistles from Cahors."

Catherine felt a constriction of the lungs, as if her riding corset had been laced too tightly, but that wasn't the case.

"Tell me the rest of it, Fournier."

He regarded her with such patience, such gentle reproof that Catherine nearly started bawling. "I believe the rest of it is for you to tell me."

He was angry. In his calm, reserved, gentlemanly way, he was angry. Well, so was Catherine. "Please get me off this horse."

He complied—no hands lingering at her waist—and tied the reins of both mounts to a low branch of a maple sapling. "We will walk and be assured of privacy."

"Until I start screaming. Deems is spying on me?"

"I know only that he is keeping watch. Nevin is most definitely bearing tales in exchange for coin." Fournier offered his arm, as if they were strolling along at a garden party rather than discussing the mess that was brewing in Catherine's life.

The new mess. "Servants gossip," Catherine said. "Nevin knows only of my recent comings and goings. I'm more concerned about my letters."

"As am I."

They came to a bench in a small clearing, an oasis of peace and greenery. "Let's sit, shall we?"

"I am yours to command."

The words were gallant, but the tone was nearly perfunctory. Catherine took a seat and sorted through conflicting loyalties and unflattering truths.

"I trust you," she said, "but I don't want to *involve* you."

"Let's make an agreement, shall we? You trust me a little bit more, and then we will decide together to what further degree to involve me."

Such sangfroid, and such a subtle rebuke. "I received a note yesterday. Four words: 'I know your secrets.' If the person who wrote that note does know my secrets, I am ruined, Marie is ruined, and your choices are to cut your losses now, or be ruined with us. I don't want you to be ruined, Xavier. I know how hard you've worked to establish your business, how careful you've been, how many people rely on you. I don't want to be the reason you are ruined."

Catherine wiped at her cheek with her glove and tried to recall the last time she'd cried, other than recent occasions with Fournier. Papa's funeral service, probably. She had not cried for Mama, but she dearly, dearly missed her mother at that moment.

"I was the reason," Catherine went on, "that my parents took one diplomatic posting after another, the reason they had to be separated as Mama was falling ill. I was the reason we lived quietly once we did return to London. They loved me, but they did not account for how much more stuffy and ridiculous Society would grow as I came of age. I hate that I caused them so much grief, and I refuse to allow you to suffer to the same degree."

Then there was Marie, an innocent child, as Catherine had once been innocent. Fournier would grasp that particular without Catherine having to spell it out for him.

He paced to the edge of the clearing and then pivoted. "Somebody knows your secrets and seeks to prey upon you because of your past?"

Catherine nodded tiredly. "I expect a blackmail demand to follow shortly, or a marriage proposal. I would rather pay a king's ransom than contemplate wedlock with the person threatening me, but love for my daughter leaves me little choice."

Fournier strode back to the bench, and had Catherine not dealt with ranting ambassadors, hysterical attachés, and childbirth, she would have scooted back.

"You know who is doing this," Fournier said, his calm unnerving. "You know the fine gentleman who is disrespecting your privacy, bribing your servants, and scheming against you. Tell me who he is, and I will kill him."

"You mean that."

"I most assuredly do."

That feeling came again, of being unable to catch her breath, of being slowly suffocated by sadness, rage, and love.

"You cannot kill him, Fournier. I cannot kill him. He is the father of my child."

Fournier strode away again. Catherine was holding back an ocean of tears, or she—who was intent on sending him out of her life—would have begged him not to leave her.

Catherine sat alone, to all appearances fairly composed, while she prosed on about being a blight on her parents' life, expecting blackmail from the father of her child, and hatching some mad scheme to marry the bastard.

"You are intent on *protecting* me?" Fournier asked, staring down at her.

"You protect many, Fournier. You took unconscionable risks in wartime to keep your vineyards producing, and that doubtless was all that saved dozens of families from starvation. You look after street urchins. You are the honorary godfather to half the émigrés in London, and when Colonel Goddard was held in such low esteem, you—his competitor—took his part. Jeanette was very clear on that."

The feelings trying to rob him of speech refused simple labels, though they made him want to both curse and laugh—and to hold Catherine Fairchild close to his heart for all the rest of his days.

"Without honor, a man is nothing. This is an eternal verity whether he is French, English, or even American. I hope I behave as a gentleman at all times."

"You do," Catherine said, bowing her head, "and that makes you vulnerable, as I have been vulnerable all of my life. You think you know what it is to be relegated to the margins, Fournier, but you don't. They will take your business, your good name, your friendships, and all it needs is a few rumors and one cut direct on a fashionable street."

Catherine wore a veiled toque, so Fournier could not see her expression, though he could hear the Toledo steel in her words.

He sank to the bench beside her and resisted the compulsion to take her hand for fear he would never let it go. "You have given this matter thought." All the while laughing at Alasdhair MacKay's jokes and pretending to enjoy an uncomplicated rosé.

And making passionate, desperate love with the man she intended to banish from her life.

"I have."

"And when not castigating yourself for an accident of birth beyond your control and not devising excuses to abandon me, what conclusions have you come to?"

"That Lord Fortescue Armbruster has decided to have my fortune, now that he has all but wrecked my good name. I have no proof that he started all the talk about me when I returned to London, but the circumstantial evidence is considerable."

"Armbruster is an ass. When the best wineshops will no longer extend him credit, he will buy cheap brandy and cheaper claret and then have his valet pour them into expensive-looking decanters. You know that Goddard and I no longer do business with him, and we have alerted our colleagues to his ways as well." Some additional fact about Armbruster tried to push through Fournier's disgust, a wisp of memory, but it refused to march into full awareness.

"You call them colleagues, not competitors."

"The London marketplace is huge and connected to much of the known world. I am most fortunate to have my piece of it, and I see no need to be greedy."

Catherine sniffled, and Fournier's heart broke.

"I love so much about you," Catherine said. "Armbruster will destroy you with a word. He'll destroy me, too, unless I marry him.

He's working up his nerve, probably trying to talk his mother around, but his scheme isn't complicated."

"And you intend to comply with it, because the only reputation he will protect as zealously as his own is that of his wife." Logical. Damnably logical. Ruthless even, and entirely unacceptable. "You expect him to accept that the child is his own?"

"The dates do not lie, Fournier, and he can pass Marie off as a by-blow with nobody the wiser as to my role. To get his hands on my money, he'll agree to that. Marie had the good sense to have blue eyes, so she won't be associated with me."

"You have been brooding on this." Brooding alone, keeping her own counsel, not being a burden to anybody. Fournier wanted to weep and uproot trees and kill Fortescue Armbruster.

Catherine sat up very straight. "I celebrated Marie's first birthday not simply because she thrived, but because the nurse reported that my daughter's eyes remained blue."

What a thing for a loving mother to have to fret about. All over, Fournier longed to wipe the blight that was Fortescue Armbruster from the earth.

"You told me Armbruster knows nothing about Marie."

"He knows that for more than a year I was unaccounted for when I left Rome, Fournier. He knows I allowed him the sort of liberties that presage conception. If he has that address near Cahors, he knows exactly where Marie has lived since the day of her birth. He'll send some runner or inquiry agent to snoop about, and sooner or later, a shopkeeper or laundress will recall that the so-called Italian widow had such peculiar eyes."

"Beautiful eyes." And this was a beautiful spot in a beautiful park. All stately maples, lush grass, and benevolent sunshine, but Fournier could not recall heartache of a greater magnitude since he'd learned of the demise of his wife and her child.

"I am so tired," Catherine said quietly, "of being the butt of whispers, of being gracious to the Dornings now that they've decided to be gracious to me. Where were they when Mama and I were whiling away one evening after another among the companions and dowagers? Where were they when I became Miss Dubious?"

From what Fournier could piece together, most of them had been trying to minimize expenses by kicking around Dorsetshire the whole year-round. Casriel came up to Town from time to time, but the average ruralizing peer was not socially adept, and his lordship's marriage was of fairly recent vintage.

"Their neglect works to your advantage," Fournier said. "You shall call upon them now to put Armbruster in his place."

Catherine rested her forehead against Fournier's shoulder, the posture of a defeated woman. "Armbruster is *Marie's father*. Married to me, he will assume that place openly. Rather than spread rumors about me, he will guard my good name."

"The estimable Lord Fart will make you miserable, neglect his daughter, and hold over your head that you kept her from him."

Catherine's glower was magnificent. "I would have sent her to second cousins in Canada had I known matters would come to this pass, and if you have another plan, I am all ears, Fournier. If I marry Armbruster, he will doubtless decimate my fortune and give me unmentionable diseases when he isn't conscientiously *seeing to the succession*. Marie must nonetheless be my first concern. If her grandpapa is a marquess, she will fare better than if she's simply Miss Dubious's dirty little secret."

That was despair talking, and mother-love. "Don't call her that, Catherine. Don't think of her like that, and never again refer to yourself as Miss Dubious." He'd lapsed into French, though the words translated easily enough.

"You are more fierce than MacKay when you speak French, and so tender."

He laced his fingers more tightly with hers. "I speak French in bed?"

"You do. Beautiful words, and they are mine to keep."

So am I. Fournier could not say that, but he could know it. "Gabriella kept me at arm's length, or off peddling my wine in

London, to prevent me from interfering with her wishes and plans. Lady of the manor was not good enough for her. She had to be lord of the manor as well. She wanted power, I wanted love. We neither of us got exactly what we sought."

"I love you," Catherine said. "I am glad about that, Fournier. Had I not known you... But I have known you, and I have known joy. I will never regret being your friend and lover."

What fool in love had asked Catherine to be honest with him? "This is a puzzle," Fournier said, watching as Bertold bowed the maple branch to crop a few bites of grass. "Because I love you too. You protect me, Marie, the Dornings, and even Armbruster himself in a sense, but who protects you?"

"The first time I overheard my governess disparaging my eye color to the head footman, I knew I'd be looking after myself, though I didn't understand the why of it then. Not even Mama could shield me from whispers, stares, and rumors. I'm used to it, though I will do anything to spare Marie the same slings and arrows."

"Even marry her disgrace of a father."

"Even marry her father."

"You will not allow me to kill him?"

"You and I are lovers, Fournier, not murderers."

He kissed her gloved knuckles. "I would dearly love to be both."

Catherine rose, and Fournier stood as well. "We have some time," she said as they returned to the horses. "Armbruster hasn't quite steeled himself to propose to me. He might make a few inquiries first, and the settlements will have to be negotiated. Kettering will take up that challenge if I ask it of him. For some of my money to go to my daughters will be expected."

"I cannot tolerate the resignation I hear in your voice." The hopelessness he saw in her eyes.

"But you cannot argue with my reasoning."

"I do argue with it. A solution which gives Armbruster exactly what he wants, while condemning you and your daughter to misery is no solution at all."

Bertold left off grazing to peer at Fournier.

"I spoke too sharply," Fournier said, untying Franny's reins. "I apologize." He boosted Catherine into the saddle and arranged her skirts when he wanted to howl with rage and frustration.

"You spoke honestly, but how do you conclude that Marie will be worse off as Armbruster's acknowledged by-blow than as my daughter rusticating away in France?"

Fournier swung onto Bertold's back and considered the question. "You assume Armbruster will allow you to live in the same household with your daughter. He might well keep you separated and use you and Marie to control each other. You love that girl, and she clearly holds you in affection as well, sight unseen.

"But let's assume," he went on, "as you do assume, that Armbruster will raise his daughter under his own roof. Think back, Catherine, to how he treated you when he was supposedly smitten with you. Was he prompt for every assignation? Did he *keep* every assignation? Did he ever apologize for having been a cad and a bounder? Did he make any effort to learn what became of you when you left Rome? Did he write you doting little notes or leave you anonymous flowers?"

Catherine made an elegant picture on her mare, but she was listening, so Fournier treated her to more of his much-vaunted honesty.

"When you returned to London, did he call on you privately to assure himself of your wellbeing or willingness to be civil to him? No, he did not. According to you, he slandered you in the churchyard and at the men's punchbowl. Now that you are wealthy and orphaned, he slinks forward, once again offering nothing but threats while he eyes your fortune and pretends to be your champion."

Fournier was making himself even angrier with this recitation, though he nudged Bertold forward at a placid walk.

"What makes you think," he said quietly as Franny fell in step beside the gelding, "that such a man will treat an illegitimate daughter well? He has treated you abominably, and you are that girl's mother. He has seduced, lied, exploited, threatened, and spied on you. I cannot accept that his reward for these trespasses will be your fortune, your hand in marriage, and an opportunity to daily shame and insult the daughter you love more than your own life."

Catherine said nothing in response, and she remained silent when they met Nevin Thurlow—sidesaddle whip in hand—at the park gates. Fournier accompanied the lady back to her stable and assisted her to dismount.

Thurlow—the traitor—led the horses away.

"Is this our farewell?" Fournier waited until he and Catherine were behind the garden walls to pose the question.

"I don't want it to be, but you must do as you see fit, Fournier. I want you to be free of whatever misfortune is about to befall me, but I can hardly appropriate the right to choose for myself while denying it to you."

He took her hand and stood too close to her, and bedamned to the various spies who doubtless took note of his boldness.

"I gradually became aware that my marriage had been a mistake. I was slow to accept the reality of my error, and when I did, I was profoundly disappointed. That grief pales in comparison to the utter fury you force upon me if you again go willingly into Armbruster's arms. The first time you fell in with his schemes, you were an innocent, but you do not have that excuse now."

"Plain speaking," Catherine said, "and not precisely fair, but what would you have me do, Fournier? My daughter's happiness seems damned no matter what path I choose."

Fournier leaned close and whispered in her ear, "Trust me, *mon coeur*. Please, for the love of God, trust me, or I will walk out of this garden and take passage on the first ship bound for Bordeaux."

Fear was not always bad, though it was always a painful experience. Catherine was full of fears, some of them for herself—she abhorred the thought of a lifetime yoked to Fortescue Armbruster. Fournier was right that when his lordship took it into his head to be arrogant, sneering, and condescending, his words could cut as effectively as any rapier.

Armbruster might, on the one hand, take any further slurs against Catherine seriously, but he'd deliver plenty of his own when in a petulant mood and private with his wife.

She feared for Marie, though until this discussion with Fournier, those fears had been predictable. Childhood illnesses, a girl's heartaches, and no mother on hand to comfort and soothe. She feared for Marie's reception in Society. Feared that a very great deal.

She feared the awkwardness of explaining to her Dorning relatives why, having acquired substantial wealth, she'd settle for a fribbling younger son as a husband.

Though in all her brooding and pondering, she'd never admitted that Armbruster's notions of parenting might be worse for Marie than having no father at all. Fournier was right about that too—adding a worse fear yet to Catherine's pile of woes.

And now he was threatening to leave—leave her and leave England—and she could not blame him and could not ask him to stay.

But could she trust him?

Fournier had been a father of sorts, had held a child's happiness in his hands. He knew how easily a bitter word or cold stare could bruise a little girl's heart. Fournier was thinking clearly, consulting hard-won experience, while Catherine was flailing about much as she had as a younger woman.

Had she learned nothing from her misadventures? Was she supposed to be Marie's sole champion as well as her own? When had she made that choice, and was it a good choice?

Fournier stood silent and patient, while Catherine tried to envision a life without him.

"I love my daughter," she said slowly. "More than anything, I want to be a mother to her, but that has been denied me. I was willing to settle for being her distant benefactress for a time, because I thought that was best for her. You are right, though, that Armbruster can add to her misery. I had not considered that." Admitting that oversight was painful, but Fournier was the one person who had never expected Catherine to dissemble.

He watched her closely, his expression giving away nothing. "I cannot make this choice for you, Catherine, but what would your own mother tell you to do?"

The question was unexpected, and worth pondering. "I wanted her to be proud of me."

"I am sure she was."

He could not know that, but the words comforted. "I want Marie to be proud of me, and that..."

"Yes?"

Behind that patience Fournier adopted like an ermine robe lay a banked passion that Catherine had seen only on intimate occasions. That same passion had fueled the growth of his business, the unthinkable wartime risks, the unshakable sense of honor that defined Xavier Fournier in all circumstances.

"If I marry Armbruster, Marie might someday ask me why I chose such an arrogant buffoon for my husband, despite my having the means to live anywhere. She might ask me why being Lord Fortescue's by-blow was such a great privilege, when she'd been happy and loved in Cahors amid a far more tolerant society."

Weariness of heart threatened to steal the rest of Catherine's admissions, but mother-love was a force of nature and more determined than even Catherine had known.

She was not the girl she'd been in Rome, neither was she Miss Dubious. She was Marie's mother, and Fournier's beloved.

"If I marry Armbruster," Catherine went on, "I will tell Marie that my choice was made out of love, but in truth, if I become Armbruster's wife, my choice will have been made out of fear. I am afraid of Fortescue Armbruster, and for that, I hate him. He and I need not be enemies, but he has comported himself as precisely that. He has enjoyed my ruination and doubtless thinks himself quite clever for scheming against me yet again. I might deserve him for a husband, but Marie does not deserve him for a father."

"One is compelled to agree with only that last bit."

A smile tugged at Catherine's heart. "So self-possessed. I wish I had one-tenth of your savoir faire, Fournier, because it's one thing for me to say I cannot marry Armbruster and quite another for me to know what to do about him. He has power, and not a kind of power I can fight."

"You have power too," Fournier said, "and you have me. I daresay you have a regiment of Dornings at your disposal and more than a few diplomatic wives. Will you allow me to fight this battle at your side or will you go meekly to the fate Armbruster has in store for you, your daughter, and your fortune?"

Catherine thought of endless evenings chatting meekly among the wallflowers, more evenings meekly sitting out dance after dance. That fate was the best Marie would look forward to, if Catherine married Fortescue Armbruster. Slighted, ignored, overlooked, or—worse—insulted and helpless to defend herself.

"We fight," Catherine said. "I don't know how, where, or with what weapons, but we fight." That choice felt right—also terrifying.

Fournier's gaze lit with unholy determination. "The very first thing we must do when planning this campaign is gather every available scrap of information we can about the foe and only then develop our strategy."

Catherine wandered to the bench beneath the lime tree and patted the place beside her. "You have the energy for this fight. That's good, because I'm not sure I do."

"You have carried the standard on your own for far too long, chérie. Time to call up the reserves and put the enemy to rout. We French excel at strategy, and this cause is dear to my heart."

Catherine remained talking quietly in the garden with Fournier as the sun rose. The discussion required her to focus on matters she'd rather ignore. She was terrified for her daughter and not a little worried for Fournier.

What sustained her, though, was the simple comfort of Fournier's presence. He put his nimble mind and shrewd intelligence at her disposal and listened intently. He was a tender and passionate lover, also inventive and tireless, but this... this taking Catherine's fears and happiness to heart, posing hard questions and listening to her replies, this was utterly precious and a balm to her soul.

Fournier's friendship was worth fighting for.

CHAPTER FOURTEEN

"We are gentlemen," Fournier said pleasantly, "in as much as English Society allows one to use the word in an informal sense. Be a gentleman, Deems, and come with me quietly."

Fournier had approached the former butler alone on the street, taking a calculated risk. Deems was of advanced years, and a butler's job did not typically hone a man's pugilistic skills. Still, the encounter might be remarked by Armbruster's other spies.

"You raised your voice to Miss Fairchild in the garden," Deems retorted. "I could hear you from the mews. You are no gentleman."

"The lady raised her voice to me as well, but that is none of your affair. Come along, and you and I will have a civilized conversation on the walkway, where you need not fear I will menace you physically. You will tell me, for example, if you are in Lord Fortescue's pay."

Deems gave Catherine's front door one last look, then set a dignified pace in the direction of The Boar's Bride. "And if I were?"

"I would offer you more to betray him than he could ever offer you to betray Miss Fairchild."

"An English gentleman's loyalty is not for sale, something I would not expect a foreigner to understand."

"We all need somebody to feel superior to, don't we?" Fournier asked, tossing Victor tuppence at the corner. "And losing your post deprived you of that."

"You know nothing about it."

"So enlighten me, though you must admit, anybody who would spy on his employer while taking her coin has parted with all pretensions to an Englishman's honor."

Deems lost none of his poker-straight posture, but something defeated came into his gaze. "It's that damned Nevin Thurlow who's spying. When Lord Fairchild hired me, he warned me that a diplomat was a target for all manner of mischief. The household must be run to the highest standards of propriety and security and no effort spared to safeguard the ladies. I tried, by God, but there's Thurlow, panting after the French chit and his next pint and slacking by the hour. Of course he'd take Armbruster's bribes. Thurlow is stupid and lazy, and that makes him an easy dupe."

"You are former military?"

"What of it?"

"Lord Fairchild trusted you, and I gather he was a discerning man. You were at something of a loss when it came to managing his wine cellar, though, so I gathered your abilities lay in more practical directions."

They crossed the intersection, and Fournier could feel Deems reassessing his strategy.

"You think I'm former military because of how I kept the Fairchild wine cellar?"

"Exquisitely tidy, not a speck of dust on even the plum cordial, which we all know to be a gift given at Yuletide by impoverished aunties and former governesses. You overstocked the clarets and all but ignored the lighter wines suitable to an invalided lady or her young daughter. Your inventory was correct to the bottle, though.

That suggests a quartermaster's eye for details and ledgers and no familiarity whatsoever with genteel ladies and London socializing."

They walked along in silence, while Fournier silently sent up a prayer for patience. Throttling aging butlers on the street was not prudent, but oh-so-tempting.

"The last thing his lordship asked of me," Deems said, "the *only* thing he asked of me, was to look after the ladies. He alluded to difficulties encountered while serving on the Continent, though he was never specific about whether the difficulties involved Miss Fairchild or her mother. His lordship assured me the situation had been handled quietly, though my continuing discretion was imperative. I respect a man who puts the welfare of his family first, sir, and if your intentions toward Miss Fairchild are anything but honorable, I will do all in my power to thwart you."

Ironic that a sacked butler was more loyal to Catherine than the man who sought to marry her.

"Then it was Lady Fairchild who warned you specifically against Armbruster?"

Deems nodded briskly. "After she was widowed, when it became apparent even to me that her health was failing, she said on no account was I to trust Lord Fortescue, or even admit him to the household if he should call. Her ladyship wasn't one to take up against others, but she hated Armbruster."

"She had her reasons. I despise him as well, for even more reasons. Miss Fairchild's sentiments toward Armbruster make her tirade against me in the garden look like a poetry recitation. He seeks to marry her now that she has come into wealth, and he will use missteps in her past to force her to the altar."

"If I were twenty years younger," Deems muttered, "ten years younger, I'd treat his lordship to some pointed explanations regarding proper conduct toward a lady."

"If I were a bit less French, I would not be reduced to accosting former retainers in the street. I could simply call him out and rid the world of him. Instead, I must learn all I can regarding Lord Fortescue if I am to aid Miss Catherine."

"Ask the almighty Dornings. They know half of polite society, and the other half comes through the doors of Sycamore Dorning's fancy club. They will put out the word, and you will soon know more than the man's tailors know about him."

"I will do exactly that, Deems, but I'm looking for the sort of information that even the lofty Dornings won't come across, the sort that passes from kitchen to kitchen and mews to mews. I already know Armbruster doesn't pay the trades and lives from quarterly allowance to quarterly allowance. Who are his enemies, and how can he be brought to heel?"

Deems's pace slowed as they approached The Boar's Bride. "I don't care for talk and did not encourage it among the staff. Murmuring and grumbling between households only breeds discontent and slacking."

Low wages and long hours were usually the cause of that grumbling. Fournier kept that observation to himself.

"Think, Deems. Lady Fairchild alerted you to the threat Armbruster posed, so you took particular notice of anything relating to him. Any scrap of information could be useful—the name of his tailor, a club that would not admit him, a horse he lost in a wager."

"He curries favor with his mother," Deems said slowly. "I forget where I heard that."

"Every son ought to curry favor with his mother."

"The marchioness pays his lordship's valet," Deems said. "Somebody mentioned that over darts. She can't rely on Armbruster to see to the fellow's wages, so she pays him directly. Nothing but the finest Parisian gentleman's gentleman would do for her darling boy, and those fellows don't come cheap."

And just like that, the sunshine was more golden, and the *clip-clopping* of a passing carriage became a cheerful tattoo.

"The valet is *French*?"

Deems peered at the plain handle of his walking stick. "I believe he is at that, sir. You will call upon the Dornings on Miss Fairchild's behalf?"

"Discreetly, and your vigilance on the walkway will no longer be required. I will send young Victor to you when I have more to report."

Deems nodded and turned to go, then eyed Fournier obliquely. "Why'd she sack me?"

Fournier could fashion a lie about years of loyal service deserving a reward or young women taking odd notions. Deems deserved the truth.

"Miss Fairchild's trust has been sorely abused in the past, and she mistook your vigilance for judgment, or something worse. She is not nearly as self-confident as she appears, Deems, for all that she is brave. Young Harry is struggling to fill your shoes, and if you'd share an occasional pint with him, I'm sure he'd appreciate any wisdom you cared to pass along."

"Harry's a bright lad. No harm in a pint on half day."

Deems touched a finger to his hat brim. Fournier bowed slightly and then turned in the direction of a certain coffeehouse in Soho favored by Frenchmen in service to lordly English households.

"I have bested the great Worth Kettering at strategy," Sycamore Dorning said, raking in a pot of chips. "My fortune has become bottomless."

Casriel tossed down his cards. "We play for farthing points, Sycamore."

"Victory is still sweet," Sycamore replied. "The question of the moment is how we are to see Catherine victorious over her foe. I'm for a pointed discussion with Armbruster in a dim alley."

"You and your knives," Ash Dorning muttered. "This is serious, Sycamore. Catherine has finally given us leave to assist her, and you speak of larking about after dark. I want to hear what Fournier has to say."

As did Kettering.

Having been raised with only a single, rather reserved brother, Worth Kettering had learned to appreciate his Dorning in-laws as one would appreciate a performance at Astley's. The conversational brawling, verbal dueling, ribald humor, and silent glances wove layers of meaning and significance Kettering still found mostly baffling.

These people understood one another, while Kettering could translate only the most obvious aspects of their familial patois. They loved fiercely, differed fiercely, and were fiercely loyal. Beyond that, he relied on his darling Jacaranda to parse the subtleties of her family's interactions.

"Fournier," Casriel said, "you have the floor."

"*Merci.*" The Frenchman passed Kettering his cards as coolly as if this was not a counsel of war, but rather, just another desultory hand in an evening of tedious play. "To ruin Armbruster is possible. Even his valet's wages are late, and that fellow is paid by the marchioness. The whole family is in difficulties."

Kettering, by virtue of lurking about on 'Change and sending his clerks to share a pint with other clerks, had taken two weeks to reach the same conclusion. "Late wages can be bad management rather than insolvency."

Fournier ran a fingertip around the edge of his brandy glass. "*Oui*, but Colonel Goddard and I have both been on the wrong end of commercial transactions with the marquess's household. We had the usual quiet conversations with our fellow merchants and decided to cut off his lordship—and his sons—rather than put vanity before common sense."

"So you can buy up Armbruster's vowels and send him fleeing to Calais in the grand tradition," Sycamore said, shuffling the deck deftly. "Not very original, but effective."

"I will not buy up his lordship's debts," Fournier said, "and I ask that you gentlemen refrain from doing so."

Kettering took a minute to sort out that logic. "You want all of Bond Street, Piccadilly, and the Haymarket to come after him."

"All of Mayfair too," Ash Dorning said. "Armbruster has personal obligations, old wagers, and debts of honor. He'll have just got his quarterly allowance and paid most of those off."

Fournier gave a slight shake of his head, the gesture somehow Gallic. "Armbruster's valet informs me that his lordship is sending an inquiry agent to France. That exercise will cost money, as spying on Miss Fairchild has cost money. The inquiry agent is to travel quickly rather than cheaply."

Casriel, who weathered familial storms with heroic calm, posed the obvious question. "Why send a man to France?"

Fournier examined his brandy with exquisite calm. "To gather information of a socially damning nature about Miss Fairchild. Need I explain?"

The three Dorning brothers exchanged looks, but for once, Kettering grasped the significance. "The ladies have noted that Miss Fairchild left Rome more than a year before she and her mother returned to London. One suspects the explanation for that gap lies in France."

"The explanation," Fournier said, nosing his drink, "is thriving in France, about two days' journey from my château in Bordeaux. Lord Armbruster has been kept in ignorance of the full consequences of his dishonor toward Miss Fairchild. His spies recently alerted him to the need to investigate, and he has both the means and motivation to do so."

"Thriving?" Casriel asked.

Fournier nodded. "No expense has been spared."

Sycamore riffled the cards into a neat stack. "Blood will tell."

Ash hit him on the arm.

"Well, Catherine's a Dorning," Sycamore retorted, "as plain as the eyes in my head, and Dornings are prone to vigorous animal spirits."

"Sycamore, *hush*." Kettering, Ash, and Casriel spoke in unison.

Fournier smiled, and damned if he wasn't devilishly dashing when plotting an English lordling's comeuppance. "I must leave for France immediately to see the child to safety, and I come bearing orders for you from Miss Fairchild."

"Thought you'd never get around to it," Sycamore said. "We're ready, willing, and able to assist, as are the ladies."

"To ruin Armbruster is not sufficient," Fournier said. "For me to marry Miss Fairchild, as lovely as that prospect is, will also not be enough. To ensure the child's safety, while necessary, is also not the limit of my ambitions."

"You aren't ambitious," Casriel said. "You are demented."

"I am determined." Fournier handed out assignments, sketched possibilities, and rehearsed scenarios for the next hour.

"We will use only the weapons Armbruster has turned on Miss Fairchild," he said in conclusion. "Guile, gossip, spies, and good manners."

Kettering was happiest when managing complicated financial schemes, and this scheme pleased him not at all.

"You want to bring him down by a thousand cuts," he said. "That plan will take monumental patience and not a little luck."

"Is Miss Fairchild supportive of this approach?" Casriel asked. "You were heard having a very loud discussion with her in her own garden not three days past."

"That altercation was for the benefit of her staff. The under-groom and very likely the housekeeper spy upon Miss Fairchild for Armbruster. They present themselves as aunt and nephew, but they are, in fact, mother and son. Armbruster somehow knows of this and uses the information to ensure the loyalty of his minions."

"How is it you know of this?" Kettering asked.

"I have formed an alliance with the former butler, and he conveyed the intelligence in a note yesterday. He assumed Miss Fairchild was aware of the situation, but realized her mother had never confirmed that. Miss Fairchild will convincingly appear to become interested in Armbruster again and receptive to his charms. His spies will confirm his dearest aspirations."

"Remind me again," Ash Dorning said, "how we defeated the Corsican?"

Fournier set down his empty glass. "You made sure Napoleon had no sleep for nearly a week, and thus he forgot his own military advice."

Sycamore poured another scant finger of brandy into Fournier's glass. "What advice would that be?"

"Never allow your forces to become too scattered. Keep your reserves close by, not miles away on the eve of battle."

"And off you go to France?" Kettering muttered. "How is that following Napoleon's proven strategies? A thousand things could go wrong with this plan of yours."

"First, the plan is not merely mine. Miss Fairchild's imprimatur is on every detail, else I should not be here explaining those details to you. Second, I am bringing a thousand Dornings and their connections to bear on the situation. If matters go awry, you must set them right."

Sycamore looked puzzled. "You are trusting us?"

"Catherine is, and trusting your womenfolk. She does not trust her own staff or her solicitors, who also happen to be Lord Armbruster's men of business. See that you do not disappoint her."

Ash Dorning, the quietest of the siblings, spoke. "See that you don't either."

Fournier rose and bowed. "We understand one another. I am for the docks, and you have a precious sister to guard."

The Frenchman strode out, leaving his drink unfinished.

"Man knows how to make an exit," Sycamore said, downing the brandy. "I suppose we relay these developments to the ladies?"

Kettering rose. "I don't like the whole situation, but I do like him. He's..."

"Smitten," Ash said, "and if Catherine has fallen in with this plan, that is all we need to know. I'm off to brush up on my bonhomie. Gentlemen, good night."

Sycamore departed soon after—he had a club to supervise, or so he claimed—leaving Kettering in Casriel's company.

"What?" Kettering asked, tidying up the table. "You have something to say."

"We failed Catherine before. We cannot fail her again."

Kettering circled his hand. "And?"

"We will owe Fournier when this is over, regardless of the success of the plan."

Kettering began blowing out candles. "I think it rather the case that we already owe Fournier. The question becomes what to do about it."

Casriel rose. "You heard him. Gossip, guile, and good manners. As it happens, I excel at the latter, my brothers have the guile, and you are a noteworthy gossip."

"I am no such thing."

Casriel yawned, picked up a carrying candle, and—only because Kettering was anxious to discuss the situation with his darling wife—was permitted to have the last word.

The fellow traveled under the *nom de guerre* Armand Ablesdorf and spoke with a convincing French accent. His watchful dark gaze and exorbitant price pronounced him to be a citizen of the great state of unprincipled ambition, though if Ablesdorf was competent, Armbruster would meet his terms.

"This is a letter," Armbruster said, passing a folded document across the scarred table, "dated years ago and acknowledging the child as mine. I state my fervent intention to be a father to my offspring in every regard, supporting and loving same et cetera and so forth."

Ablesdorf's swooping dark brows drew down. "The letter has been very well preserved, my lord."

Because it had been written yesterday, of course. "I assure you the signature is genuine. I can replicate that signature if you like."

Ablesdorf sat in the snug of the lowly Prince and Pony Inn and read the damned letter, while somebody started an argument in the kitchen about dogs, and a pair of old women cleaned their pipes by the fire. The Frenchman fit in here—above medium height, but not too tall. Medium build, regular features that somehow weren't quite handsome, and clothing that suggested a comfortable but unpresuming existence.

A forgettable man, at least when he chose to be. Ablesdorf folded the letter and tucked it into a coat pocket. "You do not mention the gender or name of this offspring to whom you are so devoted."

"I'm being discreet. The point is, the letter is clearly addressed to the child's mother and acknowledges the child as mine. That gives me rights." Not quite how the solicitors had put it, but close enough.

Ablesdorf examined the direction on the missive, as best Armbruster had been able to recall it from his days in Rome.

"This is a copy of a letter, my lord. Anybody can see that it has not been through the post."

"A gentleman employs a clerk whose job consists entirely of making fair copies of all outgoing correspondence. One doesn't want to send the same tattle to the same party twice."

Ablesdorf sipped his ale, not as an Englishman, Swede, or a German would partake, but as a Frenchman condescended to risk putting his lips to inferior potation.

"You expect this copy of a letter to convince French authorities that I retrieve the child on your behalf?"

"Not entirely." Armbruster passed over another missive. "This is my sworn explanation to anybody in an official capacity. You will note the watermark—my titled father's coat of arms—and the seal replicating the family crest. If that doesn't win you free of official complications, this should."

Having a purloined stash of Papa's official stationery had proved invaluable at public school, and Armbruster still kept some on hand for exigent circumstances.

He parted with a small bag of coins, though it broke his heart to do so. The trades knew precisely when the quarterly payments came out, and they had already started lurking at both the front and back doors to Armbruster's lodgings.

"Spend that on official cooperation if you must, but only if you must. I need you back here as soon as possible. Three weeks should be enough. A month at the latest."

Ablesdorf regarded Armbruster as if he'd demanded circumnavigation of the globe by Wednesday next.

"You expect me to make this arduous journey with a small child. I will need to hire some sort of nursemaid, my lord, if not a nursemaid *and* a governess. I must take the child's tender years into account when arranging our travels, lest your precious offspring fall ill from the rigors of the road. Unless you expect me to purloin the child's clothing, storybooks, and toys, such items will have to be purchased. To effect this undertaking in three weeks is impossible."

Armbruster took back the bag of coins. "You need two weeks under sail between Bordeaux and London—a week in each direction —and another week to travel overland and back to Cahors. Time is most assuredly of the essence. If you cannot manage such a simple task, I will find somebody else to do it."

The solicitors had recommended Ablesdorf highly, praising him particularly for his thoroughness and discretion relating to all matters Continental. Nobody had mentioned that he was arrogant and peevish.

"My lord, you do not know if there even is a child," Ablesdorf said, his words freighted with long-suffering patience. "You do not know if the child enjoys good health or has a delicate constitution. The Bay of Biscay is notoriously difficult sailing—a week between London and Bordeaux is an absurdly optimistic assumption—and

English stationery will not carry much weight with French authorities. I wish you luck with your attempts to find the child."

Ablesdorf rose, and Armbruster nearly shoved him back into his seat by main force.

The Frenchman put some coins on the table. "I can doubtless determine whether a young lady with violet eyes gave birth to this small person, but kidnapping the child is by no means assured, no matter which inquiry agent you send and no matter how quickly that agent travels. You ought to have hired a woman for this job, but I understand that you expect the very weather to accommodate your whims, and I come highly recommended. One would think, however, that a loving father would have a care for the child's wellbeing rather than insist that he or she be hauled across the countryside like so many crates of cheap brandy."

Armbruster got to his feet and wished he stood more than a mere inch taller than Ablesdorf.

"I would have doted on that child had I known there was a child, damn you." That much was true. Instinct told Armbruster that Catherine had given birth to his baby. To keep him in ignorance of the child's existence spoke very ill of her.

A man had a right to know such things and to take a hand in them if he so desired. Perhaps Catherine had been holding the facts in abeyance, to be sprung upon Armbruster like an ambush at the time of her choosing.

Well, two could play at the ambush game.

As these thoughts coursed through Armbruster's head—not for the first time—Ablesdorf regarded him with something like pity. The presuming toad needed to be taught a lesson.

But no. Eye on the main chance, as the saying went. Everything in its time. He who controlled the child controlled Catherine, and he who controlled Catherine controlled her fortune. Besides, she should thank him for rescuing their only begotten son—or daughter, but a son would be better—from the care of strangers in the French hinterlands.

Armbruster shoved the coins at Ablesdorf. "Bring me the child, or I will see to it that you never again work for any reputable solicitor in London."

An idle threat, but Ablesdorf took the money. "I will need a month at least, and if my expenses exceed what you've allotted, you will pay the difference immediately upon my return whether I am successful or not."

So the issue was money, not some high-minded regard for the brat. "Of course."

"You will speak with me again, my lord, tomorrow afternoon. I have questions regarding the child's mother."

"I'm to meet the fellows at Tatts tomorrow. A colt rising four is to go on the block. Bay with four white stockings, said to come from the Conyers Arabian line. Worth a fortune if he can throw speed."

Ablesdorf consulted his watch.

Time is most assuredly of the essence. "I suppose sacrifices must be made," Armbruster said. "Tomorrow, then. Besides, they'll save the colt for last, and I honestly don't know all that much about Miss Fairchild. She inherited pots of money, and she lied to me in a most despicable manner."

"All would agree you have been sorely victimized, my lord." Ablesdorf pocketed the money, bowed slightly, and took his leave.

Armbruster resumed his seat and congratulated himself on a successful negotiation. A month from now, he would be in anticipation of a very advantageous match. If not, Catherine Fairchild would learn how it felt to be kept in ignorance of the smallest detail regarding her child.

"How did you—?" Catherine forgot the question as Fournier drew her into his arms.

"I leave on the midnight tide," he said, between kisses. "To all appearances, I took a packet to Calais yesterday morning. Tonight, I sail directly for Bordeaux."

To be in his arms again, to hear his voice. "Who is off to Calais?"

"Jacques. We are of a height and bear a resemblance. Put him in my clothing, put him on Bertold's back, and let him exaggerate his accent and natter on about winemaking. Nobody looks twice. He is a cousin at some remove and was integral to my wartime subterfuges and ruses. I needed to see you before departing."

Catherine clung for one more moment before stepping back. "I want to do much more than see you."

Fournier smiled at her crookedly and glanced at the library sofa. "Alas, I have only a few moments, and such an undertaking requires far more than that. Armbruster is sending an agent to France."

"We expected him to try something like that." Nonetheless, the news was terrifying.

"Sit with me," Fournier said, taking Catherine by the hand and leading her to the sofa. "The agent is no fool, a Frenchman named Ablesdorf—he has other names—whose path crossed mine more than once during the war. Ablesdorf is shrewd, and that works to our advantage."

"How?" Catherine sank onto the sofa and hugged a pillow to her middle. "He will find Marie, he will confirm my relationship with her, and he will bring back proof that I have a daughter."

Fournier rubbed her back in slow circles. "He will be thorough and careful, for his own sake, if not for Armbruster's. He also charges exorbitantly for his services. If I take you to France so you and Marie can flee Cahors one step ahead of Ablesdorf, he will pursue us, and he excels at pursuit. Whether or not he finds you immediately, he can still bring back affidavits, copies of records, and other evidence Armbruster will use against you."

Catherine tossed away the pillow and curled into Fournier's side. "I want to run, Xavier. I want to beg you to take me to France so I can disappear with Marie to some obscure Canadian frontier town."

He looped his arm around her shoulders. "We have a plan, *mon coeur*, a good plan. One that keeps Marie safe, puts Armbruster to rout, and preserves your standing, your freedom, and your fortune. We can do this."

Catherine burrowed closer, drawing comfort from Fournier's calm. "I have longed for somebody to call my own, somebody to confide in and lean on. Mama loved me dearly, but I always felt I must not be a burden to her, must not impose on my parents any worse than I already had."

"And now," Fournier said, lips near her ear, "you have my utter devotion, and the idea that you must trust me to safeguard your child is intolerable."

"Difficult," Catherine said, "but how much more difficult if I were still trying to manage the situation on my own? I am prepared to marry Armbruster if I must. I don't want to."

"You shall not marry that man, Catherine. He does not deserve you, and if you demand that he have the banns cried for the requisite three successive weeks, I should be back before he can march you to the altar."

Fournier was reminding her that they had time, in other words. Not a lot of time, but some time. Enough time, God willing.

"Kettering is meeting with Belcher and Sons tomorrow," Catherine said, "and effectively removing them from involvement with my affairs. Lady Casriel and Lady Trysting are to look in on me the day after. I have made it known to Mrs. Trask that if you call here, I am not at home to you."

"And if Lord Fortescue condescends to visit you?"

Catherine recited the answer that comported with their agreed-upon plan. "I will be reluctantly—very reluctantly—charmed and flattered by his attentions."

"You are the bravest woman I know, Catherine Fairchild. Be brave a few weeks longer, and we shall prevail."

Nobody had ever referred to her as brave before. As a schoolgirl, she'd been outspoken, headstrong, and difficult. Facing London Society, she'd become quiet, unassuming Miss Dubious, and then she'd had to summon something like stoicism as her mother's illness had progressed.

"I don't think of myself as brave."

"To bear a child takes courage, to part from a child takes enormous courage, to watch a loved one die takes courage, to maintain composure in the face of Society's judgment takes courage. You are brave, Catherine, while Armbruster is arrogant, weak, and greedy."

Catherine peered at her lover. *Weak?* The word fit and fit well. "When you put it like that, I am not as afraid."

Fournier kissed her cheek. "I thank the merciful God that Armbruster was so stupid as to abandon you when he could have had your devotion for the rest of his life. He is to be pitied."

Catherine smiled, and it felt good to allow a thread of genuine humor to leaven her worry. "I wouldn't go that far."

"I would," Fournier said, sitting up. "I was a fool for love, ages ago. I see now that it's better to be a fool for love than a fool for vanity and coin. I was naïve, Armbruster is an ass. I have Armbruster to thank for showing me this distinction, so yes, I do pity him."

"Pity him when his creditors have hounded him from London." Catherine rose, when she wanted to cling and fret and melt into a puddle of anxiety. "You have a point, though. I have Marie to thank for any fortitude I claim, and in a sense, that means I must thank Armbruster as well."

"There," Fournier said, springing to his feet, "we have been philosophical and wise and gracious, none of which means we will spare Armbruster the fate he deserves. Kiss me for luck, and then I am off on the fastest sloop ever to carry contraband between London and Bordeaux."

Catherine wrapped her arms around his waist. "How is it you claim a berth on this sloop?"

"I own it, a necessary competitive advantage in the wine trade. Wish me fair weather and a swift journey. I shall dream of you."

She imprinted on her mind the sense of safety and comfort she found only in Fournier's embrace. "Tell Marie I love her, and I will come to Bordeaux to see her as soon as I can."

"The château staff will rejoice to have a child underfoot again, and, Catherine?"

She drew back. "Xavier?"

"I learned to say the words, during the war, and that takes courage too: I love you. I love you madly and sanely, with my heart, soul, and body—forever. I was still very much at sea, even as I peddled my wines and donned my fancy Bond Street waistcoats. You have brought me home. I will not fail you."

He'd said she was brave, and Fournier would never lie to her. "I love you too. Madly and sanely and forever. Go to my daughter, Fournier, and get her to safety."

Catherine opened the French doors. Fournier offered her a bow and a smacking kiss, and then he disappeared into the darkness.

CHAPTER FIFTEEN

"Where is my sapphire cravat pin?" Armbruster peered at the jewelry box Henri held open before him. "Sapphires do marvelous things for my eyes."

"I believe that pin had to be taken to the Ludgate jewelers for repairs, my lord." Henri had more dignity than the queen mother and more discretion than a ducal butler. He also had just a hint of a genuine Parisian accent, as all the best valets did, and touch of hauteur, as befit his station serving a marquess's spare.

He was also a terrible liar, for which Mama doubtless treasured him. "Told you to pawn it, did I?"

"Last autumn, sir, and such a fine piece sold before I could retrieve it. Perhaps the amethyst will do?"

"Amethysts will remind all and sundry of my intended's eyes, Henri. Good choice."

"Are felicitations in order, my lord?"

Even an English valet might have presumed to ask such a question. The marriage of a peer's son was a matter of universal interest, after all.

"Soon, my good man, soon." Armbruster raised his chin so Henri could affix the pin just so amid the folds of Armbruster's cravat. "Mama must be brought 'round, but Papa has agreed to take on that task."

Henri stepped back. "Speaking of your mother, sir..."

Armbruster fluffed his cravat and examined his reflection in the cheval mirror. The dressing closet was the usual chaos of discarded cravats, rejected waistcoats, and unsuitable gloves, though Henri would set all to rights as he waited up for his employer's return. The fellow would be bored to tears without shirts to press or boots to polish.

"If Mama has been remiss with your wages again, you must take that up with her lady's maid. I've told you and told you, Henri, finances bore me. I'll need the chocolate hat and matching gloves."

"With an amethyst cravat pin, my lord?"

"What would you suggest?"

"That depends on your destination, sir."

Oh, delightful. Now Henri was in a pet, and all over a few pounds that would doubtless show up by the end of the week.

"I'm to meet Ash Dorning for a hand of cards at the Coventry. He's the melancholic, or so the gossips claim, and I intend to add to his woes by relieving him of some coin over a friendly game or two."

"Mr. Ash Dorning is said to be quite proficient at cards."

"He is, or was, part owner of a gaming hell," Armbruster said, fluffing the curls Henri had spent half an hour styling. "Of course he'll have a good reputation at the tables, but he's only an earl's third or fifth spare. He'll lose to me to curry my favor."

Henri held out a dark emerald hat. "I am at a loss to fathom the complexities of Mayfair Society, my lord. Why would Mr. Dorning curry your favor?"

"Because he is my prospective in-law, Henri, though one doesn't speak openly of that. Miss Fairchild has received me twice in the past week and agreed to drive out with me Tuesday next, weather permitting. Proper courtships proceed according to a plan, and this one is adhering wonderfully to the plan of my choosing."

"Ah, I comprehend, my lord. The banns will soon be cried, and the lawyers will hold long meetings with their respective clients." He set the hat just so on Armbruster's head, though no hat would ever fit quite as exquisitely as the gray had.

"You are learning," Armbruster said, tilting the hat a half inch lower to the left. "But we won't bother with crying the banns. I applied this morning for a special license, and by this time next week, I should be rehearsing my make-me-the-happiest-man speech. Within a fortnight, my new wife and I might well be starting on our wedding journey."

"Paris, my lord? Paris in springtime is all the rage."

"Perhaps. A wedding journey in France would be a delicious irony." Also far cheaper than wandering about the New Forest or squandering coin on some fashionable seaside watering hole. But then, married to Catherine, even Brighton would become the affordable—a cheering thought.

Armbruster pulled on the matching emerald gloves and left Henri to deal with the mess. The damned special license had cost five bloody pounds, which meant winning some coin off Dorning was all but imperative.

Tedious, though Thurlow had reported that Miss Fairchild had stopped receiving Fournier, and Fournier had apparently nipped off to France to lick his wounds. The plan was moving along nicely, and that was another exceedingly cheering thought.

~

"Two weeks," Catherine muttered, stroking Caesar's silky ear. "He's been gone seventeen days, and not a word."

Caesar rested his chin on her knee and sighed. The morning was glorious, as only spring mornings could be, with a promise of gracious warmth from the beaming sun. In Catherine's heart, all was storm clouds and worry.

"A thousand fears haunt me," she murmured. "What if Fournier's sloop sank? What if Armbruster hired brigands to waylay him? What if Fournier ran afoul of the customs authorities? I am losing my mind."

The last time she'd been prey to such worry—*What if my baby does not live? What if my baby is sickly? What if my baby hates me?*—she'd had her mother's reassurances and the support of a kindly and loyal staff in Cahors.

Now, she had Fournier's promises.

"There you are." Beatitude, Lady Casriel, accompanied by Jacaranda, Lady Trysting, came through the garden gate. "Has no one told you that being out of doors without your bonnet will ruin your complexion?"

"My ladies." Catherine rose from her bench and curtseyed. "I am well aware of the perils I face without my bonnet. Shall I send for a tray?"

"No time for that." Lady Casriel was blond, brisk, and entirely devoted to her family. Catherine had liked her on sight, in part because her ladyship thought nothing of taking her husband's hand or whispering in his ear when among family.

I want to be like that with Fournier. Unselfconsciously besotted.

"You did not tell us that you know Lady Castlereagh," Lady Trysting said. "Very bad of you to forget an acquaintance with the foreign secretary's wife."

"Mama knew her," Catherine replied. "I suspect they were allies more than friends. The diplomatic corps is still mostly the province of aristocrats and younger sons from titled families. The ladies had to form alliances as best they could."

Catherine's guests exchanged a glance.

"Lady Castlereagh is one of the patronesses at Almack's," Lady Casriel said gently. "The one most likely to affirm rules and uphold standards."

Catherine sank to the bench and gestured for the ladies to be seated as well. "I knew that."

"You knew that," Lady Trysting said, taking a wrought-iron chair, "but because your entire being is focused on Fournier's safe return, you took no notice of your long-standing connection to one of the most powerful people in London."

"My late mother's connection." Caesar's comforting weight pressed against Catherine's leg. He was doubtless getting dog hair all over her skirts, and *she did not care*. "We should have heard from Fournier by now. He promised he'd send a pigeon when he reached Bordeaux."

"He did," Lady Casriel said, extending a hand for Caesar to sniff. "But his mews in Bordeaux has fallen prey to some sort of pigeon malaise, or a rash of pigeons in an interesting condition. He had to use a bird from a neighboring estate. The message took some time to deliver on the London end and reached Kettering only this morning."

Worry that weighed more than Caesar and Franny put together lifted from Catherine's heart. "How long did his crossing take?"

"Ten days," Lady Trysting said. "Kettering claims that's not unusual, though it's hardly a swift crossing either."

"He estimated nine days, given the time of year, and every day lost matters. Armbruster is wasting no time pressing his attentions on me."

Another glance passed between the ladies, this one easily deciphered. They were as worried as Catherine was.

"If he attempts to compromise you," Lady Casriel said, "seven adult male Dornings will line up to call him out, as will Kettering."

"And then Miss Dubious's name is involved in a matter of honor," Catherine retorted. "Lady Castlereagh will offer me the cut direct if she even recalls who I am."

Caesar gave her a worried look and nudged at her hand.

"Do you care?" Lady Casriel asked gently. "Do you give a stale bonbon what polite society thinks of you? The whole family will stand by you, as will our relatives and friends."

"Armbruster's entire family is rolled up," Lady Trysting added. "Kettering has been nosing about, and nobody has his instinct for financial matters. If he says a marquess is in dun territory, then the fellow is all but sinking in the River Tick. Armbruster doubtless sees himself as the knight-errant waltzing forth to save the family fortunes —with your money."

"And such a bid for his family's gratitude will only make him more desperate," Catherine said. "He called on me twice last week and would have taken me out driving yesterday, but the weather was foul. I have always loved rainy days. I positively adored yesterday's downpour."

"You adore Xavier Fournier." Lady Trysting made that a statement rather than an accusation.

"I do, and Lady Casriel has put an interesting question to me: Do I care about polite society's good opinion? The answer is, at long last, no. I do not. My parents took far-flung diplomatic postings, endured separations, and organized their lives around me, around the limitations of my birth, and then around my lapses in common sense. They went to those great lengths because they wanted me to eventually take a place in Society."

Catherine rose and shook out her skirts. "That place was to cower among the ferns, fetching punch for the dowagers and admiring the dresses of the wallflowers. As far as the rest of Society knew, I had done nothing wrong, but they judged me anyway."

She pivoted at the sundial and stalked back to her guests. "Why, why on God's green and bountiful earth, should I care what a lot of small-minded, vicious hypocrites think of me?"

"You don't?" Lady Casriel said.

"I do not." Catherine tested those words for false bravado and found none. "But I would rather not see Miss Dubious's legacy visited upon Fournier, whose business depends on polite society's approval, or upon my daughter, who is truly blameless, or upon my Dorning relations, who have been kind to me when I most needed kindness."

"You aren't Miss Dubious anymore." Lady Trysting extended her hand to Caesar, who took a delicate sniff of her glove and settled on his haunches at her knee. "You are Miss Desirable."

"Miss *Desirable?*"

Lady Casriel nodded. "I like it. I suspect this was Fournier's idea. I heard it from Lady Bellefonte, who heard it from Her Grace of Clonmere, who heard it from her French lady's maid."

"Kettering heard it at Martin's bakery," Lady Trysting added, "and Martin is an émigré. His English clientele has grown exclusive in recent years, but most of London's better French households do business with him too."

Miss Desirable. "Fournier had best get safely back to England, for I have much to say to him."

"He'd best get back to England for all manner of reasons," Lady Casriel said. "Armbruster has applied for a special license. He should be in possession of it any day."

No. No. No. A special license was not in the plan. "We cannot be married by special license."

Caesar regarded her with sad, worried eyes, as did both ladies.

"We can be married by special license," Catherine said softly. "If I must marry that man to keep my daughter safe, I will marry him."

"It won't come to that." Lady Casriel's assurance rang with more hope than certainty.

"It might," Catherine replied. "Armbruster kissed my cheek last week. I wanted to retch into the bushes, but I bore it. I can bear much to keep Marie safe."

Both ladies rose. "You need to change your dress."

"I do?"

"You do. If we are to call upon Lady Castlereagh, you must appear in the first stare of tastefully subdued second mourning fashion. Obviously, you have no interest in vouchers while your loss is so recent, but you are Miss Desirable. Her ladyship will want to reclaim her acquaintance with you."

"Right," Catherine said, pushing to her feet. "I am Miss Desirable, and scared to death, and missing my daughter terribly, and worried sick over the man I sent to keep her safe, but by all means, let

us make a social call. I am a very accomplished caller, as will doubtless soon be known to all."

Catherine, Caesar trotting at her heels, led her guests back into
the house, though she still wanted to retch into the bushes.

"Mademoiselle Fairchild asked that I also give you this." Fournier
passed the governess a likeness of mother and child. Catherine's face
had been rounder and her eyes tired, but the love in her gaze as she
beheld her baby made his heart ache.

"I sketched that." Miss Drawbaugh looked from the sketch to
Fournier. She was English, surprisingly youthful, and clearly devoted
to her charge. "Miss Fairchild's letter says I am to accompany you to
Bordeaux with Marie. She does not elucidate how I am to explain
this journey to the child."

Fournier spoke English because Miss Drawbaugh spoke English.
From behind the garden wall, a childish voice sang a little tune in
French about dancing in circles on the bridge of Avignon.

He wanted to snatch up the child and bolt for the carriage
waiting by the front steps of this commodious farmhouse, and he
wanted to lie down on the good French earth and sleep for a week.
His head pounded, his eyes were scratchy, and his neck ached from
looking over his shoulder the entire distance from Bordeaux.

"I will explain the situation to the child," he said, "while you pack
her effects. We must be away immediately."

Miss Drawbaugh handed him back the sketch. "Mademoiselle
does not say that we should bring Claire, but we should not think of
traveling without a nursery maid. Etienne will worry if Claire travels
to Bordeaux without him, and he's quite good with the child too. By
tomorrow noon at the latest—"

"Miss Drawbaugh, I apologize for my blunt speech, but we do not
have until tomorrow. Within the hour, I will be on my way with that
child, whether you can accompany us or not."

Miss Drawbaugh gave him a very severe look, in the best tradition of her profession. "Why this great haste? This is the only home Marie has known, and children do not deal well with upheaval."

Fournier kept his voice down only because Marie was happily dancing on the bridge of Avignon not four yards away.

"Children deal adequately with upheaval if the adults around them deal with it. Miss Fairchild has come into money. By underhanded tactics, Marie's father now knows of the lady's fortune and of Marie's existence. He thinks to use Marie as a pawn in his greedy games, and if you dither and dawdle, he might well succeed. Will you be the reason mother and child must become fugitives?"

A worse possibility had occurred to Fournier amid the exhausted blur of recent days: Ablesdorf might steal the child. His reputation included thefts of many varieties, and he was a competent forger. If he got his hands on Marie, she would soon become Josephina Dupont or Evette Garnier, and she would disappear with Ablesdorf until Armbruster wanted her found.

Miss Drawbaugh's Governess of Doom frown became an intelligent woman's careful perusal. "Miss Fairchild says I am to trust you and yield to your guidance in every particular."

"You are an English governess. I do not expect miracles in the yielding-to-guidance department."

"Marie's first language is French, but her English is nearly flawless. Speak to her in English, and she will more strongly associate you with her mother. Send your coachman and grooms to the kitchen. Etienne will water the horses and see that they have some grain. Give me thirty minutes, and then have your grooms fetch the valises."

"My thanks. You will introduce me to the child?"

Miss Drawbaugh stuck her fine English nose in the air. "You may introduce yourself. I have a valise to pack." She stalked into the house, another tempest wreaking havoc on Fournier's careful plans.

"The Bay of Biscay was worse," he muttered, trying to compose himself for an encounter with a small child. A small girl child who occupied the center of Catherine Fairchild's universe.

The coach had nearly lost a wheel, one of the horses had come up lame, and the sky was threatening a serious spring storm, but none of that mattered.

Fournier ran a hand through hair much in need of combing and let himself into the garden.

The child stopped singing and dancing in a circle with a stuffed bear. She had dark brown hair that glinted auburn in the sun, her mother's chin and nose, and blue, blue eyes.

"*Bonjour, Mademoiselle Marie. Je m'appelle Fournier.*" He'd forgotten to speak English.

She gazed up at him with the same serious reserve that so often characterized her mother. "Drawbaugh was out of patience with you," she replied in French. "She is often out of patience with me. Were you naughty?"

"I am very tired, and worried."

"You need a snack and a nap?"

"*Oui.* Yes. Marie, your mother has sent me to fetch you."

"Mama sent you? Will you take me to her?" Such careful hope lay in that question, such hard-earned caution. Fournier's heart broke to see that legacy of caution already taking root in the child.

"Eventually, your mama will come to France, but for now, we will go as far as Bordeaux. You must not be worried, because Drawbaugh and I and Claire will take very good care of you."

Fine blue eyes considered him with more gravity than a small girl ought to possess. "Etienne must come, too, if Claire comes. And Berthold."

An image of a long, horsey face came to mind. "Who in God's name is Berthold?"

"My bear—*Bear*-told, you know? Half French and half English." She smiled at him, swinging the bear by the arm, and the resemblance to Catherine was again uncanny.

"I have a horse named Bertold. He is also half French and half English."

Marie spun around. "You have a horse? Is he very big, and all white, and can he leap the moon?"

"He is a fine fellow, and I hope one day you can meet him. Let's see about that snack, shall we? Bordeaux is at least two days' journey, and we must start very soon."

The child proved an agreeable traveler, and the young fellow Etienne was indeed good with her, with the horses, and most significantly, with Miss Drawbaugh and the nurserymaid, Claire.

As they prepared to leave the innyard on the second morning of their journey, Etienne pretended to pick the hoof of the offside wheeler.

"He's back," Etienne said quietly. "You see him, monsieur?"

"The tinker," Fournier replied, studying the sky. "He was a parson yesterday."

"He stays always one hill behind us, and he does not have the eyes of a man of God."

"You are armed?"

"Knives only, but I can handle a gun. Napoleon made soldiers of us all."

You are just a boy. Except that Etienne might well be one-and-twenty, meaning he would have been of age to be conscripted when Napoleon was in power.

"We travel on," Fournier said. "Our friend has not had time to arrange for an ambush, and he will not want to bring down the authorities. The plan is for us to get the child to Bordeaux, and that is what we shall do."

That was, in fact, what they did, fourteen nerve-racking, dusty, muddy, interminable hours later. Marie seemed to sense the urgency of the situation and had traveled with only a few, quiet questions or requests to use the necessary.

Fournier's guests were tucked up in their respective beds at the château, and Fournier was desperately looking forward to a bath when his housekeeper passed him a note.

"From Delacourt, or from your friends in London using

Monsieur Delacourt's pigeons," she said. "Don't fall asleep in the tub, monsieur."

"I fell asleep two days ago. Since then, I have walked, ridden, cursed, and driven in my sleep." He unfolded the tiny note.

Armbruster has spec license. Make all due haste to return. Casriel.

Fournier cursed in English, which earned him a curious glance from the housekeeper. "Trouble, monsieur?"

The plan was coming undone, and thus a new plan would have to serve. "I sail on the morning tide. I know it's late, but please send word to the harbor."

He left the housekeeper gaping at him and managed to get himself undressed and into the tub, where he did, indeed, fall fast asleep.

"Mama tells me you called upon Lady Castlereagh last week," Armbruster said. "I would have been happy to escort you, my dear."

I am not your dear. Catherine offered him her hand and remained seated. "Lady Casriel and Lady Trysting accompanied me. A conversation about England in springtime and Paris in winter could hardly have interested you, my lord." It had not interested Catherine much either, but that had not been the point of the call, or the half-dozen others Catherine had made.

She had been from home—honestly from home—twice when Armbruster had called. She well knew what he could do, given five minutes of privacy with a lady. She was careful to meet with him out of doors or in public as much as possible, though today he'd ambushed her in the garden.

He took a seat in a wrought-iron chair and pulled it nearer to Catherine's bench. "You look quite recovered from your... I forget what it was. Megrim? Head cold? Bout of indigestion? I know your game, Catherine."

In truth, the sight of Fort Armbruster, the sound of his voice, or the scent of his cinnamon shaving soap was enough to make Catherine bilious.

"My game?"

"You have resumed socializing so I have less opportunity to catch you at home. You never cared for the Mayfair whirl, and you don't care for it now. You are taking evasive maneuvers."

His tone was polite, but his gaze drifted over Catherine's person in a less than respectful manner. Not exactly lustful, but possessive. Covetous.

"I socialized," Catherine said. "I socialized mostly as my mother's companion, true, but one cannot be a diplomat's daughter without an appreciation for friendly civilities. Much to my surprise, I find many of Mama's former acquaintances are delighted to include me in their social circle."

And that delight seemed genuine, though a few of Mama's old friends had also dropped some matchmaking hints.

"Your mother could not trust you to go about on your own," Armbruster said. "If I, the proverbial impecunious younger son, could turn your head, then she knew your judgment was questionable."

He'd offered that insult with a self-deprecating smile, though the watchfulness of his gaze struck a chord of memory.

"You used to do this in Rome," Catherine said. "Insult me with such charm that I told myself I'd imagined the slur. I was being too sensitive, too immature. And yet, a man who cared for me would never make a jest at my expense, would he? Is it not the case that your judgment as a gentleman, as my senior by several years, as a guest under my father's roof from time to time, was the more seriously flawed?"

Armbruster sat back. "I was frustrated in love. Of course I suffered an occasional attack of pique. Fortunately for all concerned, I am older and wiser now, as are you."

"I am older and wealthier," Catherine said, giving him the same sort of smile he'd given her. Jovial to appearances, with a sneering undercurrent.

This was what marriage to him would be like, if Catherine condemned herself to that hell. Sniping, insults, innuendo, and games. Intimate warfare. Fournier had been correct that raising Marie amid such animosity would only wound the child—further wound the child.

Catherine marshaled her patience accordingly. "If you press your company on me too enthusiastically, you will be labeled a fortune hunter, my lord. Looked down upon as a grasping younger son with no prospects and less pride. I have been looked down upon my whole adult life, and that fate is harder than you'd think."

He seemed amused by this olive branch. "You are not home to me half the time when I call. You declined an outing to Gunter's. You flit about with your Dorning relations willingly enough, but ignore my overtures, though you well know that I am courting you."

He was, or he was trying to. All the focus and devotion Catherine had longed for from him in Rome had become her worst nightmare over the past several weeks.

"I know the lawyers are talking," she said. "I know you seek marriage, and..."

"And what?"

And I do, too, but not to you. Never to you. "Settlement negotiations fail all the time, my lord. Engaged couples then have to 'find that they don't suit.' The lady becomes an object of pity as her family renews the matchmaking campaign mere days later, and the fellow is abruptly required at the home of some distant uncle in the north. I am already Miss Dubious, and I refuse to become the butt of more unkind speculation if you catch the eye of a wealthier heiress next week."

"Your actual appellation was the Diplomat's Dubious Daughter. I thought the alliteration rather a nice touch, myself."

The anxiety Catherine had borne since Fournier's departure twisted into a clammy snake of fear. "*You* gave me that name?" She'd suspected as much, but not that he'd casually admit his perfidy.

"I was protecting you from your wayward nature. If you were

shunned, you were less likely to share your favors again, also less likely to be believed if you started talk about me. I am not stupid, Catherine, and you underestimate me at your peril." He crossed an ankle over a knee, probably intending to look rakish. "I have sent a man to France, specifically to Cahors. I know your secrets. I have known the generalities for some time, and I will soon have the specifics *in hand*, as it were. Don't make this any more difficult for yourself than it has to be."

I know your secrets. A jingle of harness beyond the garden wall added an incongruously merry note to the quiet of the spring morning. Nothing had changed outwardly. The day was still sunny and pleasant. Catherine was still in good health and possessed of a sizable fortune.

But her dreams were shattering like wine glasses dropped to the hearthstones, just as they had when she'd realized Armbruster would not marry her. That he would come along and wreck her life *again*— this time by forcing her to the altar—gave her a measure of renewed determination.

She was Marie's mother and Fournier's beloved, *and the fight was not over.*

"I am willing to marry you," she said slowly. "We can cry the banns as soon as Kettering tells me the settlements are resolved."

Armbruster considered her as he would a supposedly valuable painting that might be a forgery. "No banns," he said. "I have a special license, and you have pots of money. The settlements will be agreed to within a matter of days." His manner left *or else* wafting about on the morning breeze.

Or else you will not see your daughter ever again? Fournier had seen that possibility more clearly than Catherine had.

"A special license makes the whole undertaking look hasty," Catherine said, rising. "Of all brides, you must know I should not be hurried to the altar."

"Of all brides, you must know that maidenly vapors and further deceptions will only try my patience, Catherine. You are lucky that

I'm willing to bother with you. And no, the child will not be raised in our household. Some parson in the Midlands will take it off my hands for a modest annual sum, I'm sure."

It? Before Catherine's outrage got the better of her tongue, she realized that Armbruster did not yet know the gender of his own offspring. Either his hired kidnapper had failed, or he had yet to get word of his success to Armbruster.

"I will speak to Kettering," Catherine said. "The settlement negotiations will conclude soon."

Armbruster rose and prowled toward her. "See that they do. I am not an unreasonable man, Catherine. Had you handled matters differently years ago, I might have taken pity on you then. As matters stand, you will have your pin money, and the child will be adequately cared for. That is much more than many men would do. And you will hack out with me every morning until Kettering has ceded the field, weather permitting, because we are a courting couple. Agreed?"

The park was safe early in the day, provided enough Dornings lurked in the undergrowth. "All those years ago," Catherine said tiredly, "I did not know where you had gone. I had to leave Rome for obvious reasons, and I know for a fact that you never wrote to me. I realize you left a horde of unhappy creditors behind, but I would hardly have announced your whereabouts to them."

Armbruster stalked closer, though if he expected Catherine to cower, he was in for a disappointment.

"You will learn proper respect," he said, "or—"

The garden gate opened, and Nevin sidled through. "Beg pardon. Did not know the garden was occupied. I brung the morning post, miss. Shall I take it to kitchen?"

Catherine took the packet from him. "His lordship was just leaving, Nevin. Please fetch his horse."

Nevin looked from Armbruster to Catherine. "You're sure there's nothing else, miss?" Armbruster's own spy regarded him with veiled contempt.

"That will be all, Nevin," Catherine said. "My lord, I wish you good day. I will meet you on the bridle paths, as the weather permits. Excuse me for the nonce. I have correspondence to see to."

"Until tomorrow at first light, then." He turned his back on Catherine without bowing and marched off to the gate.

"He ought not to speak to you like that," Nevin said. "We heard him, out in the stables."

"You spied for him," Catherine said. "Why take my part now?"

Nevin had the grace to look abashed. "Said he were sweet on you. Said he hadn't much coin and needed any advantage over the other fellows if he was to win your notice. Said you were his first love. I know what it is to pine, to be reduced to wheedlin'. I ought not to have taken his money, though, and I'm sorry for that. You can sack me now."

"I could, but I won't, unless your slacking continues unabated. Armbruster's charm has fooled others who should have known better, and you can tell your mama I said so. Another lapse of loyalty, though, from either of you, and you will be turned off without a character."

"You won't sack us?"

"I won't, but I'm apparently to be married within the week, so consider my clemency for what little it's worth."

Nevin gave her a puzzled look. "Means a fair bit to me to be given a second chance. Will mean a lot to Ma as well." He strode off toward the stable, his step uncharacteristically brisk.

Catherine took the packet of letters to the library, where she intended to at least sort through them. Instead, she stared at the cold grate and wondered if there was any place on the entire earth where a mother and daughter could be safe from the child's father when he was bent on menacing the people he was legally bound to protect and cherish.

A graveyard, perhaps. She batted that thought aside rather than give way to hysterics.

Stay busy, Mama had often said. *Occupy the hands, and the mind won't wander as far afield.* Catherine took up the stack of letters, noting that the first was an invitation to a duchess's card party. An invitation she would have rejoiced, not long ago, to receive.

The second was... a simple note with a plain seal, the penmanship a precise, elegant hand. *Safely returned. Biding with friends. Bertold longs to renew his acquaintance with Miss Franny on the next suitable morning.*

Heaven forfend. Fournier intended to meet her in the park, and she would be there—with Fortescue Armbruster at her side. Catherine barely made it back out to the garden before she was sick all over the blooming myrtle.

CHAPTER SIXTEEN

The equine Bertold was in great good spirits, while Fournier was exhausted. The crossing from Bordeaux to London had been swift but rough. Worse yet, Ablesdorf had been standing on the quay in Bordeaux, looking formidable and determined, as Fournier's sloop had glided from its berth.

The news in London as reported by Sycamore Dorning was discouraging. The special license had been granted and delivered. Armbruster was making a regular pest of himself to Catherine, and Kettering's every demand at the negotiating table had been met with cordial assent.

Such agreeableness meant Armbruster was certain of Catherine's complicity after the marriage with whatever schemes he had for her money. Matters were dire indeed.

And yet, when Fournier caught sight of Catherine upon Franny, his heart leaped.

"Is that her?" Marie whispered, sitting up straight where she perched before Fournier in the saddle. "Is that—?"

"*Oui.*" Fournier continued in French. "She is not expecting you to be with me, so remember what we talked about."

"Je me souviens, monsieur." So solemn, probably as her mother had been solemn from a young age.

Fournier made sure his reinforcements were in their appointed locations and then sent Bertold on a path to intercept Catherine and her escort.

"Mademoiselle Fairchild, *bonjour.*" He tried for his charming émigré smile and probably failed miserably. He was simply too delighted to behold Catherine again. "My lord, good day to you."

"Fournier." Armbruster's horse danced a few steps to the side. "I thought you had disappeared to France."

"I am back, as you can see, and I have brought home with me this most darling child, who has been parted from her family for far too long."

Catherine sat upon her mare, to all appearances in command of her usual gracious reserve. Her gaze lit upon Marie, though, and stayed there.

Armbruster hauled on the reins until his horse ceased fretting. "You brought that child back from France? From Cahors?"

"We sailed from Bordeaux, didn't we, *petite mignonne?*"

"*Oui, monsieur.*"

"That is not your child," Armbruster said. "That cannot be your child."

Fournier had explained the situation to Marie, as best one could explain adult foolishness to a child, and she had appeared to understand what was needed. She twisted in the saddle to send Fournier a questioning glance.

Right. They'd had a plan for this outing, and he was missing his cue.

"Armbruster, my wife and I were blessed with a daughter, as is known to all. The French document these things with relentless exactitude. My affection for this child must be obvious to the very birds of the air. Perhaps you have been going short of sleep."

"You need a nap and a snack," Marie said in slightly accented English, "and your horse does too."

"Be quiet," Armbruster snapped. "Children should not speak unless spoken to."

"As far as I am concerned," Fournier said, "this precious child is free to speak her mind in any civil manner she chooses."

"She is not your daughter," Armbruster all but shouted. "That is... Catherine, what the hell is going on?"

Catherine petted her mare. "War and other exigencies apparently separated the girl from her family, but the war is over now, and she can be with those who love her. A happy occasion, one would think."

"Just so," Fournier said. "The child's earliest years were made difficult by all manner of tribulations, but that is all behind us." He hugged Marie, and she cuddled into his embrace with a giggle.

"You cannot do this," Armbruster snarled. "Tell him, Catherine. That is not his get. That is your daughter, and you cannot allow this, this... wine peddler to steal her from you."

Catherine nudged Franny closer to Bertold and turned her gaze directly on the child. "My dear, can you recall seeing me on any occasion prior to today?"

"*Non, mademoiselle*, though you are very pretty."

Minx. "There, you see?" Fournier said. "Armbruster, you must compose yourself and apologize to Miss Fairchild for your wild imaginings."

Four horsemen—Casriel, Kettering, Sycamore, and Ash—had sidled closer to the discussion. They halted their steeds a few yards behind Bertold, and the look in Sycamore's eye in particular should have shut Armbruster's stupid mouth.

"Catherine has agreed to marry me," Armbruster said, his horse once again fidgeting. "That is her daughter, and if you persist with these outrageous lies, I will ensure that she never sees that girl again."

"Calm yourself," Catherine snapped. "That is no sort of talk to air before a child. The settlement negotiations are not concluded, and if Monsieur Fournier says he is the child's father, then who are you to gainsay him?"

Armbruster's expression became murderous, and yet, he did not admit his own role in Marie's life. The Dornings chose that moment to advance a few more steps, which only caused Armbruster's horse to begin wringing its tail and propping.

"I agree with Miss Fairchild," Fournier said. "This is not a discussion to have in the presence of the child for whom I would give my life and my fortune. Compose yourself, Armbruster, and apologize to the ladies."

Armbruster gave the reins a vicious jerk. The horse kicked out, then stilled. "I will do no such thing. Miss Fairchild has either played me false or lied monstrously. I am the wronged party here. If you say otherwise, then I will have satisfaction from you, Fournier."

Finally. Marie stretched up to whisper in Fournier's ear.

"I am instructed to be patient and polite," he said, "as you should be. You may continue your tantrum some other day and go have a snack and a nap. My friends will see Miss Fairchild home."

Armbruster seemed to notice the Dornings for the first time. "You shall meet me, Fournier, else I will put a notice in the *Times* that you are the veriest poltroon and your wine isn't fit for French hogs."

Some Dorning or other cursed quietly, and a few passing equestrians had noticed that a situation was brewing. Catherine sat as cool as a barberry ice on her mare, and Marie had begun to braid a swath of Bertold's mane.

The ladies had confidence in Fournier apparently. What a fine thing, to be needed and valued and trusted by the people he loved most in the whole world.

"I won't let monsieur kill you, my lord," Catherine said. "Fournier, you have been challenged. I believe the choice of weapons is yours."

Armbruster looked at her as if she'd slapped him with her own glove. "You are enjoying this."

Catherine's beautiful eyes acquired a hint of deviltry. "Half of Hyde Park will soon be enjoying the spectacle *you* have created, my lord."

And that would not do, for a lady's name to be involved in a matter of honor. "I choose the rapier," Fournier said. "My little darling and I are off to enjoy a fine breakfast. Mr. Ash Dorning and Mr. Sycamore Dorning will serve as my seconds. Our outing is concluded, *ma petite*. The park grows too crowded for a good gallop, and Bertold longs for his oats. Lord Casriel will see Miss Fairchild safely returned to her home. His brothers have matters to discuss with Lord Fortescue."

The child waved her farewell to Catherine, who waved back and sent Franny toddling down the path beside Lord Casriel's fine gelding. Fournier directed Bertold toward the gates, while Kettering, Sycamore, and Ash went about the delicate business of setting up a discreet, private duel such that the male half of London would know exactly where and when the combatants were to meet.

"You were supposed to leave Marie at the château," Catherine said, arms lashed about Fournier's waist. "You brought my darling girl to me and presented yourself as her father. Why on earth would you go to all that trouble in addition to the trouble I asked you to take on?"

Fournier stroked her hair, and some of the tumult of the past weeks subsided at his touch.

"We were pursued, *mon coeur*. Nanette at The Boar's Bride apparently told Armbruster the wrong address, but she could not tell him the wrong town. Ablesdorf caught sight of my coach as I was leaving Cahors with Marie. He trailed us to the château, and spiriting Marie out of France became the wisest course."

"And telling Armbruster she was your daughter? We did not discuss that, Fournier. That was very bold of you."

"Are you angry?"

Catherine drew back, her expression severe. "I am so grateful, so impressed, so agog at your audacity and generosity and sheer bravado... If heaven granted me three wishes, Xavier Fournier, they would all be that my daughter had you for her father."

She leaned into him again, holding for dear life, lest she succumb to tears yet again.

"One hoped you would approve." A slight catch in his voice suggested Catherine was not the only party in the grip of strong emotion. "Marie is a bright, dear child, and very much like her mother. Did she enjoy the gardening?"

In defense of parental dignity, Catherine allowed the change of subject. She had spent the past hour repotting ferns with Marie, who along with Fournier had been enjoying Sycamore and Jeanette Dorning's hospitality.

"She has the family penchant for growing things," Catherine said. "She will quiz you about the vineyards without mercy."

Sycamore had suggested that help with the gardening would be appreciated and then had quietly withdrawn. Marie had become engrossed with dark earth, green plants, and her mother's company. She'd chattered about bears, seagulls, Etienne's boots, and the size of the ocean. She flitted from English to French with an occasional dip into Italian and German, and her imagination was limitless.

If we can speak with the English or the Italians, why not with the rabbits and cats? Surely an animal as wise as a cat has a language known to other cats?

Why is the sky blue sometimes, or the ocean green?

Why is winter cold and summer hot?

Marie refrained from the more vexing questions. Why had her mother left her in France? Was that shouting, nasty man really her papa?

The time for those questions would come, and Catherine would delight in answering them, as difficult as the topics might be. When Miss Drawbaugh insisted that Marie return to the nursery for a change of pinafore, Catherine had not wanted to allow the child from her sight.

Fournier had taken her hand, as if he'd known the struggle in her heart, and the instant they'd been alone in the garden, he'd wrapped her in a hug.

"Will your fiction hold up?" Catherine asked, drawing Fournier into the gazebo that sat at the foot of the Dornings' garden. "Are there documents that name you as the father of a girl child of Marie's age?"

Fournier's eyes were ringed with shadows, his mouth bracketed with grooves of fatigue, but he seated Catherine with his usual courtesy and took her hand when he came down beside her.

"Children come in many shapes and sizes. Mignon's hair was lighter than Marie's is, and she might have been born a few months earlier than Marie. I have the documents recording Mignon's birth with me. Her death came during the tumult at the end of the war and was not to my knowledge officially noted. Her grave, may she rest in peace, is unmarked." He kissed Catherine's dirty knuckles. "I should have asked you before I assumed even the fictional honor of Marie's paternity, but..."

He stroked her fingers, his gaze going to the ferns repotted on the gazebo's steps.

"But?"

"If the problem we faced was keeping you and the child safe, then I could marry you and turn the château into a fortress, but that is what your parents did. They kept you safe—from the gossips, from scandal, from your own ambitions—until all that safety made you reckless. I decided to solve a different problem— how to reach for both safety and happiness with you and your daughter."

Catherine considered that version of events and the rich dark earth beneath her fingernails. "You are not wrong. Mama and Papa did what they thought was best for me. The result was that polite society's censure came to loom in my mind as a much more dire fate than it is. Still, I would not wish that gauntlet on my daughter. If Marie is *your* daughter, officially, then she need not fear the fate I dreaded. You are very generous, also courageous, Fournier."

"I am emboldened by love and a bit devious of necessity."

She kissed his cheek. "I've learned a few other things in your absence, my bold fellow."

"Did you learn that you missed me? I missed you terribly. A thousand times, I wished I could show you a beautiful vista, a sunset at sea. I longed to walk the vineyards with you, to introduce you to the wines that a Bordelais bottles for his own pleasure rather than for export. I love France, Catherine, and I love you. If I did not love Marie when I rose today, I certainly became enthralled with her when she told Armbruster he needed a nap."

"His lordship needs a good hiding. You love France?"

Fournier nodded. "I have avoided going home to Bordeaux for anything but necessary business, because the memories were difficult —the more recent memories. They were recollections of heartache, loss, and failure. I have a great deal of money to show for my years in London, but what does the money matter when I have nobody to make happy memories with? I am tired, Catherine, and I have been tired for too long. I would like to *go home and rest*, and I would like you and Marie to come with me."

"You will tell the world she is your daughter?"

"If you and she will allow it. Between us, a less comfortable truth can be acknowledged. You gave Armbruster a chance to admit his relationship with the child, and he declined that very great honor. Perhaps he hopes the child is not his. I want to kill him for that, but he is too pathetic. Tell me you missed me."

"I missed you," Catherine said, leaning into his side. "I missed you terribly, and I would love to bide in France with you. You cannot kill Armbruster."

"Ah. You will allow me to disfigure him, *non*?"

"No, Fournier."

"Merely a small scar across his arrogant nose. He insulted you and Marie and deserves to be held accountable."

"Fournier, we had a plan, and Marie coming to London doesn't change the rest of that plan."

He sighed, though in that sigh, Catherine heard a touch of

humor. "Stubborn woman. Yes, we have a plan. I shall wield my rapier with my usual skill, and Armbruster will lose, though I shall not so much as pink him. I might allow him a few passing touches, the better to inflate his confidence."

"You will enjoy the whole business. Armbruster is to be pitied."

Fournier rose and drew Catherine into his arms. "He should be relegated to the heap of memories best allowed to fade. While I am teaching our daughter the wonders of winemaking, and you maintain your voluminous correspondence with the Dorning aunties, Armbruster will be alone, on foreign shores, with nobody to love him. Nobody to care when he suffers the penalty for cheating at cards, living beyond his means, or trespassing on another lady's trust. One makes choices, and he has made his."

"So you won't wound him? He is the father of my child, Fournier."

"He is not Marie's father in any sense that matters."

Catherine pondered that as a childish voice drifted down from the open nursery windows. Marie sang a jaunty tune about dancing beneath the moonlight on a summer evening.

"Do as you see fit, Fournier. *Tu as raison.* Armbruster is not Marie's father in any sense that matters. I trust you, and I have missed you unbearably. Perhaps you would like a tour of the Dornings' potting shed?"

"I have just now developed a towering fascination with potting sheds. Lead on, *mon ange*, and we shall invent new pleasures amid Sycamore's seedlings and grafts."

Fournier offered his arm, and Catherine allowed him to escort her across the garden at a decorous pace. When they reached the potting shed, she locked the door behind them and threw all pretensions to decorum straight onto the compost heap.

"I don't understand," Sycamore Dorning said. For once, Mr. Dorning had the sense to keep his voice down.

"I am not to draw Armbruster's blood," Fournier replied, slowly bending from the waist to touch his nose to his knees. Thank God he'd been bored enough at sea to maintain his stretches, and thank God the male half of polite society could not resist a good spectacle.

"How do you prevail in armed combat without wounding your opponent?" Sycamore asked, kicking an acorn across the grass. "Or will you lose in some convoluted plot to see Armbruster revealed as the opportunistic bully he is?"

Fournier rose on a slow inhale. "He is an opportunistic bully, also a cheat and a cad. I suspect those fellows,"—he nodded in the direction of the growing crowd ringing the clearing—"know him for what he is and have lacked the standing or wits to call him to account."

"Then he's cheated a bloody lot of younger sons and shopkeepers," Sycamore said.

Fournier began a series of stretches that started from the lunging posture, one foot forward, the other back at a right angle.

"Kettering, Oak, Willow, Casriel, and the others are among the crowd," Ash Dorning said. "They will follow orders to the letter. Fournier, are you concerned about the legalities?"

"*Non.*" His left hamstring was being its usual contrary self, so Fournier spent extra time coaxing the muscle to relax. "I will be off in France, where English authorities cannot reach me. That the first man to draw blood is technically the aggressor and the other fellow thus acting in self-defense is a silly affectation of English law."

Sycamore grinned. "You promised Catherine you wouldn't kill him, but if you pink him, you might get a little carried away."

The hamstring eased, and Fournier remained in his stretch for an extra three breaths, because that particular muscle sometimes seized up at the worst times.

"I do not get *carried away* when trouncing a bully," Fournier said, allowing himself a small smile. "Catherine has made her wishes known. I am not to wound Armbruster with my blade. The wounds will come from all the talk even now circulating among the spectators. I am not to scar him, nor even to draw blood."

Ash refolded Fournier's coat over his arm. "Then what are we *doing* here?"

"We are enjoying the fresh morning air." Fournier unbuttoned his waistcoat and passed it to Ash. "I brought that back from France on this last trip. I would hate to see it ruined."

"The workmanship is exquisite."

"The work-*woman*-ship is French. If you would indicate to Armbruster's seconds that I am ready to begin, we can see this matter concluded."

Sycamore strode across the clearing, to where Armbruster was alternately nipping from a flask and bouncing into shallow pliés.

"He's going to pull a muscle," Ash Dorning muttered.

"Let us hope he pulls a muscle in his groin," Fournier said, untying his cravat. "Though pulling a hamstring will leave a man lamed for ages. He accepted my terms?"

"Duel to the death or until a combatant concedes. Fournier..."

"My affairs are in order. Catherine is my heir. Goddard will manage the wineries for her in exchange for reasonable remuneration, which he does not need and will spend on his urchins. A sum has been set aside for the widows and orphans of other émigrés and another sum put in trust for my daughter. Kettering, Casriel, and Catherine are her trustees. Custody and guardianship of my daughter goes to Catherine. A duplicate original of my will has been sent to my lawyers in France."

"You have been amazingly thorough for a man who intends to prevail."

"I am always amazingly thorough." From the sound of the murmurings at the edge of the clearing, the Dorning brothers were being amazingly thorough as well.

"I've held Lord Fart's vowels since Yuletide," one fellow muttered. "He owes my brother even more."

"He borrowed my phaeton," the man next to him replied.

"Lamed my cattle and sent the vehicle back to me with a dented wheel. No sort of gentleman does that."

"My mother won't invite him to our house parties," a third man volunteered. "The maids would quit en masse, and the footmen would defend them for doing so."

"If his father weren't a marquess..." the first man said.

"That ought not to matter where debts of honor are concerned," a fourth spectator observed. "Why have we left it to a Frenchie to see Armbruster put in his place?"

"A Frenchie who makes good wine, by the by."

A series of bets followed, and Sycamore returned from his errand. "Armbruster is ready, or thinks he is. You aren't wearing even a shirt?"

Fournier pulled his shirt over his head and passed it to Ash. "Clothing can become entangled in the blade, and accidents result. Besides, that is a French shirt."

"I have a fiver on you. Fence in the altogether if that's what it takes to win."

"Don't encourage him," Ash muttered, folding the shirt neatly over his arm. "Let's be about it, shall we?"

Armbruster, wearing both shirt and waistcoat, took his place opposite Fournier. At the signal, the fencers saluted, and then the circling and feinting began.

"Armbruster knows how to wield a blade," Ash muttered as a slashing riposte nicked Fournier's forearm.

"That was on purpose," Sycamore said. "I used to let you older brothers get the first hit in, because then you got all cocky and dropped—"

Fournier's return opened a long cut in the sleeve of Armbruster's shirt.

"—your guard," Sycamore said. "This promises to be interesting."

The crowd grew silent as Armbruster did appear to become confident. He attempted a slashing attack, but somehow in the middle of his advance, his other sleeve was torn. Within minutes, his shirt was hanging about him in ribbons, and he was in a heaving sweat.

Fournier, by contrast, half naked with blood trickling along his arm, looked utterly composed.

"What the hell are you about, Fournier?" Armbruster called. "My shirt is not your opponent."

"Your shirt isn't fit for the rag-and-bone man," somebody retorted. "Just like your promises to pay your debts."

That started up a murmur, and Armbruster reengaged Fournier, who allowed himself to be backed around the clearing in a wide, slow circle.

"Tiring Armbruster out?" Sycamore whispered.

"Up to something," Ash replied. "Mark me on this, Fournier has simply been playing with him."

Armbruster pinked Fournier again on the same arm, but that somehow resulted in a rip down the front of Armbruster's breeches. A length of pale thigh showed, though Armbruster wasn't bleeding.

"What the hell, Fournier? These are new breeches."

"I beg your pardon. Most clumsy of me."

"Damnedest bit of clumsiness I ever saw," the fellow with the dented phaeton said. "Do it again, Fournier, and you can have my matched bays. I want Lord Fart's gray though. Poor beast deserves a decent home."

Fournier again sliced Armbruster's breeches without drawing blood, saluted to the crowd, and reengaged, until offers of vehicles, riding horses, boots, and saddles were flying in all directions. The mood shifted to include calls for vengeance.

"Broke my sister's heart, if you know what I mean. Make him pay for that, Fournier."

"Nearly bankrupted me, and me an honest tailor. Teach him a lesson, monsieur."

"Fournier has done it," Kettering said, coming up on Ash's left. "The scoundrel is being torn apart by his own pack. Oh dear."

Fournier's latest flourish had somehow resulted in the seat of Armbruster's breeches gaping to reveal a manly fundament.

"Gracious," Sycamore said. "My virgin eyes."

"Fournier!" Armbruster tried to hold up his breeches with his left hand and brandish his sword with his right. What the devil are you about?"

"Do you concede, Armbruster?" Sycamore called. "Or will you entertain us further, your pants around your ankles, your sword on display before us all?"

"Never even pinked you," somebody shouted. "Don't know when I've seen finer skill with a blade. Give it up, Armbruster. You are no more a swordsman than you are a gentleman."

"I do not concede!" Armbruster bellowed, coming at Fournier from a slight angle. Fournier pivoted, did something with his wrist, and the falls of Armbruster's breeches were abruptly missing the buttons on one side.

"Foul!" Armbruster cried. "I say foul!"

His second looked embarrassed. "He drew no blood, my lord. Not technically a hit. Combat may continue."

"I can't watch this," Ash said.

"You couldn't *do* this," Sycamore said. "I couldn't. Nobody else could. You are a wizard with your fists, and I know how to throw a knife, but this... This is genius, and we are here to see it with our own eyes."

"I would rather not see that."

Fournier's latest flourish had left Armbruster's breeches gaping from the waist. To keep his pants on, Armbruster had to choose to hold up either the front or the back, leaving at least some part of his anatomy in view.

"Concede," one of his seconds called. "You are bested, Armbruster, and if this is what Fournier can do when he takes it into his head to assault your tailoring, then I fear for your unborn children should he decide to attack your person."

Concede became a chant taken up by the crowd, while Fournier stood, sword held out to the side, and merely waited. He'd worked up a sweat and made an impressive sight, muscles glistening in the morning sun.

"Oak should paint this," Ash said. "Give it a heroic title, like Honor Vindicated."

Armbruster, his fine clothing in tatters, his chest heaving, tossed down his sword.

The tip of Fournier's sword was under Armbruster's chin in the next instant. "The price of defeat remains to be paid."

Armbruster's gaze swiveled about the crowd, most of whom were glaring daggers at him. The seconds had the grace to stare at the ground, and somebody's horse chose then to pass a prodigiously ripe blast of equine gas.

"The girl is your daughter," Armbruster said quietly. "I did not mean to imply otherwise."

Fournier eased his rapier away. "Then I wish you good day. Thank you for a fine morning's exercise." He bowed with a flourish of his sword and moved to the side of the clearing.

Nobody approached Armbruster, not even his seconds. He limped off, clothing flapping in the breeze, as money changed hands, and muttering turned to taunts and threats.

"I believe he's pulled a muscle," Ash said. "Getting onto his horse will be agony."

"One should always take one's carriage to a duel," Fournier said as Sycamore poured the contents of his flask over the scratches on Fournier's arm. "One might well be wounded and need the conveyance to return home."

"He probably didn't want anybody claiming his coach for repayment of a debt," Ash observed as Casriel and Kettering assisted Armbruster to don his morning coat over his ruined shirt and waistcoat.

"I booked his lordship passage to Rome," Fournier said as Sycamore bound a plain handkerchief around his forearm. "His valet will present the ticket as the last courtesy of a gentleman's gentleman whose wages are a month overdue, along with a packed trunk and a few coins. Catherine insisted that I facilitate the villain's departure, lest the matter grow into an unnecessarily large scandal."

"Rome gets beastly hot in summer," Sycamore said. "A medium-sized scandal ought to get the job done, if the talk from the spectators is any indication."

"I don't believe Armbruster speaks Italian," Ash added, tying Fournier's cravat in a tidy *trône de l'amour* knot. "Though he'll have some Latin—and a lot of enemies here in England."

Fournier shrugged into his waistcoat. "As long as Lord Fortescue leaves me and mine in peace, I have no quarrel with him. I am famished, though, for some sustenance and for the company of my darlings. Shall we to breakfast, gentlemen?"

"You make me wish I was part French," Sycamore said, gathering up the swords. "This was quite well done of you, Fournier. Not too violent, but memorable. Most assuredly memorable."

"Your wife is half French," Fournier said, donning his coat. "We may thus have some hope for your children, *non?* Let us collect the family lordships and begin embellishing our stories for our respective ladies."

Ash guffawed, and Sycamore Dorning, for once, was left with nothing to say.

~

"Now, this," Sycamore Dorning said, "is a wedding breakfast." At the top of the terrace steps, in full view of the assemblage, he slipped his arm around his wife's waist and bussed her cheek.

"And this," Jeanette replied, saluting with her glass, "is exquisite champagne. If Orion hasn't broken out his best vintage, then he has some nectar of the goddesses stashed away in his warehouse."

Fournier suspected the Dornings had some French blood stashed generations back. They were affectionate, ferociously loyal to family, and they knew a fine champagne when they sipped it. They had also turned the Richmond estate garden into the perfect venue for a large, merry wedding breakfast.

"*Le champagne*," Fournier said, "*est magnifique*. As is the noise."

"Get used to it," Jeanette muttered. "This family is always noisy when happy."

The Earl of Casriel, who along with Worth Kettering had stood up with the happy couple, appropriated Sycamore's champagne, offered the glass to his countess, then took a sip himself.

"We Dornings do love a garden, and your wife is a Dorning, Fournier."

Sycamore snatched back his glass, which was empty. "Catherine wasn't a Dorning for too long, but she is now. Dornings thrive in the out of doors and in gardens in particular."

Catherine chose that moment to catch Fournier's eye, while the young Marquess of Tavistock babbled away beside her, looking earnest and handsome. She was at the table beneath a white awning that stretched down the center of the garden, and one by one, the Dorning family members and guests were paying their homage to her.

She'd sent Fournier after her shawl, though the day was warm, almost as if she'd known that he needed the activity.

"If you ask me," Casriel observed, "when Catherine gazes upon her husband, she's entirely a Fournier."

Fournier winked at his wife, who was bearing up with good grace under this riotous show of familial support. She looked all of a piece with the blooming irises, billowing lavender, and majestic delphiniums—also with the adoring swains. The youngsters racing about underfoot, and the mastiffs gamboling about with them, bothered her not at all.

I needed this. The thought cascaded into Fournier's mind as bright sunshine illuminated old cathedrals and ancient forests. *I needed this joy, this celebration, this exuberance, and most of all, I needed the smile from Catherine that says without a single word that she understands me.*

His imagination carried him forward in time, to more loud, happy family gatherings, some of them at the château. Catherine would smile at him exactly thus, and he would smile back, and his heart would ache with love for the woman who had brought him home from the wars.

"Catherine is her own person," Fournier said, "and it is my greatest honor to be her devoted spouse. If you will please excuse me, I must relieve my wife of a smitten marquess."

"Talk to him of grapes," Jeanette called. "Tavistock has become mad for grapes."

Tavistock, in a display of tact and good manners that had doubtless served him well on both sides of the Channel, excused himself as Fournier approached Catherine.

"His lordship is charming," Catherine said. "He very much enjoys France and will return there when the Season is over."

Fournier slid into the seat the marquess had abandoned. "We will call on him at the end of our wedding journey. Have you had enough to eat?"

"Yes, and drink."

Catherine had declared that, for the weeks of courting, intimacies were to be suspended. She'd used the time to begin easing her way into Marie's life, while allowing Fournier all the affection he could have asked for.

Which, of course, had made his longings only more intense.

"You are content that Deems will manage the warehouses in your absence?" Catherine asked, holding a petit four up to Fournier's lips.

He bit off half—lemon-flavored—and Catherine popped the other half into her mouth. Foolishness. Wonderful, married foolishness.

"Deems was born to manage inventories, and he will tolerate no slacking. You are prepared to travel with me and Marie from Bordeaux to Champagne?"

Their wedding journey would be a means for Fournier to become reacquainted with his homeland—and acquainted with his daughter.

Marie fascinated him, so like her mother and so much her own person too.

Catherine waved to Marie, who was dodging around tent poles with one of Lady Penweather's boys giving chase and Caesar tagging after like a canine nanny.

"I am prepared," Catherine said quietly, "to start that journey in the next five minutes. The breakfast is lovely, our family is lovely, but I am your wife, and I would very much like to begin enjoying the honors of my office."

"While I," Fournier replied, "am wild to explore with you the fascinating English term 'wedded bliss.' When I excuse myself to fetch your shawl, MacKay will escort you into the greenhouse. He will ensure you can meet me in the side garden in five minutes. We will make a very leisurely progress back to Town in my traveling coach, and MacKay will offer our excuses to the host and hostess."

Catherine leaned close to sniff the petite irises affixed to Fournier's lapel, and temptation nearly overcame his determination.

"Xavier, we shouldn't."

"I am assured that for the bride and groom to make a discreet exit from the melee is something of a Dorning family tradition. One can understand the origins of such a practice, because this bacchanal will clearly last for the next three days."

"They do look happy," Catherine said as, over by the fountain, Worth Kettering smacked Ash Dorning hard on the shoulder and got a sound whack in return from Lady Della. Della grinned and waggled her fingers at Catherine, then made a little shooing motion with her hand and blew Catherine a kiss.

"We are excused," Fournier said, "and MacKay approaches. Five minutes, my dear, and not one moment more if you value your husband's sanity."

He did not kiss her, lest his sanity give way right there before the barbarian horde.

"My husband," Catherine said as Fournier helped her to her feet. "How I love the sound of that. *Mon très cher mari. Cinq minutes.*"

"Four and a half." Fournier placed Catherine's hand on MacKay's arm—the Scotsman cut quite a figure in his kilt—and set a brisk pace for the back terrace steps. Lady Casriel caught his eye, and if her spouse knew what Fournier was about, he had the good grace to keep his smiling, lordly mouth shut.

MacKay was as good as his word, delivering Catherine to the side garden in something over four minutes.

"We'll bring Marie and Miss Drawbaugh back to Town with us tomorrow afternoon," MacKay said. "Do get some sleep. One should be rested when embarking on a journey—or an adventure." He kissed Catherine's cheek and strutted off, kilt swinging.

"You brought the traveling coach," Catherine said when Fournier had escorted her around to the porte cochere.

"The most comfortable of our conveyances." Also the one designed to turn into a rolling boudoir.

He handed Catherine up, instructed the coachman to make only the most leisurely progress toward London, and joined his wife inside the vehicle.

"Lady Jacaranda passed along some gossip," Catherine said, unpinning a cluster of violets from her chignon. "She's Lady Trysting in formal company, but family still calls her Jacaranda."

"My love, gossiping is the last thing on my mind at the moment." He took the flowers from her, set them on the opposite bench along with his top hat and gloves, and kissed his wife.

She kissed him back, rather thoroughly, then removed his boutonniere lest her enthusiasms crush the delicate blooms.

"This gossip says Lord Fort will remain on remittance in Rome indefinitely. His mama claims he needs time to grow up."

Fournier slipped Catherine's gloves off. "If that man lives to be a hundred, he will not grow up. What the marchioness refuses to admit is that his lordship's debts exceed the family's willingness or ability to pay. I will spare my pity for the merchants and younger sons whom he has cheated, but, Catherine, might I pity them *later*?"

He emphasized his request by pulling the shades down, one by one.

"This is a very comfortable coach," Catherine said, as if noticing the deeply padded benches and the pillows stacked near Fournier's hat for the first time. "Are you sure you don't mind that Marie will accompany us on our wedding journey?"

How could she think, how could she even...? Except that Catherine was Marie's mother, and the question was genuine.

"I could not part you from her," Fournier said. "All too soon, she will be a young lady and have no use for her old parents, but at present, you and she belong together. She is my daughter now too. You are the love of my life and the mother of my children. We will travel together, beginning as we intend to go on, as the English say."

Fournier did not have to add that he was unwilling to part from his wife, or his child, ever.

Catherine cupped his cheek against the warmth of her palm. "*Children*, Xavier?"

He took her hand and kissed her fingers. "One can hope and trust to good fortune." And commodious coaches and marital devotion.

Catherine kissed him again slowly, almost solemnly. "One can love and ensure that the door to good fortune is always open."

Fournier agreed with that thought, but it wasn't until a very lucky, sweet, married hour later that he was able to communicate his agreement to his wife... with words.